DIFFERENT SHADE OF WYNTER

STORM BLOODLINE SAGA: BOOK 2

EMMY R. BENNETT

DREAM SCRIPT MEDIA

Published by Dream Script Media LLC

1st edition Library of Congress 1-7670897051

2nd edition Library of Congress 1-12663882187

Line edited by Rebecca Jaycox

Copyedited and proofread by Gail Delaney Editing Services

First Edition 2019

ISBN: 978-1-950501-00-7 (paperback)

ISBN: 978-1-950501-01-4 (ebook)

Second edition 2023

ISBN: 978-1-950501-13-7 (paperback)

ISBN: 978-1-950501-14-4 (ebook)

Get new release updates and exclusive content by signing up on Emmy's

mailing list

DEDICATION

To Daddy: I miss you.

WYNTER'S THOUGHTS

If someone had told me a month ago that my evil grandmother would capture me and breed me for my gifts, I would've told them they belonged in a nut house. Since then, I've learned the world is much more sinister than first believed.

War is coming...

1

THE DAY AFTER

MUCH OF MY RECENT life has me feeling like I'm in a tailspin as I reflect on the last few days. I peer through the teleporter, observing the other side, which reveals a meadow of bright colors of purple, blue, fuchsia, and oranges. The vibrant green grasses wave in the wind, welcoming me to its land: Ladorielle. All my training this past week has prepared me for this moment—to venture to another world and locate the Sword of Valor. It's rumored Dragonscale will know the whereabouts of its existence.

Now, as I stand before the portal in the loft, details of recent moments surface, of events that took place the day after my birthday. I reflect on the past and my training up to this point.

"THE FIRST STEP," DAD said, "is to learn to control your emotions. You must remember that, okay?"

I nodded and focused on his valiancium steel sword, then back to his facial expression. His eyes narrowed, waiting for me to make the first move. I lingered too long, and he stepped first, prompting me to lean forward at the wrong time. He stuck out his foot and I tripped, which sent me sailing into the bushes and my weapon reeling through the air, giving him prime opportunity to aim the tip of his sword at my throat.

"And you're dead." Dad laughed. "Wynter, you must concentrate. Know when to move and when not to."

"I'm never going to get this down, am I?"

Giving me his hand, he helped me to my feet. "Never is such a strong word, my dear. I like to call it 'practice.' Now, go get your sword, and let's try again."

My mother Isalora cut in, bringing hot cocoa with her. "I'd say that's enough exercise this morning, Jeff. She needs to know how to use all her gifts."

"My dear love," Dad said, "people of our world have swords. She must learn to wield one."

Mother smiled. "Ignore your father, Wynter. Sometimes, I think he wishes you were born a boy," she teased and handed me my mug. "Here, this should keep you warm."

My dad scoffed. "Absolutely not. I'm merely teaching her to fight. She needs to know shadows are lurking everywhere."

"Fair enough." She gave my father a stern look and passed him his cup. "As for you, sir, how do you know she won't have the magical touch like her mother?"

Dad shrugged. "Can't fault a father for hoping his daughter is the warrior kind." He took a sip. "Mmm, well done, my sweet. The perfect taste of a well-brewed mocha."

"We will not know where her true talent lies until she crosses over to Ladorielle," my mother reminded him, flirting back.

They acted like a couple of teenagers. Gawd, it was so sickening I turned away to keep from blushing.

I noticed Cory through the fir trees, standing down by the river alone, and I made my way toward him. The snow remained in small drifts with patches of pine needles, rocks, and dirt peeking through the layer of white. It had snowed hard last night, but one wouldn't know because of the thick wooded terrain.

I snuck up behind him, but even the sound of my footsteps betrayed me. "Hi, there, Wynter." His senses were too keen.

"Ah damn, a good scare ruined, I suppose. I don't think I'll ever have the skill of surprising you, will I?"

He snickered. "You will in time, I'm sure." He grabbed my hand and laced his fingers with mine, and asked, "How's practice going with your dad?"

"I don't know. He seemed fixated on teaching me sword fighting, how to hammer a nail, and other jobs a father would normally teach a son. I have no desire to learn any of this. I remember growing up and wanting to wear pretty clothes and play dress up with my dolls, but he would tell me it was a waste of time, and that I should be learning how to get along in the 'real world.' Funny, what exactly is the real world anyway? I mean here we are—all of us preparing for the journey into a new realm."

"It will all work out in the end. He's just trying to get you focused on the battles we face ahead." Cory's voice drifted into a mumble as he stared absently at the flowing river.

Something seemed off like he was in a faraway land. "Hey, are you okay?" I touched his shoulder hoping to break his trance.

He turned. "Hmm?" His smile brightened. "I was daydreaming a bit, wasn't I?"

"Is everything okay?"

"Yeah, fine, why wouldn't it be?

"You seem distracted."

"Am I?"

His dazed look had me concerned. "Cory, what is it?"

"It's nothing."

"Something is bothering you—tell me."

He hesitated before answering. "It's just that... I haven't been to Ladorielle in a long time, and I'm worried that the world will look different."

"How so?"

"When I last left there—"

This new adventure we were about to go on seemed to have stirred distant memories, and he took a few seconds to finish his thoughts.

Cory's voice shook as he spoke. I sensed a bit of fear. "This place we're about to visit is a very mountainous domain divided into three island kingdoms, with each realm having its own House serving on the great council. The species of plants, animals, and atmosphere is very different from the world you're used to seeing. And magic, powerful magic."

"It's surreal hearing you say 'magic' like it's a normal thing. Until recently I would have thought it was all nonsense."

Cory grunted. "Magic is all around you, Wynter. Even here on Earth. The difference is most humans don't know how to use it properly."

"What do you mean?"

"Take psychics for example. Their gifts are magical, but the magic only works for those receptive to receiving the messages."

"I see your point, but what about Aunt Fran and her ability to heal? Or me, for that matter? How do you explain that to an ordinary human?"

"True. This is why we as magically gifted people, must hold our secrets close to us. The ordinary public wouldn't understand."

"What are you trying to say, Cory?"

"I'm saying that Ladorielle is a magical place full of wonder but in the same breath incredibly dangerous for the one who cannot protect themselves."

I turned around to where the house hides behind the trees. I couldn't see the structure through the thick woods, but I can see the area where Dad and I were practicing. "That's why he's teaching me how to fight, isn't it?"

"Yes."

I took another sip of my hot cocoa before I asked, "Can you enlighten me on what you mean by Houses?"

"We're 'The House of Storm' and the current reigning monarchy of Ladorielle. Then there are the Ladorielle territories and Dragonscale Island."

"Who are the others?"

He turned to look at me. "There's the House of Deagon and the ruling kingdom of Dragonscale Island." His mind drifted a moment as though he didn't want to continue, but did anyway, saying, "Then there is the House of Zhir, Vothule's ruling kingdom—although he resides on the sister planet Elleirodal."

"Wait, you mean Vothule is on the council? How is that even possible?"

"It's what you call the balance of power."

"That makes no sense to me at all."

Cory scowled. "I agree, and I think many oppose him being included in any decision. He should have been removed long ago."

"So why hasn't he?"

"The Order of the Twelve Council is set in place to keep the balance of magic in check. The evil rulers are against the good ones. Dragonscale is the deciding vote should something end in a tie." He firmed his lips. I can tell he doesn't like this diplomatic setup. "There are rules everyone must abide by."

"And this council, what do they want from me?"

"Nothing. It's Sarmira that wishes you harm."

"And you think we'll find this Dragonscale?"

"I honestly don't know. He's not exactly easy to find." Cory walked down along the river, and I followed, listening to his story. "The Ladorielle Territories are slowly being taken over by Vothule and his allies, and Dragonscale has managed to keep the three islands balanced, somewhat."

"And you think Vothule is involved somehow with Sarmira?"

Cory laughed. "Definitely."

"You seem pretty sure of yourself."

"Vothule is Sarmira's father."

I gasped. "What?" I thought back to when Moyer attacked me in the basement and my necklace zapped her. She mentioned she was going to see Vothule. "No wonder Moyer has so much magical pull, the good ol' father/daughter duo."

Cory arched an eyebrow and gave me one of those looks. The kind that makes a girl's heart stop. "It's all very complicated, isn't it?" he asked. "At any rate, not only do we have to stop Sarmira and release Moyer from her possession, but we now are also going to have to be on the lookout for Vothule and his allies."

"How can we protect ourselves?" I looked beyond the trees thinking this voyage will be more dangerous than living at the manor.

He stopped to take my hand. "Wynter, there's something else I need to tell you."

A twig snapped behind us and we turned to see Fran walking up. "There you two are," she interrupted. "Lunch is ready, and your mother asked me to come find you. Your dad has set up the tree, too. I think your mother is excited. It's her first Christmas with you."

I smiled. "I'll be right there, Aunt Fran." I turned back to Cory. "What were you going to say?"

"It's nothing. I'll tell you later. We better get inside," he said, and together we walked back to the cabin.

By the time we reached the steps of the cottage, the snow had begun to fall again. "Do you think another snowstorm is on the way?" I asked.

Cory shrugged. "We'll be snug and warm if it hits us." He opened the front door and we were both knocked with the smells of gingerbread cookies baking in the oven and a yuletide fire burned in the hearth.

"Mmm, smells delicious," I said. More steaming hot cocoa awaited on the dining room table.

A noble tree has been placed in a corner near the fireplace, with the needles bare, waiting for ornaments, tinsel, and garland. "A dream I've always wanted," Isalora murmured. She came to greet Cory and me as we took off our jackets. "I never thought I'd have the opportunity to celebrate the holidays with you." She hugged me and tears formed in her eyes.

I smiled, thinking of the absent years. It's weird calling her my mother. Maybe in time, I'll get used to it. "Well, this Christmas we'll make up for lost time."

Her excitement grew, leading me to the assorted boxes scattered across the floor. "I brought out seasonal decorations from the basement."

For the first time in my life, we celebrated Christmas together as a family.

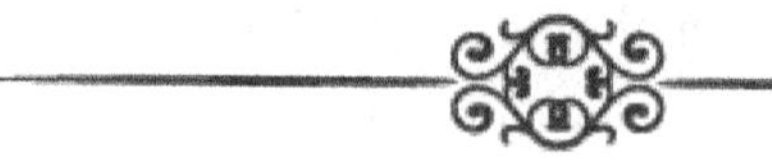

"ARE YOU READY FOR this?" Cory asks, bringing me back to the present.

"As ready as I'll ever be, I suppose." I look behind me. Dad, Isalora, and Aunt Fran all stare, smiling, as if they're waiting in anticipation for my reaction to stepping into a new world. All the grueling training is about to be tested once we pass through to the land on the other side. A part of me doesn't feel ready.

"Believe me, you're more than ready," Isalora says in my head. *"Remember what you've learned and apply it. Your memory will come back to you, I promise."*

"There's those promises people keep committing to," I reply.

Her eyes cloud in tears, and she smiles. *"The longer you are exposed to familiar things, the sooner it all will come back to you."*

Isalora stiffens, stating aloud, "Ashengale is the city of dragons, and the adventure awaits the four of you."

I peer at the portal window again. The sun shines bright in the blue sky. Taking a step backward, I glance over the balcony where Stella still sleeps on the living room sofa below. "I was hoping she'd have woken by now to see us off," I whisper.

Isalora stands next to me. "Dear child, she doesn't know a world like Ladorielle exists."

"And yet she won't know what happened to me either."

"Not to worry, I'll take care of her," my mother says.

A couple of days ago, while making another rescue attempt to free Cole from Moyer's grasp, Dad, Aunt Fran, and Isalora, found Stella in the basement chambers. According to Dad, Stella was hanging by her wrists in chains like all the other victims Moyer has tortured. Stella's the one person who doesn't know the truth about Storm River Manor, and it angers me that Moyer retaliated against me, through her. Perhaps she intended to lure a Storm and ensnare them. If that's the case, it didn't work. Dad wrapped Stella in his coat and brought her to the protective comforts of the cottage.

I remember that day clear as a bell:

THE FRONT DOOR SWUNG open on Christmas Eve when Dad called for help as Stella was unconscious in his arms. "I found her in chains while searching for Cole. Quick, help me set her by the fire."

Cory and I moved the couch near the hearth, and Dad laid Stella down. "The Shadow Walkers are everywhere inside the manor," he added. "If not for the last invisibility potion you gave me, Cory, we wouldn't have gotten out alive."

"How many are there?" Cory asked. "Are we still safe staying here in the cottage?"

Dad looked concerned. "For now, yes. I believe we are fine." He nodded to Stella. "I'm more concerned about her." He knelt and checked her forehead. "It's more dangerous out there than we first anticipated. It's as though Moyer went out into the world to hunt for an army, selecting each victim with a purpose." He brushed the hair out of Stella's eyes.

"What are you saying?" Cory asked. "That she's gone into the urban cities hunting for humans?"

Dad nodded.

"Dad, what does this mean?"

"It means Moyer's upped her game."

I looked at Cory, and he looked just as worried as my dad.

"We may have one last shot, the day after tomorrow," Dad said. "We can try again, but after that, we will have to go to plan B."

"Plan B?" I asked.

"He means we will have to go to Ladorielle without rescuing my brother." Cory sank into a nearby chair and cupped his hands to his chin. "Where's Isalora and Fran?" Cory asked.

"Not far behind me. Your mother and aunt distracted them while I raced to the cottage, shielding us from *her* evil sights. Isalora assured me Stella would be okay and I should run as fast as I could to safety."

"Them?" I asked.

"The Shadow Walkers," Cory answered.

The howling of wolves disrupted our chat. "I'm guessing it didn't go unnoticed though." I raised a brow at Cory.

Dad stared at us as though he might have thought the same thing. "She won't find us," Dad says with confidence. "Trust me."

"Moyer must be seething with revenge that her precious plans are falling apart," I said.

"What about Blair, Chad, and the others?" Cory asked.

Stella shivered in her sleep, so I went to the closet and brought out an extra blanket to cover her.

"They insisted on staying behind, claiming they'd be the eyes and ears on the inside until we were ready for battle with Moyer. Besides, Blair has no intention of leaving Cole there alone, nor Casey for that matter."

Now, I didn't see that coming. "Why Casey?"

Dad smiled as though I should've known better than to ask it.

"My older brother," Cory answered.

I stared at him in shock. "You never told me Casey's your brother."

"Now's not the time to explain that story, Cory," Dad said, quickly changing the subject. "Will you go grab more wood for the fire, please?"

Knowing I won't get my answer this evening, I asked another question. "Did they say anything else? Like how to get them all out safely?"

"Chad did mention something about that." Dad hesitates "There are keys that will unlock the valiancium cuffs bound to all the Storms."

Cory dropped the logs into the fire and directed his attention to Dad. "You mean there is a way to get this wretched thing off?" He pulled up his pant leg, showing the cuff around his ankle.

"Apparently, but Chad didn't say where to look or where they're located. For all we know, they're locked away somewhere down in that hell hole of a basement." Dad huffed with frustration.

"Is that why they wouldn't leave?" Cory asked. "Because of the cuffs?"

"Mainly, yes. Blair said something about Moyer being able to track anyone that wears the cuffs."

I felt a bit of panic, and bile rose in my throat.

Dad noticed and assured me with a smile. "She can't find us as long as we remain close to this house, remember?"

“I’m guessing none of you know where the keys are?” I asked.

Dad shook his head.

“If we find those keys, it will definitely give us an advantage in defeating Moyer at her own game,” Cory said, as he poked the fire, rearranging the logs.

“Look on the bright side, the jewelry we wear, shields the evil magic Moyer casts. At least she can’t read our minds like she can the others,” Dad said.

“Except Cole and Casey,” Cory said.

“Yes, you’re right, they don’t wear any enchanted items.” Dad walked to the kitchen and got out a mug from the cupboard. “We will get them out, Cory, I promise you that. For now, the rest of our family network will remain undercover, working both sides until the Storm family is free.”

As I pull myself back into the present, still gazing over the balcony watching Stella sleep, I question if she’s truly okay. Her regenerating process seems slower than the rest of them—the vampire side, that is. She doesn’t have the same symptoms, leaving us all puzzled. “When will she wake up?”

“Don’t worry. She’s in good hands,” Isalora says, placing her hand on my shoulder.

Turning to face the rest of my family, I say, “It’s been days since she’s been like this. How are you going to protect her? She’s going to remember everything. What if Moyer placed a memory stamp on her, too? Like she did with me. Moyer’s going to know—”

“I have a few memory stamps of my own,” Isalora interrupts. “When Stella comes to, she will know everything. What Moyer has done, how she got here, and why she’s changed. She will have no secrets. Except maybe knowing who you really are. And as far as the memory stamp is concerned, Moyer doesn’t know there is still someone magical enough to cast a powerful counteraction spell.”

Deep down I know Isalora is much more powerful than she's leading on. "Who am I really, Mother?" I ask, not intending to sound facetious. It's a wholehearted question.

"You will find out soon," Isalora says, smiling.

I glance again at the open portal with its outer edges glowing bright, waiting to pass through it. This journey to the unknown has me rethinking everything.

More moments from the past slowly appear again.

"IT WILL SHOW ITSELF in time, trust me, Wynter," Aunt Fran said. "As time goes on, more of your powers will be revealed. Especially once you enter the world from which your lineage is from. The key to understanding it, is learning to control it. The magic has laid dormant in you for so long that you may not know how to adjust right away, but I assure you, the magic will find you."

"What magic, Aunt Fran?"

Shock permeated her face. "Wynter."

My question wasn't meant to offend her but I was so tired of not knowing who I was. Too late to back out now. "Okay, so I have some sort of 'magical power,' but I *see* nothing—" I turned away, annoyed, looked out the window, and watched the water trickle off the frozen icicles and drip into the river. "And sure, so I see ghosts... yay, me. Oh, and let's not forget I can heal, too."

"Wynter, you have amazing gifts," my aunt said, attempting to calm me with her tone.

"Do I though?" I turned to face her, frustrated. Like a spoiled brat, I'm sure, but, for eighteen years I've lived a lie and it's really messing me up. It's amazing Aunt Fran doesn't lose patience because mine is gone.

Fran gathered both my hands in hers and smiles. "Sit with me." We took a seat on the bench that sat against the large bay window. "You're the first one in centuries we have seen able to heal others."

I shook my head. "Centuries." I took a deep breath, still trying to wrap my head around the fact that I wasn't from this world. "That's what I mean, Aunt Fran. I feel like I'm a lost soul."

She gently squeezed my hand. "You're not a lost soul. And seeing ghosts, well, you're the first for that, too. Everyone else must use a spell or make a drinking potion."

Aunt Fran gave me a concerned look. "As you acquire memories of lost discoveries on Ladorielle, you will become more emotional. These feelings will become intensified, and may even enrage you, but whatever you do, you must keep them in check. For if you allow them to carry through, the dark side of you will take over."

That remark sent goosebumps up my spine.

"Don't worry," Cory intervened, "I'll be there to help you if it becomes too overwhelming."

"You can't keep coddling her, Cory," Fran said. "She needs to learn how to balance her abilities. Only then will she truly be *in control* of herself."

"You all make it sound like I have this monster inside me, waiting to come out." I was half-joking, but a part of me was serious, and from the look on their faces, they were worried.

"Hiding you from magic took a toll on your father and me," Fran said. "It was the only way to keep you safe from Sarmira. She's gone to great lengths to find you. We mustn't allow her to win. This will require an 'all hands on deck.'" She looked at Dad, Cory, and Isalora, and they all nodded in agreement.

Fran narrowed her gaze to my necklace. "That will reveal more to you than what you know already. Continue to wear it, and don't take it off. It will also shield your location."

I touched my chain. *What if we can't pull this off?*

"You mustn't think like that," Isalora answered. *"I would go with you, my sweet daughter, if I could. The Reveal Spell allowing me to take human form renders me weaker than if I stayed in ghost form. Besides, you're in good hands."*

I smiled at her. *"And you have to take care of Stella."*

"There, see, now you're getting it. We all have a role to play."

"It's going to be fine. We will be right behind you," Dad says, bringing me back from my memories.

"Take care of her," Isalora states. "You don't want to answer to me if she's harmed." Although I can tell she's joking with my father, her tone says she's nervous.

"Don't worry. I see the future, remember? She will come back unscathed, my love," he assures.

"Yes, but your views are subjective. It can change." She kisses him, and he holds her close. It still amazes me how solid her body looks and not translucent like a ghost. If one saw her on the streets or sidewalks, they might think she's just another person and not a spirit.

"She's my daughter, too, you know," Dad says.

"My biggest concern is you're not back in time before the Super Blue Blood Moon eclipse. If the evil Underworld releases during—"

"It won't happen. I won't let it," he swears.

The rest of us look away, trying not to impose on their candid moment.

"Okay, come on. The portal isn't going to stay up for much longer. Let's go," Fran calls out and steps through the portal, disappearing out of sight.

"What's with Aunt Fran?" I ask, looking at Dad and Isalora. They both stay quiet, and Cory gives a slight shake of his head.

Isalora smiles. "All in due time, my dear."

"Right," I remark, "all of you will explain later... I got it."

Ignoring my comment, Isalora says, "Oh wait, I almost forgot." She darts downstairs and pulls up the floorboards.

"What are you doing?" Dad asks.

"Just a second." When she's finished, she brings with her the mysterious second box that hid in the hole below along with the one Cory and I had found behind the hearth at the manor. "Please take this with you," she says, giving it to me.

"What's in it?" I ask.

She smiles. "Something Nyta has been searching for, for a long time." She pauses, adding, "Will you please give it to her?"

"Of course."

There is a mystery in her eyes, and I know deep down she's holding back information. I'm about to press for more answers when she says, "Now quick, you must go before the portal closes."

And so, the adventure awaits.

2
SONGBIRD MEADOW

I HESITATE TO GRAB Cory's hand while looking through the portal gate. "It'll be fine," he says. We take the step together.

A tingling sensation crawls up my fingers and through my arms as I cross the threshold with him. An odd, warm lull flows throughout the veins of my frame, as though my body is asleep, yet, I'm wide awake. All thoughts of my entire life flash before me. The light from the gated portal is so bright when we pass through, I must close my eyes.

Passing over the gateway feels like it's taking days if not months to go through, except it's only been seconds. "That was so strange."

"You've experienced the phenomena of time manipulation, Wynter. You'll get used to it."

Immediately, I notice birds singing beautiful melodies and the need to take a nap overwhelms my body. My eyes grow heavy and my mind clouds with confusion. I look down at the soft plush patch of green grass and let out an unexpected yawn. Gentle wisps of snowflakes fall from the sky, and although a cold chill grazes across my skin, I still feel the urge to lie down and sleep. Dropping to my knees, I touch the green meadow, twisting the blades between my fingers, ready to curl up in a ball and drift off to a blissful slumber. "Cory, I feel so tired." I look up at him and smile. My eyes sting, as I try to fight to keep them open. It's been a long eventful morning, one small nap isn't going to hurt anything.

"No, Wynter. Stay awake." He swears under his breath, but it doesn't faze me. He pulls something from his pocket and places an S-shaped object in both my ears. "The birds will put you to sleep, and we will end up going nowhere until nightfall."

My urge to fall into a delightful snooze evaporates as the sounds from the birds become faint. "What was that?"

"Magic songbirds." Cory offers a hand to pull me from the ground.

I push the plugs further into my ears to give them a tight fit. "What other wondrous things have you forgotten to mention, Cory?" I look down as I graciously take his hand, watching the long blades of grass sway back and forth, leaving no evidence that I once laid on this exact spot. "What in the—"

"The grass cocoons its victims like a blanket, sending them into a blissful sleep. Being caught within the beds of these meadows is dangerous," Cory explains. "This place is Songbird Meadow of Unrest. It's designed to protect the portal. I'm sorry. We forgot to tell you about the earplugs with all the excitement of preparing for a new world—"

Before I can argue with him about forgetting to tell a crucial point in our survival, we both are distracted by Dad passing through the portal. He comes over to join us, asking, "Where's Fran?"

Dad's question prompts us to scan the area. Seeing Dad go sheet white and the expression on both their faces makes me wonder what other odd features this new world I'm in has in store for us.

"I—I—" Cory is at a loss for words. The look of worry in his eyes concerns me.

"We need to find her." Dad steps forward, calling out Aunt Fran's name.

A snowflake falls onto my nose giving me a slight chill. I look up at the sky and notice three planets. One is directly opposite of the one we are on, hovering in space, with a hole in the shape of an eye. The illumination is so bright it would blind me in my human form, I'm sure. It looks much like Jupiter, except the planet is blue with lavender and green stripes. On either side of this planet, sits two others. One is grayish blue while the other is reddish orange. All three appear as though there will be an eclipse soon. "Now there's something you don't see every day."

"That is planet Elleirodal. Our planet's twin," Dad says. "The other planets are moons. The blue one belongs to Elleirodal, and the red one is ours. When they all align together, it becomes night. In the morning, you will not see our red moon, and their moon will be on the opposite side and out of our view. The hole you may have seen that is in the shape of an eye is made of molten liquid, which is our replacement 'sun' and we have one on this planet you cannot see."

"It's truly amazing."

Dad walks ahead. "There's a coating around both planets that protects us all from the eye — our sun. Should that coating be destroyed, the planets would shine so bright it would burn everything in sight."

I secure my pack to follow. "So is this 'eye' the galaxy's sun? How are we to see? I mean, wouldn't our eyes burn?"

"Yes, the eye is our sun and no, our eyes won't burn," Cory says. "Imagine Ladorielle wearing a gigantic pair of sunglasses." He smiles. "The protective shield around this planet shades us from the brightness."

"So, the planets don't rotate around the sun?"

"No," Dad answers. "Long ago, the council discovered our sun was dying, and they figured out how to collect the essence of the sun's energies, forming into what you now see as a molten eye. There's so much you'll discover, but first, we need to find your aunt."

"I'm just going to throw this out here, guys, but doesn't it stand to reason that if we are on a planet Fran grew up on, that she shouldn't be lost?"

"Precisely," Dad says, "which has me concerned."

The peaceful sound of silence is deafening as the flakes intensify. I mean, yes, the birds are still faintly chirping through the earplugs, but it's strange that in the nothingness of silence, Dad and Cory are heard as plain as day.

The snow falling from the sky becomes more prevalent, and the flowers on the ground seem to relish the icy temperatures. They become brighter and grow larger right before my eyes.

A white layer of snow blankets the ground. "I'm sure she couldn't have gotten far."

"That's exactly what I'm afraid of," Dad says on a huff. "Cory, can you see her visions? I mean, can you see what she sees?"

"No, she must be asleep, otherwise I'd see pictures in her mind right now. It makes me think she's forgotten to put in her earplugs."

"Why would she be so careless?" Dad argues. "She knows better."

The two of them look around, appearing anxious and it begins to give me a panic feeling. "What's going on? Has she been hurt or taken?"

Dad points toward the trees. "It appears the birds plan to have Fran for dinner. The grass will cover you like a blanket once you lie down."

"Right, Cory mentioned that." I look over at him. "That's what the earplugs are for." I touch the strange mechanisms in both my ears. "And you think Aunt Fran forgot to put these in?"

"Yes," Dad says. He and Cory step around in the grass, moving slowly. "The earplugs you wear are intended to withhold the temptation of the melodies the birds sing."

"I can still hear faint sounds of them, though."

"Yes, and you will," Cory adds. "You may also feel a sense of fatigue, but not at all like what you experienced a few moments ago. The earplugs are handcrafted, and not many own them."

"Have you been here before, Cory?" I wonder what else he hasn't told me.

"Yes," he says, bowing his head.

Dad wanders on the other side of the path, carefully walking through the grass.

"When?"

"Once, a long time ago when Cole and I were little. Blair and Chad brought us to this lovely place when we had an opportunity to escape the wrath of Madame Moyer. One of the many times we tried to get away, I might add. Moyer has an uncanny way of finding things... people." He gives a grim smile. "Once she discovered the valiancium steel weakens a Nytemire... well you know the rest. Every Storm has one on their wrist or ankle."

"Except me."

Cory nods. "Except you."

The snowflakes are huge now, and I realize at this rate the grass will no longer be seen, and a white blanket of snow will take its place. "We need to hurry. The snow is getting deeper."

We step through the grass with caution, searching for Fran. As we search, Cory continues his story. "The night you were born we all escaped. Another attempt to run away you could say. Cole and I were maybe around two. Blair, my brothers, the whole family, fled to the river where Geneviève waited to port us all to Ladorielle."

"The night I was born?"

Cory huffs. "According to my mother Blair, yes. Cole and I were two. I'm sorry I don't have much memory of that. Anyway, apparently when Sarmira killed Isalora the night you were born, it sealed the doors to the Hall of History that led to the Iron Door of Secrets. It's why Moyer cannot penetrate those doors. Even if she finds the keys, touching the barrier will burn her skin."

I shake my head remembering the moment when Cory showed me the secret doorway. I look over across the pathway watching my father tread lightly upon the ground searching for my aunt. "But my dad can see the future. Why didn't he warn our family?"

"Ah, yes." Cory sneers as though he's miffed. "The famous question everyone asks themselves. Even Jeoffrey." He stops to look at me. "Because Jeoffrey could see the future, he knew about the fate of his beloved Isalora. He told me once that ever since he got his magical talent at eighteen, he's claimed it to be a curse rather than a gift. But like I mentioned before, his visions are never foolproof."

"So, that's why Moyer hasn't come back to Ladorielle? Because of my mother's spell?"

"One of the theories, yes."

"What's the other?"

He winces. "Because Sarmira has taken hold inside Moyer's body, and if she comes through any portal, it frees Moyer's spirit. Sarmira wouldn't have a body anymore, and she'd lose everything. The empire she's built at Storm River would be gone."

"How do you know so much, Cory?"

"Reading. Lots of reading. Your Great-Grandmother Sara was very good at keeping journals."

I point toward his ankle. "Maybe there is something in her journals about those cuffs, too."

Cory smiles. "Your dad thinks a weaponsmith he knows might be able to remove the cuff around my ankle if we can't get our hands on the keys."

"Really? If we can find those keys, it will free everyone at Storm River from the clutches of Madame Moyer."

"It's going to be next to impossible to find them, though," Cory says.

"Speaking of the impossible, this thick grass, along with the falling snow, is posing a problem in finding my aunt. How are we going to find her in this?"

As though Dad hears my comment from a few feet away, he asks, "Do you think there might be a way to conjure something up that might help us locate her, Cory?"

"Wait, what?" I look at Cory. "Conjure? You mean to create something out of nothing?"

Cory grins at me, then glances at Dad. "I need something of hers to locate her, Jeff. Do you have anything?"

Dad pauses a moment, then shakes his head, continuing to gaze over the land.

Cory looks at me. "I can create things from my head. All I need to do is think of what I want, and if it's something small, it appears in my hand. If it's a large item, it sits next to me."

He laughs, and I know it's because I have a confused expression on my face.

"Do you happen to have any personal items of Fran's with you?"

"Aunt Fran used my hairbrush this morning. Will that work, you think?" I open my pack to pull it out and hand it to him. "She used it a few hours ago. Perhaps there are a couple of strands?"

"It's definitely worth a try." He sifts through the hair, looking for auburn strands, pulling them from the bristles. Then hands me back the brush.

"Why isn't Aunt Fran's hair white like mine?" I ask.

Dad laughs in the distance while still stepping through the grass searching. "That's easy. Hair color. Fran's white hair made her feel old, so she dyed it.

Cory closes his eyes and moves his fingers above his other hand that holds the hairs in his fist. Each fingertip moves like he's playing a musical instrument. The wind kicks up, and I'm not sure if it's him doing it or Mother Nature. Inside Cory's palm, a glow seeps through his clasped fingers. "What are you doing?"

He grins. "Watch." In seconds, a wand appears before me. It hangs in midair, waiting for something or someone to seize it. Light cascades from its wooden features. "Grab it, will you?"

I do as he asks and the glow stops. The wand reminds me of a dowsing rod, except it's in the shape of a Y.

"Let's see if this will work, shall we?" He puts out his hand. "May I have it, please?"

I give him the item and Cory extends his arms as he sways the stick back and forth from side to side. By now, the meadow is nearly covered in snow and the flowers have grown double in size.

We both stand in the falling snow, watching Cory as he allows the stick to lead him to Fran's location. "If Cory could've done this all along, why didn't he do this at Storm River Manor? It would have saved us all a lot of headaches."

Dad grunts. "That's simple. Magic doesn't exist back home like it does here."

Magic. The thought of destroying Sarmira with fire comes to mind. I feel my blood boil in my veins. I'm anxious to get my life back.

Cory glares in my direction. "Wynter, I feel you. Now is not the time. We will defeat *her*. You can be sure of that."

"It's not as easy as you might think," Dad says.

"What?"

He chuckles. "Killing Sarmira."

"How did you—"

Dad doesn't answer me. "Soon, my dear, you will understand."

Knowing he isn't going to give me an answer I ask another question. "How does that thing work anyway?"

"It looks for body heat. Fran hasn't been asleep for long, so I wouldn't imagine the birds have eaten her yet. But with the falling snow, her temperature will drop soon."

"What do you mean by that?"

"Don't worry, she's fine for now. The birds stay in the trees until nightfall. When all is dark the nocturnal birds come out to hunt. They feed on what they caught from the day. Most who wake by nightfall do not survive. By that time, you're awakened by the birds that have already begun feeding on you. A victim can scream, but they cannot move."

"Flesh-eating birds like vultures?"

"Something like that, yes. I suppose you can make that analogy. The difference is these birds will not eat a dead kill. They like the blood to be warm, and they're similar looking to that of ravens, except these killing beasts are songbirds."

"They sound like horrible creatures, Dad."

"Indeed, they are. Their prey is immobilized and cannot move, dying a slow death. Eaten alive, awake, and feeling every peck and rip while the birds tear into their victim's flesh. On rare occasions, some victims escape because they hear the screams of other targets. The key to surviving this horrible death is allowing your body to be awoken on its own, and not by the birds. If you're woken by physical contact, paralysis kicks in. It's essentially how these birds can kill the strongest of beasts. The birds are here to protect the portal from people passing through."

"Dad, that's horrible." I look at him in disgust. "And you know about this because..."

He glances at me with innocent eyes. "Because I raised these birds myself and migrated them here," he says, grinning. "Rather your mother and I did. Before you were born, of course. In fact, I believe your mother was pregnant with you at the time."

I'm about to question him when Cory shouts, "Found her!"

We rush to Cory's side and help him pull away the mound of snow. Frozen green blades cover her sleeping body where she huddles in a fetal position. Her knapsack is still on her back.

"I don't understand why she forgot to put the earplugs in," Dad says, dipping down to unzip her bag.

"Careful, Jeff, you don't want to wake her," Cory warns.

"I know." He searches for a few minutes. "They're not in her pack. I'm going to try for her inside pocket."

"Gently, Jeff. It might be too risky."

"We will never get her out of here if we don't try." Carefully he pushes his hands to the inner pouch of her jacket.

"This is taking forever. Can't you move quicker?" The fear of losing my aunt worries me.

"We have to do this as slowly as possible. One wrong move—"

"And she wakes paralyzed, I know."

Taking what feels like an eternity, Dad finally pulls out the earplugs. "Now for the hard part."

I huff. "If that's the easy part, I'd hate to see what's defined as difficult."

Dad gives a lopsided grin. Holding up the first plug, he places it in Fran's left ear.

I whisper to Cory, "How is he going to get to her other one?"

"Very carefully."

Dad lays down next to Fran and slips an arm under her head, which prompts her to move. She gasps, murmuring something in her sleep.

Dad stops, allowing Aunt Fran to drift back into a lulling slumber, before continuing. Taking advantage of the position he's in, with his arm underneath Fran's neck, he whispers, "Cory, take the other plug and see if you can get her right ear. I'll tilt her head, trying not to wake her."

Cory sighs, and I can tell he's nervous. "If this doesn't work, don't blame me that you killed Isalora's sister."

"It will work. Trust me." Dad brings his free arm up to give Cory the other plug. "Ready on three."

The suspense is killing me. I know one wrong move from either of them and the birds above in the trees will swoop down and eat Fran for dinner.

Dad whispers, "One... Two... Three..." He lifts Fran's head, and Cory races to plug her other ear. It all happens so fast that I didn't even know they started.

"Now, we wait," Dad says as he gingerly slips his arm out from underneath my aunt's neck. "Remember, we must allow her to wake on her own."

By this time the heavy snow has already covered her body once again. "Can't we do something about the snow?" I look over at Cory. "Put a tent over her or something?"

"That's a great idea," Dad says, looking at Cory.

"Already on it." Cory takes his hand and quickly makes a circle with his finger.

Whirling winds form right in front of us, kicking a breeze through my hair. My body gives a slight shiver.

Appearing out of thin air is a large tent, big enough to fit us all. Hovering over Aunt Fran at first, it then drops, and secures to the ground.

"Wow, how did you do that?"

"When you are within the realms of magic, powers that are innate to you, can exist," Cory says with a shrug.

"Right," I say, remembering once again, that the magic here is much stronger than Earth.

Dad unzips the side of the tent. "Let's get out of this wretched weather."

3
New Ability

We follow behind him. I'm immediately mesmerized by what I see. It feels like a fully equipped cabin, with logs surrounding the ceiling, and walls. A wood stove is centered in the middle of the room. Aunt Fran lies on a cot, sleeping, against one wall near the kitchenette, and in front of that is an island countertop with stools. To my surprise, three steaming cups of hot beverages sit atop the counter, waiting to be consumed.

"Is this for real?" I ask, astonished. "How is it possible that we are still in a tent?"

The two of them look at me, smirking. Dad says, "Kind of hard to explain but you can consider it a protection layer."

"Like the cottage at Storm River Manor? A protected shield from Moyer?"

"Something like that, yes. You have much to learn and I don't expect you to understand it all at once. Soon, perhaps, your true memory will come back. Make yourself comfortable." Dad drops his pack next to a chair sitting near the woodstove and takes a seat. A magazine sits on top of an end table, and he begins to read. "Who knows how long it will take before Fran wakes."

Cory places his bag near the entrance of the tent, walks over and grabs all three steaming beverages, and hands me one. "Wynter, have some hot chocolate."

"Thanks." I take a sip. The cocoa soothes my body. "Mmm, this is so good."

He takes a sip of his before setting the third cup near my dad. "Drink up."

Dad nods. "You two should look for firewood before the snow deepens."

I squint. "What about you, Dad?"

"I'll wait here with Fran. Someone should be near when she wakes."

Cory nudges my arm. "Come on, it'll be fun."

We hurry and finish our beverages and head out into the freezing temperatures. "Where are we going to find wood in a snowy, wet mess like this?"

Cory points in the distance but I can't see much beyond my nose from the falling snow. "There's a dead tree we can chop a few feet away."

"Can't you conjure some wood of your own, Cory?" I ask.

"I could, yes, but it won't be as effective as real wood. It would be like burning a newspaper."

"I see."

"When we passed through the portal, you might have noticed a dead tree overhanging at the entrance. It should give us plenty of logs for a little while. We can trim a few branches and chop them up." He conjures a saw and an ax. "Here, take this." He hands me one of the items.

We reach the tree and I notice some of the branches are torn. Not a single leaf appears to sprout life from its limbs, either.

"We are rather lucky this is here, but this one..." Cory lingers. "This one has a history."

"How so?" I ask, following his lead as we cut at the branches.

"It was a story your dad told once. He was being chased by giants. One happened to be a warlock. They are mean creatures and very strong. This particular giant conjured lightning and he blasted this tree, narrowly missing your dad.

"That sounds intense."

Cory hacks down a large branch. "It was years ago."

We finish chopping and gathering the wood and stack it inside the tent. "There we are. A solid pile of it now," he says, sounding pleased. "There is one thing I cannot conjure, though."

"What's that?"

"Fire. Did you happen to bring your lighter?"

I shake my head. "No. What are we to do now? We can ask if my dad has one."

"No need. You already have the flame inside you."

"What do you mean by that, Cory?" I raise an eyebrow.

"You're a healer, which means you can create heat from your hands." He snickers, but I'm sure it's because I'm looking at him like he's crazy.

"Trust me." Cory takes a step toward me. "All it takes is a bit of concentration. You're in the magical world of Ladorielle now where the true magic inside you exists."

"This is nuts, Cory. I don't know how to create fire from nothing. I'm not like you."

"No, you're not. But you're a Deagon, and Deagons can create fire."

"What do you mean by that?"

"I'll leave that for Fran to explain since she can do the same thing."

"Um no, you need to explain."

"I can't, I'm not a healer. Never mind that now. We need to concentrate on not freezing to death."

I want to press the issue, but he's right it's cold, and I want to get back to where it's warm, so I cave to Cory's request.

"Concentrate as though you are beginning to heal someone," he says. "Allow your hands to glow and once you feel the burning, you'll know the fire is ready to shift to your fingers."

Leery of what he says, I ask, "You think this will work?"

He hesitates. "Maybe we should do a practice run first. Blowing up the tent may not be a good idea."

"Excuse me?" Cory's grand plan of making flames spring from my fingers is a preposterous idea. Whoever heard of such a thing, however, we are after all in a magical world and what I've seen with my own eyes so far has me about to believe anything is possible. "What do you mean by 'blow up the tent,' Cory?"

"It's a theory. We don't know how powerful the burning fire that exists inside you really is yet." He paces closer. We are inches away from each other, and I feel his breath escape his parted lips.

He takes my hand and softly rubs the tips of my fingers with his. "Remember how you felt at the cabin when you pushed your spirit out of your body?"

"Yes?"

"It's similar. Close your eyes and visualize your fingers having a flame. Bring that burning feeling to your fingertips."

"You mean like when I get angry or upset? Are you saying my emotions are tied in with my power?"

Cory laughs. "Okay, yes, but leave out your emotions. Adding the anger may fuel more sparks than you would like to."

"Well, that's comforting. Thanks for the tip," I retort.

"It will be fine, I promise."

"Remember what I said about promises," I smirk.

"Trust me, I know you can do this." He takes both his hands, covers them with mine, and gently forces my fingers into a fist. "Allow the boiling of your blood to flow to your fingertips."

I try to concentrate on what he suggests, allowing the burning sensation of my blood to flow freely. "Is this how you're able to conjure the items you create?"

"Yes. Except I don't have the burning sensation like you or Fran. Mine is more like the wisp of lightness flowing about my skin.

"You mean like air?"

"Not exactly. It's more of a feeling in my gut that guides my thoughts. I picture an image in my head, and with the help of the 'wind' as you say, my creation appears in the physical form." He grabs my shoulders, looking into my eyes, smiling. "Now, you try." He steps backward, giving me some room to work.

I focus on the sensation traveling to my fingers, and it makes them tingle. "It burns, Cory."

He nods. "You can do this, Wynter. The first time is always the hardest."

The pain stings like I placed my hand on a hot burner. "Do you feel this agony every time you do this?"

"I've had much more practice than you. Don't lose your concentration. Stay focused, or you'll have to go through the pain all over again."

The burning inside me intensifies, and I let out a scream of anguish before flames erupt from my fingertips. Then the throbbing pressure dissipates as quickly as it came.

"You did it," Cory says, coming to kiss my cheek.

I'm at a loss for words, witnessing each finger flicker with fire. My hand is numb to any pain, although I'm not sure if it's from my new magical power or the falling snow that has kicked up in the wind. This mesmerizing phenomenon has me relishing the moment. If only I had this power on Earth. My mind flies with the possibilities of how I'll destroy Madame Moyer and her malevolent minions.

"Wynter, I still see pictures in your head, remember? Now is not the time to lose focus. You will have your chance, trust me on this. Besides, you can't use your power on Earth like here... yet."

"Yet? What do you mean yet? Are you saying it's possible to have all these powers you have, I mean we..." I look around and think about Fran and Dad. "Us? Cory, you have no idea how badly I want her dead."

"I do know, remember?" He points to his temple to remind me. "So, please, put it away for now and concentrate on the task at hand—waking Fran. She needs warmth."

I work to push the anger aside, pacing as I try to focus. "What's next?" I ask, tilting my head from one side to the other, popping the stress from my neck.

He smiles and nods. I imagine he feels he's gotten through to me, but I still have revenge in my heart. For now, I'll put it away because Cory is right. It won't help Fran.

"With your free hand," he says, "make a circular motion above your fingers, keeping the flames flickering until you see a ball of fire pop in the palm of your other hand."

I do as he instructs and to my disbelief, a ball of fire appears. "That was easy. I don't feel any burning this time." The flares from my fingertips vanish and transfer into one giant sphere of fire.

"That's a good sign. It means your body is warming up to your new abilities. I bet, given the opportunity to project out of your body again, it will also not be as painful either."

Cory takes a couple of steps backward. "Okay, now go near the campfire I built," he says, pointing. A few feet away is a small fire pit. Cory probably made it while I was concentrating, and I didn't notice it until now.

"I want you to throw that fireball in your hand to that fire pit. Don't miss, else you may cause a forest fire." He chortles.

"Sure, no pressure, Cory. Don't miss... easy for you to say. I was on the track team back home, not softball." The thought of missing my target terrifies me. This flame is huge. Although, adding that there is snow falling gives me a slight confidence that perhaps if something disastrous did happen, the blaze won't be too harmful. "Here goes nothing." I fling the scorching ball in the air, and it lands a direct hit on the logs.

Cory applauds. "See, you're a natural."

The bonfire inspires a craving for roasted marshmallows with chocolate and graham crackers, but with the increased intensity of the snow coming down, the fire will be put out soon.

"Let's see how you do inside," Cory says, interrupting my thoughts. He unzips the tent, bringing with him a few logs, and places them next to the wood stove.

"How's she doing?" I ask. She looks as though she hasn't changed her position at all.

"The same," Dad replies. "I heard you outside. Do you think you've mastered the flame-throwing technique yet?"

"She wasn't bad for her first time," Cory says.

"Okay." Dad gets up, putting down his magazine. "Let's see how you do a second time."

Cory conjures newspaper, crumbles it, stuffs it into the stove, and then adds a couple of logs. "This should be easier, only need the use of one finger to spark the paper," he says, smiling.

Dad stands to the side and watches.

I close my eyes and concentrate like before. "The burning is more bearable this time."

"Because you have broken through the barrier already. Like I said outside, the first time is always the hardest," Cory answers. "You're much more in control now. You know what to expect."

My fingertips light up, one by one. Cory takes the remaining newspaper in his hands and engages the flame, tossing it into the stove. "There we go. We should all be warm in no time."

It isn't until now that I realize my whole body is cold, and all three of us can see the breath coming from our mouths as we breathe. As though a light switch turns off my senses, the fire from my fingers goes out, and my hands and face become ice cold. I shiver, and the temperature outside permeates the tent inside.

"Looks like we timed that just right," Cory says.

The wind howls and the cold intensifies. "What's going on?"

"A blizzard, I think," Dad replies.

4
WINTER STORM

ONE SIDE OF THE tent has a zipped-up window, and Cory peers out. "Can't see past a couple of feet. Looks like the campfire you practiced on is buried, too." Cory adds another log to the woodstove. "We should have heat coming soon." He conjures some blankets for each of us, and we huddle around the heater waiting for the warmth to spread throughout the tent.

My teeth chatter a bit, as I struggle to get warm waiting for the stove to heat up. "Dad, What's the story about these birds that you and Isalora migrated to here?"

Dad gives a dubious glare at Cory.

"What? You never elaborated on the story. Cory glances at me and grins. "I'd like to hear, too."

Dad sounds annoyed. "And for good reason." Dad breathes in deep, then lets out a huge sigh. "The story takes a while to tell."

"Look around, Jeff. We're not going anywhere anytime soon," Cory counters.

Dad stares at us for a few minutes as if making a difficult decision. He sits straight up and gets more comfortable in his chair. "I guess now is as good of a time as any." A blue glow in Dad's eyes tells me he's not amused. He clears his throat before starting. "When you're woken by the birds, the poison from the grass mixes with the enchanting spell of the songbirds' melody and it paralyzes you the same as the venom from a snake bite, or in this case, an Iknes Shaw."

Nora comes to mind. "Are the Iknes Shaw from here?"

"Yes, they hide out in the mountain terrain. Their lair rests beneath the surface of Ladorielle."

"You mean there are cities beneath us?" My mind whirls at the thought.

"Many cities, not just Iknes Shaw. It's where the nocturnal creatures thrive. We'll be traveling through their territory later. You may see them hiding among the shadows. They don't usually come out during the day, as the brightness of the sun minimizes their sight. They hide in the shade most of the time." Dad takes another deep breath. "Remember when we reach their territories to stay in the sun and they will not touch you."

"That's a little creepy, Dad."

He huffs. "Not as creepy as some of the other experiences of this world. You must always be alert when traveling through the Ladorielle Territories."

He pauses to get up, and paces to the kitchen, grabbing a cup of coffee from a brewed pot on the counter before turning back to us. "Cup of joe?"

"No, thank you. Maybe more cocoa, though?" I look at Cory.

Cory smiles and clears his throat. "At your service, My Lady."

I elbow him in the gut. "Knock it off."

Cory winces. "Ow." He conjures two more cups that appear next to Dad, and we take our drinks.

We gather around the warm stove again as Dad continues. "The birds, as you were told, are nocturnal. Those caught in the melodies of Songbird Meadow of Unrest are the evening meal. The difference between the Iknes Shaw and these birds is they will eat during the day if they're famished for food."

"Is that what you meant when you said those who awake from the sounds of others' screaming, it's because at that point poison takes effect?"

Dad nods. "Yes."

"So, does that mean by us talking it will help Aunt Fran wake up? I mean, how long will this take?"

"Shouldn't be long. She hasn't been asleep for more than a few minutes."

"A few minutes? I feel like we have been here for hours already."

"Well, of course, you would. You're used to the hours on Earth," Dad says. "Remember, time is different here. You can tell the time by the lining of the planets in the sky." He smirks. "I would show you, but there is a blizzard out there."

"Well, can I take out these earplugs at least? I don't hear the birds through the humming sounds of the wind."

"No. You may not hear them, but they're still out there singing through the storm." Dad sounds annoyed. "Nothing like being trapped in a trap of your own making," he murmurs as he takes a sip of coffee. "Although, I will say the snow is a new experience. The meadow doesn't get cold like this, let alone bring with it blizzard-like conditions. It boggles my mind."

"How so?" Cory asks.

Dad's posture stiffens and he hesitates to reply, "Remember the story I once told you about the giant wizard that chased me to this meadow?"

Cory nods.

"Well, someone else was with me that day." Dad gives an oppressive smile and looks at me. "Your mother."

"Yes, Cory mentioned that."

Dad grunts. "At the time, I had no idea she was pregnant with you. We had discovered the cottage was a portal hub to Ladorielle, and we needed to figure out how to protect it. It was your mother's idea, really."

"My mother's?" I ask, intrigued.

Dad nods. He looks at his hands, as though he's trying to find the words. "There's a small island near an Orc village where the birds flourish."

"Orcs? You mean like what one would read in fantasy books, or play in video games, where they are green in color and hold clubs and smash a person to smithereens?" I laugh.

Dad scowls. "Yes. Something like that. It's not a laughing matter, Wynter."

"You're serious?"

He gives a stern glance. "They're real. Their green skin comes from the elements in the ground where their city resides. It's toxic to most people. It is said that those who enter their outer territory either die from the Orcs or the fumes from the ground. For centuries the Orcs and birds have lived there, and as time went on their DNA learned to adapt to the change."

"Don't tell me you went to this place."

"Naturally, we did, yes. Your mother knew of these birds and had an idea of how to capture a couple of them. All we needed was two. A male and a female. She was convinced if we raised these birds in a new habitat, they would thrive. The ocean is on the other side of these cliffs, and we knew if we could somehow raise them in this meadow, it would essentially protect the portal." He narrows his glowing blue eyes. "That was our main objective."

"But how did you protect yourselves from the toxic grounds near the Orc city or the sounds of the birds?"

"Priestess Nyta helped." He points. "She created those earplugs you're wearing. And she alone is the one who has the formula."

"I would imagine her invention is highly sought after then?"

"I'm not sure anyone knows about it. You can imagine if it were to get into the wrong hands..."

I nod, realizing the delicate information Dad is confessing to.

Dad continues, "We avoided the city and the toxic fumes coming by boat. Wearing our earplugs made it easy." He wrinkles his forehead. "And we had invisibility potions to boot. They didn't see us coming." He takes another swig of coffee and looks over at Cory. "So, fast forward to when we encountered the giant wizard and his army, he didn't anticipate the singing birds in the Songbird Meadow of Unrest." Dad laughs. "Those birds ate well that day."

"Why were they chasing you, Dad?"

Aunt Fran stirs, mumbling something in her sleep, prompting us to bolt from our seats.

"It's about time," Dad says, as he sets down his coffee cup.

FRAN STRETCHES HER ARMS and yawns. It takes a few seconds before she realizes there's an audience. "How long have I been out?"

"Not long," Dad says. "I must say, Fran, you surprise me."

"Why?" She turns her head to look around. "Where are we?"

"Cory conjured a tent to protect us from the storm outside." Dad has a displeased tone. "Tell me, Fran, you of all people should know better."

She glares at him. "What did I do now, Jeff?"

Dad's anger builds. "Forgetting your earplugs, that's what I'm getting at."

Her eyes grow wide and she touches her ears. "I forgot to put them in before passing through the portal... dammit. How could I have been so stupid?" Throwing the blanket off her legs, she stands. "So, what happened? I see we're all snuggled up to a warm stove." She looks over at Cory.

"You didn't miss much," Dad says, turning back to pick up his coffee. "We've been waiting for you to wake." Dad's voice raises. "Apparently, we have loads of time to waste."

Fran rolls her eyes. "So, tell me what I missed." She takes the blanket and covers her shoulders. "And why is it so cold?"

"I told you, there is a storm outside," Dad says.

"It's snow," I mumble.

"How is that possible?" Fran asks. "Snow doesn't come around here."

"Yeah, we know." Dad's face looks irritated. "And we wouldn't be in this position if you hadn't forgotten your earplugs."

Aunt Fran looks stunned. "I–I'm sorry Jeff, what do you want from me?"

"Dad, come on, I'm sure she didn't do it on purpose. Cut her some slack."

"Slack?"

Here they go again. Back at the bickering charade they played at home.

"Jeff, I know you're mad, but yelling at me isn't going to change anything now." She shifts her shoulders back and tilts her neck from side to side, popping her joints. "Question is why? I would never forget to put the earplugs in, Jeff. It shouldn't have come to this. Something is wrong."

"I know. It has me puzzled, too," Dad agrees. "We've spent the last hour waiting for you to wake up."

"Thirty minutes maybe," Cory corrects.

"Clearly it hadn't been thirty minutes," I say on the inside. I bust in at Dad and Fran. "Why can't you two play nice? All my life, I have seen you two argue, scream, and yell at each other. Just once, I would like to see you get along."

All three of them look at each other, surprised. Cory appears uncomfortable. I know that feeling, too, when you witness a family quarrel right in front of you and are powerless to do anything.

"You're right Wynter," Fran says. "We have bigger fish to fry." She glances at Cory. "Thank you for finding me. I owe you one."

Dad stays quiet.

Fran takes a deep breath. "Come on. We haven't time to waste."

"And where are we going to go?" Dad argues. "I'd like to see you try and get through this storm." He points to the window.

"Oh, it can't be that bad." She opens the entry to show the snow has packed us in.

Fran turns around, glaring at Dad. "Well, we could surely use a Druid about now, couldn't we?"

"Ya think?" he says sarcastically.

"Nice. More snide comments. Some things never change," she shoots back.

Dad's eyes glow bright, and black veins appear beneath his skin, like Cory when he showed me his true form back at the manor. A growl erupts from his throat.

"You want to start that here? Now? Really, Jeff, grow up!" Aunt Fran isn't afraid of Dad's outburst.

Her words seem to cut his emotions like a knife because before I have time to react, Cory knocks Dad off his feet. "Not now!" A blue glow comes from Cory's eyes, and he, too, begins to change but not completely. Dad becomes pacified. His dazed features become apparent that Cory has somehow subdued my father from transforming into the creature I've been warned about that also runs through my veins. It's at this moment that I fully realize how powerful Cory is. Is this what the letter meant—that the three are to be one? Is this why Cole must be rescued from the clutches of Madame Moyer? Because the three of us standing together can overthrow *her* power?

I glance back at Fran. Her back is pressed against the wall, and her features have changed, too. Her skin is no longer smooth, but scaly like when Nora became angry, that day in the hall by the kitchen. Is Aunt Fran an Iknes Shaw? The difference is, Nora's were a golden yellow and in the shape of a lizard, but Aunt Fran's... are fiery red with a hint of orange. Like a bright flame of fire.

"Aunt Fran!" I shout, hoping to distract whatever it is she's about to do.

Her eyes go back to emerald, and her skin again resembles human flesh. "Wynter, I'm sorry. I've allowed my emotions to cloud my judgment. Please forgive me."

"Forgive you? What was that, Aunt Fran?" I turn around to stare at Dad. "And you... Dad, are you..." It takes all my will to not utter the words, but Dad answers me, as though he reads my mind like Cory would with seeing pictures.

"Yes. I am."

"But how? I don't understand. When were you going to tell me?"

"I tried. Believe me, I tried."

"How am I not a Nytemire?" I ask.

"We don't know," Fran interrupts. "You're definitely a carrier, though. You possess speed, hearing, and sight. But that's the only thing that has developed."

I look at Fran. "And what about you?"

"A Nytemire?" she says. "Dear heavens, no. Are you kidding me?"

Dad gets up from the ground and brushes himself off. "You were born a Storm, with Nytemire blood, like Cory, Cole, and many of the others, but unlike the rest of them, you don't seem to have the yearning to kill for food." He pauses. "At least not yet."

"Is that what you want, Dad? To kill?"

He doesn't need to answer me. His silence is loud and clear.

5

FIRE AND ICE

"WYNTER'S RIGHT. WE NEED food, or else we will kill each other," Cory says. "It's in our nature to hunt."

"Cannibalism doesn't sound appetizing, Cory. Besides, can't you conjure our food?" I ask.

"That's not what I mean. We're all agitated and hungry."

Something tells me it isn't the consumption of food, but rather Cory's need for blood that's rising. "What do you mean by that?"

I can tell Cory doesn't want to answer.

"Go on," Dad encourages, "she might as well know. It's not going to harm her memories."

"My memories?"

Fran walks to the kitchen, grabs herself a mug and pours a cup of coffee. "I'm glad you boys are about to tell this story and not me."

The tension in the room thickens. Patience isn't my strong suit, but I keep my emotions in check for now.

"Remember at the manor when you heard the screams of that woman behind the door, asking to be let out?" Cory asks. "Nora caught you, as I recall, and you were directed to the bathroom."

I nod. "Yes, I remember, but how do you know that?"

"We Nytemires—rather Shadow Walkers—communicate and report to Moyer. We all knew that day."

I hesitate, and then ask, “What happened to the girl?”

“One of the advantages Moyer has when bringing homeless girls to the manor is once she breeds them for their purpose, they no longer hold any value,” Dad explains.

“Don’t tell me. You shelf them as food, don’t you.” I glance at Fran taking a sip of coffee, and she avoids my eye contact. Dad looks down at his feet.

Cory nods. “We’re all predators to humans. I hate to admit it, but they are quite tasty. I made a choice long ago that I wouldn’t kill people. It wasn’t easy. I had to fight the urge. A good comparison I suppose would be the same craving one would get with cocaine. Human blood has a different taste than any other species. It’s like a drug. Once we taste, we can’t stop and we want more. With each kill, we become stronger. A Nytemire has an advantage over a vampire. While we crave human blood, like the vampire, we also crave the essence. Their soul. When we take the life of another, we also gain their talents, abilities, and their knowledge. We have a choice, either their blood or their essence. We can’t have both with one body.”

“That’s what Sarmira did to Moyer, isn’t it? Gained Moyer’s talents and abilities?”

“Yes, except rather than killing her, she possessed her body. Moyer was an alchemist. When Sarmira discovered what she could do, it set her plans in motion,” Fran adds. “Of course, Moyer has her secrets, and she was much more than a scientist.

I reflect on the past, remembering the car accident. “I remember there being an explosion.” I glance at Aunt Fran. “How were you able to escape?”

“That’s a little more difficult to explain.” She takes a sip of coffee.

“I’m sure I can keep up.”

She pulls away from the kitchen and comes to a comfortable place to sit down.

I don’t wait for her to answer me and push for more questions. “You have scales and I saw your skin transform moments ago. Are you like Nora? When you were poisoned, it changed you, didn’t it?”

“No. It’s not what you think at all. In fact, it couldn’t be further from the truth.”

I take in a deep breath coming to sit next to her. "Then what is it?" I can tell she doesn't want to answer me.

She stares over to Cory, then Dad, and both nod for her to go on. "I can't be destroyed by fire, nor you for that matter. At least, that's our theory." She glances back up at Dad.

"A theory?" I follow Aunt Fran's gaze to Dad and Cory. "The assumption you're all making on my life is based on a theory?" I stand in frustration.

Dad isn't fazed by my outburst, but Cory has a look of confusion. "I don't understand, Fran," Cory says. "What do you mean in theory? I thought you said—"

"I know what I said!" she shouts. She takes another sip of coffee as though it will stop the impeding confessions.

"What exactly happened with that car accident?" I ask.

Cory folds his arms, staring at my aunt. I can tell he is just as curious as me. On the other hand, Dad won't even look at me.

"After the explosion, I got up and walked away, as you know." She half smiles, setting her cup down.

"You just got up and walked away?" I ask. "As if nothing happened?"

"Please, all of you sit—"

I huff. "I'll stand, thanks." I cross my arms.

Dad lets out a huge sigh, grabs his cup, and sits back down in his chair. He takes the magazine he had before and begins reading. Crossing his legs, he looks up. "What?" Noticing he has an audience watching his every move, he adds, "I know this story already."

"Yeah, Dad, of course, you do. You were there! I hate this. You two have always left me in the dark, so why should this be any different?"

Cory takes my hand, encouraging me to sit next to him on the floor. I can feel his soothing aura try and calm my nerves. "We haven't heard the story, Fran. It would be a pleasure to listen. Besides, it's been haunting Wynter for a long time."

Dad says, "I already told this story back at the cottage, Wynter knows all about how we escaped."

"Yes, your version, Jeff," Fran snaps back.

As much as I am angry with them, I still want the untold version, so I give in to my raging emotions and say, "Go on, Aunt Fran, I'm ready to listen to your side of the story."

"Well, you're a Deagon. Legend says the family comes from a long line trailing back to dragons. Of course, nobody ever took the story seriously until—"

"Until what?" I ask.

"Until the day Sarmira attacked the Storm family. You remember the dream, right?"

"You mean the day you fell ill and the Storm family were ported to Earth to escape?"

"Yes, that's right. Your mother was still a baby. As you have been told before, the magic here is more relevant than on Earth. So, things are different. All species possess inner magic."

"You mean like gifts or a talent, yes I'm beginning to understand that." I look over at Cory, remembering the lesson he taught me earlier.

Aunt Fran nods. "So, imagine, if you will, my healing ability."

"Yes. You cut yourself right in front of me in the kitchen, and it healed before my eyes. Not exactly something I was expecting that day."

"Well..." She clears her throat. "It is said that the Deagon line holds power and magical abilities, and no matter where you are in this grand universe, a Deagon will possess those abilities. It's a matter of learning how to control it."

"Is that how you're able to have such unbelievable gifts on Earth?"

"Yes, and it's also why you do, too," she says.

"Me?" The thought that I have huge magical powers descended from dragons has me seriously questioning whether I'm still dreaming. If it wasn't for the fact that I witnessed with my own eyes flames shooting from my fingers earlier, I think I might have called Aunt Fran a fabulous storyteller.

"This must be how you were able to heal me that day in the classroom," Cory says.

Cory's comment prompts me to question more. "Are you saying you can form fireballs, too, Aunt Fran?"

"The Deagons hold different talents when it comes to fire. If you can form balls of fire with your hands, Wynter, then it appears you have taken after your Great Aunt Isobel. My gift is a little more gruesome." She pauses, as though she is trying to find the right words. "My talents are of the mind, whereas yours are more physical. You can project and heal others. I cannot do that. The gift you received at eighteen was to see the undead and be able to project out of your body. Mine is to see the future, or rather the present as it is happening. To be able to foresee someone coming. Matching with the fire magic that derives from the Deagon family line, I can get inside the mind of another and burn them from the inside out. It takes concentration, though, and it's almost impossible if I'm being chased. I'm sure if Sarmira had the chance to get her hands on me, she would have loved using my abilities for her gain."

I'm taken aback. "You mean, literally—"

"Burn a person's inner flesh. Yes," she says.

"Um, okay. Remind me never to tick you off."

Dad chuckles as he turns a page in his magazine.

"I'm stunned Moyer never captured you," I say. "So, if we have this ability, why can't we melt our way through the snow outside?"

All three of them glance at me and then at each other, appearing stunned.

"That's a brilliant idea, my dear niece. Why didn't I think of that?" She pauses, looking up at my dad. "Which reminds me. How much more daylight do we have, anyway?"

He looks at his watch. "About four hours."

"Hmm, we won't make it to Geneviève's Ranch before dark if we wait too much longer."

"No, we won't." He grimaces. "Traveling out of the meadow takes a few hours of walking."

"Who's Geneviève?" I ask.

"The Druid that ported us to safety all those years ago," Aunt Fran says.

"You mean she's still alive?"

"Of course, she is." My aunt smiles.

I look over at the doorway. "What about the compact snow?"

"We'll do as you suggested and melt it." She smiles holding out her palms. "With our hands." She gets up and walks to the door and unzips the tent entry. The doorway looks like an icy snowbank.

It reminds me of when Dad would take us skiing in the mountains of Washington State, and the highways would have walls of snow on either side of the road. "How are we going to do this?" I ask, feeling unsure of my own abilities.

"If we camp in for the night, we are vulnerable to the birds outside when they come in the evening to feed. We have to at least try," Cory answers.

"I haven't had much practice. What if the place explodes because of my unpredictability with learning magic?"

Cory barely touches the tips of my fingers with his. "It's worth a shot, right? Besides, we will all be with you." He looks over at Aunt Fran.

She nods. "You got this."

"I suppose I can try."

"No, we should wait," Dad says. "Until the wind and snow stops."

"If we wait until the storm lets up and assess our circumstances, it might be too late," Fran argues.

"Too late?" My heart pounds thinking about what they are referring to. Does she mean the birds can reach us?

Concern glazes Dad's face and he takes a deep breath. "I hate to admit this, but I think Fran is right. If we stay here through the night, we may risk the birds getting inside."

"Getting inside?" I ask in apprehension. "Can the birds penetrate this tent?"

"Through the flue." Dad points.

"How is it, that our tent isn't getting crushed right now?" I ask.

"Simple," Dad says, "this tent, although it appears to be flimsy from the outside, is as sturdy as any house you would see in the mountains. Cory's conjuring items disappear after twenty-four hours."

"And yet you're claiming the birds will be able to get in after nightfall?" I ask.

"It's my theory, yes." He glares at the stovepipe.

"Our hands can melt the snow," Fran answers. "At least in theory." She tests her assumptions and presses her hand against the wall of snow embedded around the entryway. Water begins to drip down, and Aunt Fran releases her hand. An impression is left behind. "See, it's working." She looks at me, adding, "With both of us doing this, it might get us out of here."

I nod. "Okay. Let's do this."

Fran's eyes light up. "Listen." She puts a finger to her lips. "Do you hear that?"

Silence ensues as we all heed her request. "Hear what?"

"Precisely. With supersonic ears, you all should hear the 'nothing' going on outside. I know, I for one, don't hear the whistling anymore."

Dad sits up in the chair. "She's right. Perhaps the storm has let up. We might very well be in the eye of it right now."

"How long do you suppose we have before the storm begins again?" Cory asks.

"I don't know," Dad answers. "Maybe twenty minutes tops."

"Guess we better get going then," I say.

Dad puts on his pack and throws me mine. I follow his lead, as do the others. "We need to get out of this meadow before the storm hits again."

Cory conjures up some knitted hats. "We are going to need to stay somewhat warm, aren't we?" He hands me a beanie, smiling. "It will help keep your body toasty while melting the snow, too."

Fran proceeds to hold her hands out again as she presses against the cold icy snow. It begins to melt, making a wet pool around our feet. I assist her, slowly working our way out of the makeshift igloo.

6

ESCAPE FROM FROZEN MEADOW

WE SLOWLY MELT OUR way out of the meadow, leaving behind a trail. In the trees, the deadly birds caw. "They know we're on the move, don't they?"

"You mean the songbirds?" Cory questions. "I suppose, but they don't normally attack while you're awake."

"Unless you're in a closed tent surrounded by snow," I remark.

"We didn't want to take any chances," Dad says.

Fran and I continue to melt away the snow. We're making progress because the farther we go the less deep the snow becomes.

"Where are we headed after we get out of this?" I ask.

"To Geneviève's Ranch," Fran answers. "We were supposed to reach her place before dusk."

"Why is that?"

"It's when nocturnal predators come out to play," Cory teases.

"Not funny, Cory." I nudge his gut with my elbow again.

"Ow, you have some seriously pointed joints, you know that?"

"Yeah, well, now is not the time for jokes. These birds creep me out. I want to get out of the meadow as soon as possible."

"Well, if that's all it takes to freak you out, I would hate for you to meet the other bizarre creatures ahead."

"Lovely," I say, concentrating on the task at hand. Curiosity gets the better of me of course and I ask, "What other creatures are there anyway?"

"Shadow Walkers for one." He grins.

I stop what I'm doing and look at him. "Of course there are."

Fran smirks and melts more snow.

Dad presses, "C'mon, let's talk as we go. Darkness approaches."

Getting back to thawing the snow, I ask, "Why are they here, anyway? I thought they were the creation of Moyer?"

"They are sort of. Here, they have developed their own coven. Vampires and Shadow Walkers exist together. During the last Super Blue Blood Moon, they used the opportunity to slip away through the eclipse, living here." He pauses. "Don't worry, you're safe. Besides, they prefer species like Fran." He grins.

"Shut your mouth, Cory. Now isn't a good time for taunting," Aunt Fran spouts back.

"I'm beginning to get the feeling there are some major grudges between you three," I say.

Dad huffs behind us. "Just the three of us?"

"What's that supposed to mean, Dad?"

"It's a long story going back centuries. Moyer helped it along a little bit with her… creation," he answers.

A low growl comes from Cory. "Can we please change the subject?"

I see grass in the distance. "Hey look, the snow is slowly receding," I interrupt, hoping it would smooth out the conversation at hand.

"Won't be long now before we're out of this mess," Dad says.

As we make our way out of the meadow, Dad and Aunt Fran walk a few feet ahead of us before I ask Cory, "So, what was that all about back there? I mean, there's some serious hostility between you three. I always thought you and my dad got along."

"We do. It's not your dad. It's—" He glances away from me, avoiding eye contact. "Fran."

"What do you mean?"

"It's not my business to say." He takes both my hands, placing them near his lips. "I will admit this, though. There will never be another you to take your place, should you—" He struggles to say the words.

I pull my hands away. "Die?" I finish. The silence is deafening. "Is that what you think is going to happen? Did my dad see something and you haven't told me?"

"No. No... no. Nothing like that. But when Isalora died, your dad moved on."

The snow behind us looks like it's slowly melting away, and the warm eye of the sun beats down. I walk beside Cory through the woods, saying, "I see. And Fran is angry with him."

"It appears that way. Although she has never come out and admitted it. We better keep up with them. Not the best idea to be out here alone this far apart," Cory adds, and we quickly catch up to Dad and Aunt Fran.

On either side of the trail, as we're walking, I notice palm trees lining the path. Beautiful pink and red flowers grow around the base of each trunk, sprouting soft-looking fur-like bristles from the center, resembling a lily. Distracted by its beauty, I reach down to touch one. "What a beautiful flower."

"Wynter no! Never touch the Perpalily. It will kill you within minutes. Seconds, even."

I retract my hand and fold my arms. My mind races, thinking what a wondrously beautiful but deadly place my family has brought me to. "Sorry."

Cory tilts his head. "Don't be sorry, just be careful, okay? You will discover many new things here, I suppose. Perhaps it's best not to touch anything for now... at least until you gain your full memory back."

"Singing birds that put you to sleep and then eat you, and now deadly flowers that kill with one touch. What's next, Cory?"

"You haven't seen anything yet," he says. "Your memory, I'm sure, will come back to you soon."

"And going to this place called Geneviève's Ranch has something to do with that, do you think—my memory, that is?"

"Perhaps, but only time can help with that."

"That's what Isalora said." I look up to the sky to see the two moons appear to be closer and begin to cut off some light.

"The planet is losing sunlight. The closer they move together, the closer nightfall approaches. See how they seem to be touching? Similar to an eclipse like what you're familiar with, except, this is the eclipse of the moons, and it happens every day. It tells us when the evening is near, like what your dad mentioned earlier. In the morning, you will not see the moons at all. They rotate around our planets."

"That's quite fascinating, Cory. And the moons cover the eye?"

He nods. "Our seasons are different, too, and the planet's rotation is very slow. There's a big city on the other side of this continent that has a gate, opening to the two worlds where people can travel back and forth between planets."

We leave any remnants of frozen winter behind us as the winds seem to kick up and graze my cheeks. A cold chill travels to my bones. "Is it always so cold here?"

"No. This is the first time I've seen snow in these parts."

"Come on, you guys, keep up," Dad calls. "We need to get out of the meadow and through the woods quickly. The moons will join soon."

"The storm seems to have disappeared, too. Weird," I say.

"I agree, but your dad is right, nightfall is our next threat. We need to keep up with them."

We walk close behind Dad and Aunt Fran through the woods. "I must admit having the earplugs in, it doesn't make it difficult to hear you speak. How is it possible that I can still hear you through the singing birds?"

"When Nyta made these earplugs for Jeoffrey and Isalora, she made them with clear intentions: to keep out the singing. Once the plugs settle into the ear, little feelers sprout from the nub and travel near the eardrum. Similar to what you might be familiar with as a hearing aid, except maybe the feelers part." He grins.

I trace the plug with my fingers and travel through the contours of its design. "Is that why it connects to this tube looping around my ear to the earpiece?"

"Yes. Not only to secure it but to screen out the music from the birds. It's the sensory filter." He pulls at my hand. "Come on, we better catch up. They are getting too far ahead again."

Soon we come to a hillside cliff. A huge cavern skates across what seems like miles to the opposite side of the canyon. There's a sizeable mountainous rock that shows an enormous opening to a dark cave beyond it.

A loud screech grabs my attention, and I look up to see large birds circling like scavengers.

"What are they doing?" I ask. "They are so big I almost swear they're condors."

He laughs. "Oh, they aren't birds. They're drakes, and they're searching for food. They swarm in flocks when there is a fresh kill. There must be a very large carcass in the cavern below."

"Drakes?"

"Yes, like dragons, but smaller, less sensible. One might refer to them as a cousin. They're scavengers. You never want to get too close to them, either. They can evoke a stun that knocks you back, immobilizing you, giving them the opportunity to charcoal you from their breathing flames."

"They sound pretty deadly," I say.

"Naw, they're harmless, really. They won't attack unless you attack them first or come upon their nest." He gestures with his hand, pointing in the direction of a trail leading down toward the cliff. "We better keep moving or we will lose them."

The path turns to the right, and we follow down to a carved nook in the side of the cavern.

We catch up to them as Aunt Fran climbs onto a large boulder. "This should be a safe spot to rest," she says.

I climb it too and sit next to her. The sounds of the birds are gone, and all I hear now is the drip of water, and periodic squawks coming from the beasts flying above. This brief rest allows me to soak in the sights of the lands. We're on the edge of a deep cavern and when I dip my head a bit to look, I feel dizzy. A fear of heights is something I don't think I'll ever overcome. I clear my throat and look away. Removing the earplugs, I have the opportunity to hear nature and it prompts me to ask, "So how is it that none of you remembered to warn me about the deadly songbirds?"

Fran has a smirk on her face and Dad smiles. Cory gives me a shy glance and Dad says, "It's my fault. I forgot to mention it to you. We all innately know about the meadow."

I glare. "It would have been nice to have some type of warning."

Dad steals a glance toward Fran.

I make eye contact with her, too. "How is it one forgets to put in their earplugs, if you, 'innately know,' already?"

Dad raises a brow and pulls off his pack, setting it next to the large rock, and sits. "Yeah, I too would like to know that answer."

Cory stands near the ledge looking down the cavern. "I would have to agree," he says, sounding a bit distracted by what he sees below. "If I knew I was about to enter a place that would put me to sleep until death came calling, I would make sure to be prepared." Cory turns around, takes his pack off, and sits near the ledge.

Aunt Fran rolls her eyes, as if to brush aside all our comments, and pulls a small snack from her coat pocket. "I don't know."

"Don't brush this off, Fran," Dad adds. "I mean, you were almost killed because you didn't take the time to remember what area we were entering."

"Come on, it was an honest mistake. And I didn't die. You found me. Okay? Geez, you guys. You're treating me like a five-year-old." She tears into her jerky, looking the other way. "It's not that big of a deal."

"I guess what we are all wondering is how could you forget something like that," Cory states.

She glances back at us. "I'm bothered by it, too. And honestly, I don't have an answer for any of you." She looks as though she's worried like the rest of us.

Had someone, or something, gotten to her? Another memory stamp placed upon her maybe. Why didn't she put the earplugs in? It was a rookie move and we all knew it.

7
THE BEAST WITHIN

AFTER A LONG SILENCE, I ask, "So, now what?"

"We sit and rest up a bit," Dad says, looking at his watch. "According to the time, we have a little over an hour before it's nightfall. Geneviève's Ranch is just beyond the mountains, and it looks like we won't make it. Down below this ravine is the path leading there." He adds, "We'll make camp at the bottom of the canyon. Being caught out after dark will leave us all vulnerable."

"Wait, I thought we're out of danger now. We're past the meadow."

"My dear, heavens no," Fran interjects. "There's danger everywhere, like wolves, Shadow Walkers, and Iknes Shaw. You mustn't ever let your guard down out here in the wilderness."

Realizing I still have my pack on my back, I unlatch it and search for a snack for myself. "This world is so different compared to the world I know."

"Your memory will come soon." Fran smiles, taking another bite of jerky.

I pull an apple from my lunch bag Isalora packed. "When?" I ask as I take a bite.

Fran smiles. "It will take time, my dear."

"That's all you and Dad ever say. My personal favorite— 'I'll explain later'—as if that's supposed to make it any better." I'm annoyed with Dad and Fran.

"We can't rush it. Helping you along, yes, perhaps that will work, but you, and you alone, are the one who will be able to fully allow yourself to remember everything. You might experience déjà vu. Just like the way the birds put you to sleep, you too, must wake on your own. Else your memories will be sealed forever," Fran says.

The thought of going to sleep and possibly never waking up disturbs me, just like not ever recovering my memories. I know they thought what they were doing was to protect me, but it's still frustrating. It makes me not trust any of them, including Cory. Although, at least Cory will answer questions if I ask him. "What else are you hiding from me?"

All three of them look at each other as though trying to figure out which one of them will say what's on their mind.

"See, this is what I mean." I'm determined to get to the bottom of this. "I get the feeling there is a deeper, darker secret than the mere defeat of Sarmira, so what is it?"

Fran takes in a deep breath. "The night you were born your mother placed a memory stamp on you. It wasn't me who placed the first one."

"The first one? You mean I have more than one memory stamp?"

Fran puts her finger up. "Let me finish, my dear niece. My goodness, you really must work on your patience, too. You have an uncanny habit of interrupting."

Cory snickers, and this time instead of jabbing him with my elbow, I throw at him, my half-eaten apple.

"Hey, now, let's not waste food, shall we?" he teases.

Fran eyes us both, raising a brow, proving her point. "Look who's acting like children, now?"

"Sorry, Aunt Fran, please continue," I say, glaring at Cory.

Fran straightens her posture and resumes her tale. "Your mother bought us time to keep you safe. That night, we fled Storm River Manor and met with Geneviève down by the river."

"You mean near the cottage, right?" I ask.

Fran nods. "We knew if we could get to her in time, she could port us out of harm's way."

"So, it's true. I was born on Earth at the manor."

"Yes. And probably the reason why you hold some sort of inner powers. We think there's a connection to your healing abilities and the gift of sight."

"What do you mean by the gift of sight?"

"I mean, although you have the genetic makeup of someone from Ladorielle, you've somehow pulled much more magic than any of us."

"Is that a bad thing?"

"No. But it's a complicated thing. It means without that necklace you're more vulnerable than anyone else."

"Or more powerful," Dad says.

Fran glares at Dad, adding, "The memory stamp lasted for a while but as you got older, it became easier for your thoughts to override the spell. Your dad and I knew that soon you would remember, and there would be nothing we could do to stop that."

"Hang on a second. How can a newborn remember anything? I mean, what's the purpose of this so-called stamp on a baby?"

Fran glances at Dad, and he nods at her to go on.

"This whole world you see before you is within your mind, your true memories. It already exists; you just don't have the ability to remember that part yet. And we must be careful not to trigger your memories too soon. Otherwise, your memories will never return. The memories you have of Florida, the beach, that day we fled are a mirage. That part is an illusion, sort of like a dream you remember. Florida is a memory that never existed—the place that is. The people you saw on the other hand were very much real. You were on Ladorielle the whole time. Something I left out while explaining the Deagon side of the family is that we have the ability to have memories from birth."

It takes me a minute to absorb all of what she's saying. My thoughts jumble as she speaks, and at times I'm not sure I'm listening.

"The escape from Florida to Washington State, are you saying I dreamt it?"

"Sort of? I mean— not exactly—it's hard to explain. To you, it was as real as any other memory," she says. "Like a memory of a childhood moment."

"Like when I broke my arm and Dad took me to the doctor's?"

"You went to the doctor's office, yes, and broke your arm, true, but it all happened here on Ladorielle. The faces you saw were real people to you—human looking, but they were the people of Ladorielle, with pointed ears, taller bodies—features and traits unlike humans."

"Was Washington State a mask as well?"

"No. You were really there." Aunt Fran looks at Dad. "We all were really there. We had to make you think we fled Florida."

"So, a magic memory stamp?"

Aunt Fran tilts her head as though to nod, saying, "The type of magic that can withstand Earth's elements, yes. On Ladorielle Memory stamps wear off after a couple of months—"

"But on Earth?" I interrupt.

"Up to a decade."

"When did you know it was wearing off?"

"Your sophomore year."

I glance at Cory. "Where are you in all of this?" I ask.

"I'm... well... around. Moyer has a way of influencing the people she wants. She managed to use us to her advantage in a way so convincing we caved to her doing." He looks at Dad. "Until—"

I finish his sentence, "Until Dad handed you the watches."

"Yes," Cory says, "and after I put the watch on, the real memories came back, and the memory stamp Moyer placed, faded. The details of what she compelled me to do remained, though. Etched in my brain forever." Cory's expression fades and I can see the pain in his eyes. "She had me doing things that if you found out the truth, you may never see me in the same light again."

"I'm sorry you had to go through that, Cory." My heart aches at the thought of what he's had to endure all these years under her thumb.

"I imagine Cole will have the same experience if we ever rescue him from her grasp."

"We will, Cory. I won't stop until my entire family is liberated. I promise."

Fran laughs. "I like your passion, Wynter, but I don't think you realize what we're up against."

"Oh, I'm beginning to get the hint."

Aunt Fran stiffens, takes in a deep breath, and says, "It's going to be a hard undertaking, but together I believe we can do this." She bites into the last of her jerky and chews. I can tell she is holding back more information.

"Aunt Fran?"

"Like I mentioned earlier, Wynter, some of your memories were illusions mixed in with reality. The memory stamp tricks your mind into thinking about what is real and what is not. Fleeing Florida in your mind was real, but we were really escaping from one kingdom to another."

"And that's why we fled to Washington?"

"Yes, your father has a portal hub there in the mountains."

"I was hoping to throw Moyer's men off our tail, the day of the accident." Dad grunts. "We all know how that turned out."

"Moyer didn't count on us coming back though, Jeff. Now we need to refocus our energies on the present. Getting our family free."

Memories of the car crash surface. "So, that's how she found us, isn't it? My necklace fell off, landing at the bottom of the pool at school, and I didn't put it back on for the remainder of the day."

"Yes." Dad looks at me with regret. "I should have been more forthcoming with you. "

"I remember that day clear as if it was hours ago," Cory says. "Moyer ranted about the castle, calling all Shadow Walkers forward, tasking us in preparation. She had a handle on a plan, and she didn't falter from it."

"I get it now." I look at Dad. "The day we left home you mentioned we were headed to a cabin, but that's where there is another portal. Am I right?"

He nods. "I built a log cabin around it so it didn't look conspicuous."

"Conspicuous? You make it sound like anyone can see it."

"Well, yes, sort of. I mean, if one were to stumble upon it, they will see a pedestal fixated to the ground, with a book lying on top, closed. Nobody can open the book or remove the stand because it's held by Ladorielle magic, but it will stick out like a sore thumb should someone come across its path."

"I'm going to guess that the two cottages are connected?" I ask.

"Yes," Dad replies. "It's how I was able to travel avoiding Moyer's detection. To my knowledge, she still doesn't know that the cabin exists."

His confession has me thinking of the fateful day I was kidnapped. "You were never going to fly in the stormy conditions the day they came for us, were you?"

Dad shakes his head, appearing dazed, as though he's at a loss for words.

"That explains the sudden change of mind," I say aloud.

"When I realized you were not wearing your necklace, I knew then that I'd have to take both you and Aunt Fran with me."

I feel Cory reading my thoughts again, but he stays silent.

I'm about to hurl the loudest scream of all time, because all this information is beginning to frustrate me, when Dad adds, "Remember when Fran and I told you we can see the future?"

"Yes, go on."

"Well, I saw your death. It wasn't a pleasant premonition, and I have the unfortunate gift of seeing Moyer defeat the entire Storm bloodline. The Super Blue Blood Moon approached our planet, as predicted, and the battle of the Underworld won."

"So, you're saying... staying with us and going forward knowing I would be kidnapped and putting me through the awful things I was forced to endure, was the only option? I cannot believe what I'm hearing." I don't know whether to cry, scream, or hit my father. I feel my blood boil beneath my skin. My mind clouds with irrationality, and I try to stay composed. I fight the urge to be angry, knowing, in my head—the Wynter part of me, the compassionate side—tries to break through with understanding, but this beast of rage that I feel, wants to take control and overpower my sense of logic. "What is happening to me?" My mind becomes hazy.

"Now perhaps was not the right time to tell her," Cory says to Dad.

I know what Cory means because I know he can feel the rage boiling inside me. The power I feel grows stronger and my mind races with shooting pain piercing behind my eyes. It changes my vision. Cory looks different from Dad, too. There's a sudden surge of emotions that penetrate my psyche and both of them appear as the enemy. "Did you know too, Cory?" I hiss.

This isn't like me. I can't seem to fight the rage. Steam begins to escape through my skin, yet I don't feel any burning. My skin color begins to turn gray, like I've seen with Cole, Cory, and Dad. No longer do I see the forms of people before me but animals of prey. I desperately want to burn them alive. Eat them. Devour them to the bone. I'm hungry and I need food.

"Stop her, Cory!" Aunt Fran screams, in a voice that doesn't sound like her.

My mind shifts between my human self and the beast within. My desire to kill them increases with each agonizing breath I take. I pounce at my first victim.

Someone screams. "Cory, watch out!"

My prey gets away, but not for long. A sensation of power fills my veins increasing the adrenaline. I jump at my moving target again and miss. The Wynter part of me is numb, and I feel like I can't stop the beast from consuming me completely—it's as though this being has incinerated my soul with utter hate. The sensation of flames burns me from the inside out and I find it intoxicating. Oh, the yearning I feel for this innocent soul's blood, I want him. My next pounce lands a direct hit, and I slice through his tender skin. The smell of his blood fills my nostrils with soothing gratification to devour him. The urge to kill him is almost complete. The Wynter side of me still fights the heat, the rage but I can't help it I must have him.

"Do it now!" I hear her say.

That directs my attention to her. "Do you really want to cross me?" I growl. "No matter, I can consume you, too."

A splash of water drenches my head. Fear clouds my senses, coolness spreads throughout my body, and the burning that's enveloped my flesh begins to dissipate. My insides freeze like ice as though I've gone from one extreme to another in temperature. Again, my body goes numb, but this time it's the opposite and I feel frozen. Sweat beads across my forehead, and my hair is wet, almost like icicles. Now cold, I shiver from head to toe while my stomach churns with pitted agony.

"My throat is dry," I say. "I need water, please."

The image I see before me is a man I don't recognize, and he comes forward to brace my back. His sweet smell is familiar, and his touch is gentle, but firm, as his hands hold my head up. Another person gives me something liquid, and it trickles down my throat. It burns as it goes down. The taste is sour, and I want to spit it out but decide against it because it soothes my flesh. "What was that?"

"Which part? The water you drank, or the beast that tried to consume you?" The voice that is talking is unfamiliar.

Still dazed, and not exactly sure what has happened, I ask, "Who are you?"

"What do you mean, who am I?" he says. "Wynter it's me, Cory."

"She's on the cusp of turning," another man says.

I look up at the second stranger, not able to identify any of his features, and ask again, "Who are you people?"

"I'm your dad, sweetheart. Fran's here, too." He points. Aunt Fran gives a small wave and smiles.

"Cory," Dad asks, "can you calm her?"

"I *am* calming her. She is getting much stronger, Jeff," he snaps.

I press my hand against the back of my head and feel a lump. "Ow."

"Sorry about that," Cory says.

The memories of what Dad confessed moments ago are still at the front of my mind, but I no longer feel angry. Cory has pacified me. It's probably a good thing, too. My desire to devour a soul is gone. "I'm turning into the monster all of you have been warning I might become, aren't I?"

"We're not sure yet," Aunt Fran utters. "What we do know, is you're changing faster than any of us ever have. We need to find Nyta first before seeking out Dragonscale, Jeff."

"Agreed. We must get to Geneviève's Ranch before your change is complete."

"How are you feeling?" Aunt Fran asks.

"There are no words to describe it," I confess. "I literally could feel the beast within. It terrifies me knowing I didn't recognize any of you. I don't understand what's wrong with me." I turn around and Cory is behind me. "I feel like I'm a monster being watched. Like at any moment you all believe I will attack you."

"Wynter, for the first time, you have shown your true form. All of us here now know who you truly are," Cory says.

"And who am I, exactly?"

"You will find out soon enough," Fran answers. "Out in the open is not the ideal spot to discover your hidden secret that's laid dormant for eighteen years."

My body remains calm. The anger is there bottled inside, yet it will not come out. I know it's being suppressed by the influence Cory bestows on me. "Must you continue to block my frame of mind like this?"

"Yes," Cory presses. "We can no longer risk our safety. I know you don't understand this now, but you will soon."

The blood in my veins keeps an even temperature, not allowing my frustrated anger to escape, which annoys me, but I know it's probably for the best. Besides, slaughtering Cory and eating him for dinner would not sit well with me after I calmed down. "I suppose I would have been rather disappointed had I killed you."

"Ya think?" he teases.

I look at Aunt Fran and Dad. "Thank you for pulling me back from the darkness that was about to consume me."

"Does that mean we're forgiven?" Cory asks.

I nod and grab his hand.

"Ouch." He pulls away.

I look down and see bite marks. "Did I do that?"

Cory doesn't answer.

I gently cover his hand with mine as they begin to glow, healing his wounds. "I'm so sorry. You, too, Aunt Fran." I remember everything. Tears form. "I don't know what to say." I glance at Dad.

"There isn't anything you can say." Dad furrows his brows then turns and walks off.

"I guess I'll give him some space," I say.

Still holding my hand, Cory picks up my pack and hands it to me, saying, "Come on. We should keep going. I forgive you and I know you were overtaken by the monster within. I understand because I've been there. Let your dad cool off. He'll come around. Trust me." We follow Aunt Fran and my dad, toward the valley below.

8
UNANSWERED QUESTIONS

WE REACH THE BOTTOM of the ravine where the sound of water is more prominent. "It's like a cove, except on a riverbed," I say.

Dad flashes about at super speed, scouting the area as though he's looking for something. "We must find a safe spot to pitch a tent," he says. "As I predicted we will never make it to Geneviève's Ranch in time. It's still over an hour's run to her place. We are safest here for the night rather than taking our chances through the mountains right now."

Cory looks around. "You don't think we can make a run for it?"

"Sure, we could," Dad answers, "but we still would have to make our way through Shadow Vine Forest."

"Ah, that's right. I forgot about that," Cory says.

Curious, I ask, "Shadow Vine Forest?"

"No one can get past the Shadow Vine Forest alive. It's the barrier that protects Geneviève's Ranch from enemies," Cory answers.

I gulp. "That sounds terrifying."

"Through that crevasse there," Cory points to a pathway between two cliffs. "is the way out of here. The problem is we must go through there when there is no shade. And more importantly during the day." He looks up, and we all follow his gaze to see the moons nearly joined. "As said previously, when the darkness approaches, the nocturnal species come out." And as though his words conjured meaning, wolves howl.

Dad smiles. "We most certainly wouldn't survive to the other side. Too many predators. We'll wait until tomorrow when the sun is warm."

"Dad, what are you not telling me? You have more to say, I can sense it."

"That's a loaded question, now, isn't it? Don't you think you have learned enough for one day?" His tone reveals irritation.

"Yeah, about that. I'm sorry, Dad. I don't know what came over me. But whatever it is, Cory has it handled." Something tells me he doesn't think I'm sincere.

"Does he?" Dad glares at Cory and then back at me. "Wynter, you don't seem to understand. Your power is gaining momentum, and we don't have the ability to stop it. We're running out of time."

His tone has me scared for the first time. Not like before when I didn't wear the necklace or when I experienced the car accident. The fear in his eyes puts fear in me. "How do I control it, Dad?"

He looks at me with his glowing blue eyes. "With fewer explanations right now." He glances at Cory. "And with as much pacification as possible because we know compelling won't work with you."

"Dad?" Tears well up in my eyes as I feel the stinging pain of his words cut through to the core. My heartbeat pounds, but somehow, I fear he doesn't hear it. "What do you mean by that, Dad?"

"I mean no more stories. No more reminders of who you really are. It will have to wait. You're becoming too dangerous, and for the safety of us all, you will have to keep the questions to yourself for a while." He takes a couple of steps backward. "I'm going to scout the perimeter. Fran, you take the other side." She nods and runs off. "Cory, find a place where we can set up safely out of view from predators." Dad, too, races out of sight.

Cory looks up to the mountain above us. "Your dad's right. The sun will be blocked soon. We must find a place to set up shelter before they come out." Grabbing my fingertips, he says, "Stay close."

We walk in and out of trees and along shrubs. Many times, I think we find a great spot to set up, but Cory keeps giving reasons as to why it isn't ideal. Finally, we come to an alcove carved into the side of the mountain. "It's almost like a cave."

"It's a great spot," he says. A boulder slightly hides the entrance. "I can make a tent to camouflage the large rock."

The rustling of leaves kicks up, sending me chills. "Cory, I'm scared."

"Why? We will be safe once I set up camp." His confidence reassures me.

"It's not that. What I'm becoming concerns me. What am I? A wolf? A vampire?" I blurt. *Or, an unknown beast that Moyer possibly concocted, and nobody has confessed the truth yet?*

"I can't answer that, Wynter. I'm sorry."

Another howl sounds off. "The wolves seem close," I say, feeling a little nervous.

"They are hunters. Don't be scared. I'll have us set up soon."

"I'm not afraid of the wolves. I'm talking about me." Pointing to my heart, I say, "Who am I?" Tears again glaze my eyes.

"Don't worry." He comes closer, taking my hand and placing it on his heart. "I got you. And no matter what your dad thinks, I won't let anything happen to you."

"How can you be sure?"

"Because I know you, Wynter. There is good in you. You can fight this, and we'll win. There is someone on Ladorielle, I know, who can teach you. But for now, your dad is right. No more stories. You must allow your memories to take hold naturally. It's way too dangerous for all of us right now." He cups my cheek, gently kissing me. "We will get through this together. I promise."

"Making those promises again?" I joke.

"Haven't broken any yet, have I?"

I smile at him. "No."

"Come on. Let's get to work."

More growls come from beyond the brush ahead of us. "Cory, what is that?" I ask. I'm reminded of that same growl at the manor. The sound of Redmae when she had me pinned to the ground about to take her next meal.

"Dire wolves," he says. "They're closer than they seem."

We both glance around to find a hint of their location, but all that's revealed from the hungry pack are snarls that hide behind the thick brush.

"What do we do, Cory? I don't see them anywhere."

"Hold still, and don't move an inch. They strike on motion, waiting until the last second before attacking. Most victims don't see them coming."

"Are these the same kind of dire wolves like at the manor?"

"Yes, however, these are wild ones and not trained." Cory turns his head not heeding his own advice, and without warning one of the beasts rushes out of the bushes, knocking him to the ground. Snarling teeth froth with burning saliva. While Cory fights the dire wolf, another one descends from the brush, exposing fangs, and makes eye contact with me. The memories of Redmae come to the surface. It has silver eyes, and not red like Redmae's, which has me wondering why hers were different.

"Don't move," Cory warns, struggling with the other beast. More growls come from beyond the shrubs and trees, but they stay back.

"What do I do?" Panic strikes.

"Use your fire skills," Cory calls and punches the beast he's fighting in the neck, stunning the creature.

He's right. But I feel fear this time, not anger. A cold chill brushes my skin as I notice snowflakes float down from the sky. Numbness travels through my veins and I feel colder than normal. A sensation of coolness encases me as though I'm in the Arctic.

"Wynter, snap out of it!" He kicks the animal, sending it flying and it gives him time to regroup. "What are you waiting for? Use your magic," he orders.

The wolf recovers, leaping into a defensive stance. Cory and the animal circle each other, and Cory turns into the creature he has fought so hard to control — a vampire. His teeth protrude as he prepares to pounce.

The second wolf that has its eyes on me seems to lose patience and dives forward. Out of instinct, I put my hands up in a defensive position. Instead of the animal devouring me, it is encased in ice. "Did I do that?" I say, stunned.

I glance over to Cory. He's killed the wolf that battled with him and is eating it. It's almost like he doesn't notice me, or rather doesn't care about my existence at this moment. Is that what it's like when the beast consumes you? That there's no going back until the hunger is fulfilled?

No longer do I hear the other wolves hiding out in the brush. Silence follows and the singing of crickets begins to sound off. *They've retreated.*

Cory finishes his meal. It's the first time I have seen this side of him. His eyes are bright blue, his skin is gray, black veins bulge, and blood drips from his lips. He conjures a towel and wipes his face.

By the time he reaches me, his features are back to human form. "Are you okay?" he asks.

I'm still in shock from what I witnessed. I hug my arms across my chest. "I—I think so?"

He views the frozen dire wolf. "Did you do this?" His tone of shock surprises me.

"Apparently." I take a step back. "I don't know exactly how. It all happened so fast. One second, I'm bracing for impact, and the next second this animal is frozen."

"Wait until your dad sees this."

"Do you think he's going to be mad?"

"Mad?" Cory grins. "No, I don't think so."

"Guess one less mouth to feed now." I point to the carcass of bones lying on the ground.

"Right," he murmurs. "Sorry you had to see that."

"It's inevitable. Sooner or later, I would have. Just didn't expect it so soon." I look at the wolf encased in ice. "I'm sorry, Cory, but these animals don't make me hungry at all. If anything, I'm beginning to feel sick."

"Yeah, well. It's not what I prefer, either. But I don't exactly see humanoids around, and you're certainly not an option for me." He teases.

"Nice, Cory. Glad to know I mean something to you."

"Hey, the feeling is mutual. You wanted me for lunch earlier, remember?" he jabs back.

"How could I forget?" I kiss his cheek.

The snow sprinkles down in small flakes. "What is up with this weather?" he says. "Snow doesn't come around these parts."

"Don't look at me. I have no memory of this place."

Cory squints, as though he knows more than what he's letting on. "We better get back to making camp."

He makes a circle with his fingers like before when he's conjured items out of nothing and creates a tent that bolts to the ground and blends itself between the boulder and the side of the mountain. The color and contours of the makeshift tent look exactly like the large stone next to it. "I can't see where the real boulder and the tent merge. It looks like one giant rock, Cory."

"Welcome to your five-star hotel suite, My Lady," he teases.

I nudge his arm and he laughs.

"We should gather wood for a fire," he says. "Especially since it's snowing again."

Once the wood is collected, we bring it inside and pile it next to the stove. The place looks exactly the same as the last tent Cory conjured, except it's bigger this time. Four cots are set against the back wall. To one side of the faux tent is a kitchen and a table. A living room is pieced together around the wood stove centered in the middle of the room, like last time, too. "How do you do it? I'm in awe each time."

"Do what?"

"This," I say in amazement. "Too bad this kind of magic couldn't be created on Earth."

"You have this kind of magic, too, Wynter, just in a different form."

His comment brings me to the rage I felt earlier when I wanted to kill my entire family. "Cory, how do you deal with it? I mean, you warned me that something like this might happen, but I didn't expect it to be so soon."

I sit down in a nearby chair. "I remember everything about how I felt—how instinctual it was to look at each of you as prey. At that instant, I didn't care who any of you were. All I wanted was a fresh kill. The horrible part is I remember every bit of it, too. What's wrong with me, Cory?"

He drops the stack of wood he's carrying by the hearth. "I don't know. It's almost like you have the same tendencies as a Nytemire, but yet there is something else stirring. I wish I could tell you, but I can't." His face looks worried. "And that popsicle pup outside," he adds, "I've not seen someone do that before, Wynter."

His expression prompts me to ask, "What are you not telling me, Cory?"

He hesitates. "Whatever it is Wynter—the beast inside you—is much stronger than anticipated. I had a hard time getting you to calm down on the hillside when you... changed. I predict soon even my soothing powers will not stop you."

"And going to this place... wherever it is we are going, can help with that?"

"Sort of." He pauses. "There is a transporter that will take us to Ladorielle's castle. That's where we will find the queen of this realm, and hopefully, she can tell us what is stirring inside you."

Cory conjures a newspaper and crumbles it, sticking it in the stove. "In the meantime, we must seek the priestess at Geneviève's Ranch." Picking up a couple of logs, he stuffs them on top of the paper. "She's one of the last survivors of Queen Sara's court."

"Sara, you mean my late great-grandmother?"

"Yes. It's said that during a great battle, the priestess fled in hiding. Her powers are so extraordinary that if her abilities fell into the wrong hands, it would be devastating to this world."

"I see. And my dad knows where she is?"

"Yes." Cory comes over to sit next to me. "No more stories until we see her. You're going to have to trust me. All of us. But I know for sure wearing that necklace now is more important than anything. And I don't mean just to protect you from Moyer, but to protect you against yourself, too."

"Cory?"

"It's a theory, but I think I now know why you must wear it always, besides the obvious reasons your dad gave," he says, pointing to my neck. Cory perks up. "They're back.". He gets up and goes to the door of the tent. "Don't mention what we talked about. It might worry them, or you may press them for answers, and your rage may kick in again. We can't take any more chances."

I nod, knowing how much rage stirs inside, I must find a way to rein it in or it will control me. "What about the frozen wolf?"

Before Cory can answer, Dad and Fran enter the tent. "Is everything okay?" Dad asks.

Fran follows closely behind. "What's with the frozen dinner outside," she jokes.

"Yes, fine," Cory replies. "We had a run-in with a dire pack. Seems they became the hunted."

"I can see that," Dad retorts. "So, it appears you have another layer of magic that's building, Wyn."

"I don't know how I did it, Dad, honestly," I plead with him, but for some reason, I feel it goes unanswered. He glares with his glowing blue eyes. I know that look. It's the stare of anger.

"Dad, please don't be mad."

"I'm not mad," he assures. "Honestly, I'm nervous about what's becoming of you. Furthermore, this part of you, the ability to freeze, isn't something I've foreseen coming."

"What are you saying, Jeff?" Fran cuts in.

"I never saw in the future where Wynter would freeze things."

I get it now. He's not mad at all. He's frightened of what I'm becoming. Something must be shielding him from seeing my true self.

"Are we safe?" I gulp. "I mean are we safe—from me?"

"For now." He removes his gloves. "We will rest up, and in the morning pick up where we left off." He pats my shoulder. "Everything will turn out fine."

Fine? It's not like Dad to be so quiet. I wish I had the power to see what he's thinking.

"Wynter," Cory says. "Can you light the fire?" He brings with him a crumpled newspaper and eliminates my inner thoughts of anxiety.

I look at him, my eyes blurry from tears. "Of course," I say and light the edges with my fingers.

"It's going to be fine," he whispers, "just like your dad said."

9
GIANT COUNTRY

THE NEXT DAY I wake to a loud thud. Not knowing what's going on, I bolt up to find Cory, Dad, and Fran gone.

Crushing sounds continue to bounce off my ears and vibrate the ground. I hear a loud, unfamiliar growl.

Unzipping the tent, I see Cory conjuring something.

"Hurry, I can't hold him off for long!" Aunt Fran yells.

Cory throws a quiver set to her and conjures another for himself. Dad wields a sword.

A lofty, human-like creature with massive strength smashes the ground with a club he's brandishing. Towering over all of us, a low growl rumbles from his throat. Just as Aunt Fran takes aim, whatever is holding the giant's feet to the ground breaks free. The beast takes one massive leap forward with the spiked weapon in his hands and hits the ground, narrowly missing all three of them.

I focus on Cory as the creature stomps toward him.

"Cory, look out!" I scream.

Aunt Fran casts a magic spell on the ogre. The ground oozes with mud and wraps around the giant's ankles preventing this thing from taking another step.

Fear consumes me once more, and my hands go numb. I feel cold, but I push back the chill. I must help them. I should probably keep my abilities at bay, but I won't let this thing hurt my family. Rage replaces fear and I focus on the fire Cory taught me yesterday. My blood boils in my veins once more, but this time it's different, rather than anger controlling me, it's my fear of losing my family in an unknown world. The combination of the two emotions seems to bring out my skills to manipulate the power.

Maybe the cliff behind the giant will help. If I can somehow blast magic at him, making it lose its footing, perhaps he'll fall down the ravine. For a split second, I think about the aftermath.

Cory notices I'm behind him. "There wasn't any time to wake you." He sees the fireball in my hands. "Go ahead, throw it."

"Nothing like a morning wake-up call from a giant," I holler. "Any other surprises?" I raise my hand in position to launch my flame.

He raises a brow. "Might be a few more," he replies, grinning. "We can't hold him off much longer," he says, as they all leap like frogs at every swipe from the giant.

"Throw it!" Aunt Fran yells. "Hurry up before he calls more to come!" She, too, has a ball of fire in her hands.

It's the confirmation I need. The fire within engulfs me and the ball grows in my hand, glowing bright orange. I fling the fireball into the air at the same time as Fran, both hitting our target, but it doesn't seem to do anything except make the giant angrier.

"Well, that backfired," I mumble.

Fran casts another immobilization spell, and the mud around the giant's ankles thickens, drawing his attention to her rather than me. It gives me the chance to create a bigger fireball. I hurl the flames toward the giant, pushing him backward, closer to the cliff, breaking the spell that has fixed the beast to the ground. The giant teeters on the edge, but the beast steadies himself to keep from falling over. His attention switches, and he takes an immense leap forward, nearly crushing me. The force pushes me backward, and I lose my footing.

Dazed for a moment, I gather my thoughts. Cory grabs my arm and pulls me behind a boulder before the giant has a chance to swing his spiked club again. With his attention diverted, it allows Fran enough time to cast a third spell immobilizing the beast once more. We escape from behind the large rock.

"It won't hold him off for long!" Dad yells, running toward our tent. "Time to vacate." He comes back with our packs. "Quick, we don't have much time. Follow me."

It doesn't take long before we hear the sounds of a horn.

"What was that?" I ask.

"He's calling more giants," Dad says. "We should have killed him when we had the chance."

The pounding on the ground feels like an earthquake as more giants come running. One of them takes a huge leap into the air and lands near us and the ground beneath us cracks.

"Run!" Dad calls out.

Then a second giant takes another leap right into our path. But we're quicker, jumping to the side. I turn around and run in the opposite direction when I realize I'm facing a canyon.

"Fran, hurry up with that bow," Cory yells.

The giant runs toward me, and I have nowhere to go but closer to the edge. He leaps again, but this time, an arrow strikes his neck, and he slips on a rock, causing him to lose his footing.

"Wynter, watch out," Dad screams.

As the giant loses his balance, he grabs the back of my pack trying to take me with him.

I release my sack just in time to see the creature fall into the ravine below.

"That was fun," I say, trying to catch my breath.

"We're not done yet," Cory says, nodding toward three other beastly giants appearing also to be fixated on the ground.

"The lucky thing about your Aunt Fran is she's blessed with the ability to keep a creature rooted to the ground," Dad says.

"I figured we would be safe and far enough off the trail," Cory says. "The tent clearly was hidden. He must've smelled us. We were eating the thawed-out wolf left out overnight."

"You okay?" Aunt Fran asks.

"Yes, fine. My pack, however, is gone." I pause, realizing there is more than just the sack we lost. "The coffer was in there, too."

"Then we must get it," Fran insists. "Your mother's heart is in there." We all stare at her in shock. "Long story," she says.

"Give us the shorter version," I assert.

"Rosie gave it to me. I'm the one who placed the coffer under the hidden floorboards." She veers toward Dad and Cory. "You're not the only ones that know about the hiding spot, you know."

Both men look dumbfounded. "How do you propose we get the box? That spell won't hold the giants for long. More will surely come, too," Dad says.

I peer over the edge of the cliff.

"Be careful, Wynter, it's a long fall," Cory cautions.

"I see it," I say, ignoring his warning.

"You mean your pack?"

"Yes, look." I point. "There, on the tree limb. It's hanging by a tree branch. Do you think we can get to it?"

One of the angry giants calls on the horn again. "More will be coming," Dad warns. "We need to hurry up."

"We can hold them off," Fran says. "The coffer can't be left behind. We have to fight to protect it, at all costs."

The anger on Dad's face changes to worry, or is it fear? I can't tell. "I can climb down to get it," he says. "Cory, can you conjure a rope?"

"No, Jeff. You're too heavy," Fran says. "Wynter must do it. She's the lightest of us all. That tree won't hold you. Besides, who else will help me kill some giants?" Fran grins.

The ground rumbles beneath our feet, warning us more are approaching.

"I can hold them off with my immobilization spell like I did with the others. We can pick them off one by one." Aunt Fran winks. "You can do this, Wynter. I've already taught you what you need to know."

"I get why we went to those rock-climbing sessions, now." I look down at the ravine below and my stomach churns. "I'm still afraid of heights."

"No, you're not. It's all in your head." Aunt Fran points to her temple.

Cory ties the rope around a large rock nearby, then around me. "I agree with your aunt. You can do this. I'll hold the rope and keep it steady for you."

The tremors vibrate beneath our feet, and I let out a gasp.

"Just focus on the task at hand," Cory says as he helps to lower me down.

I nod and try to concentrate while hearing the bellows of several giants echo from above. I pull on the rope. "A little lower, Cory."

A small ledge sticks out from the side of the mountain, allowing me to settle firmly on the solid rock. The satchel hangs from a tree branch growing out the side of the cliff. This isn't going to be an easy task at all. "I'll need to climb the tree to grab my pack," I call to Cory.

More growling bellows from above. The sound of Dad's sword clangs against what I assume is a weapon from his opponent. A loud groan resounds then the ground shakes again from a fallen ogre beast.

"Do what you have to," Cory yells. "Just hurry."

Pushing aside the fear, I climb the trunk toward the tree branch that clasps my bag. One wrong move and I know I will plummet to the cavern below. It takes a couple of tries before I'm able to inch it forward. A loud crack from the base of the limb behind me disturbs my concentration. Realizing the branch I'm on isn't going to hold my weight, I give one last-ditch effort to grab the strap of my pack before it breaks away from the tree. I lose my footing and fall with the tree limb, screaming.

"Wynter, I got you!" Cory shouts.

The rope attached to my waist and legs tightens, saving me from death. Still holding the strap of my pack, I attempt to throw it over my back but fail because of my awkward position.

"Just hang onto it," Cory calls. "I'll have you up in no time."

"Cory, I need to swing to the ledge to get my bearings. Can you help me?"

"Yes, go. Go!"

Managing to gather momentum, I swing my body around the tree trunk, which allows me to manipulate the strap of my pack, and I swing it to my back. My feet grab the tip of the ledge allowing me to gain some footing. Tugging at the rope, I yell, "All set."

"Well, that was an adventure," Cory says as my hands land on the soil near his feet. He grabs my arm to help me up.

"Not as much as the one we're having now," I reply, staring at a few dead giants lying on the ground. One is still fixated on the terrain. His horn is a few yards away and out of his reach.

"We got the bag!" Cory yells.

"Good, then let's get out of here," Dad replies. "This giant isn't going to be trapped much longer. We should make a run for it while he's rooted."

"Or kill him where he stands," Fran says, and she forms a ball of fire.

"Not now," Dad cautions, "we need to save our stamina for the travel through Scale Rock."

"Wait," I interrupt, pointing to the horn, "shouldn't we at least throw that thing over the cliff?"

"She's right," Fran growls. She badly wants to finish off the beast. "At least he won't have the luxury of calling the others when we flee."

It takes three of us to toss the enormous horn over the edge. When we're finished, Fran recasts her rooting spell to keep the last giant planted to the ground.

"Now, let's get out of here," Dad says.

"We have about a three-minute head start," Aunt Fran replies.

"Remember to avoid the shaded areas."

We follow Dad and Fran, weaving in and out of trees. It's the first time I've gotten to experience the swiftness of a supernatural being. The heightened senses of smell, sight, and sound have innately changed and without any conscious effort, my body is fully aware of my surroundings. *So weird.* Every inch of my skin experiences the brush of wind and I see the most microscopic of organisms. This must be why creatures avoid a face plant into a tree.

As we reach the opening to the other side of the vast cavern the walls appear to close in on us. The ravine is dark and dreary. I hear hissing noises behind me, something wicked and threatening.

"Don't look back!" Dad yells. "Keep moving."

"What are those noises?"

"Iknes Shaw," Cory answers. "This valley is their home, and they live in the mountain caves. Their alliance is with the giants. And they know we've escaped their grasp."

As though Cory has tapped into my mind again, he answers another question I'm about to ask. "The cove we were in is the nesting grounds of the Iknes Shaw. The giants live among the trees and the lower caves, while the lizard-like creatures hang out above, near the heat of the sun. They normally sleep during the day and are nocturnal. The giants patrol during the day while the Iknes Shaw patrol at night. They roam these parts, patrolling the trails leading down to the cavern below. It's probably why those drakes you saw yesterday were circling above. A dead giant is a huge meal for the drake."

A loud thud rumbles under my feet. "What's that?"

"Sounds like the giant is loose," Cory says.

"Keep running," Dad says.

Not stopping to see what I hear behind us, we continue through the deep cavern until we reach an open field.

"Looks like this guy isn't going to give up so easily." Dad stops to take a sword from behind his trench coat, wielding it as though he has done it many times.

"Told you I should have finished him off!" Fran yells.

Cory looks to Fran. "Seems you did, indeed, irritate him more." He grins. "Shall we take him on?"

"Do we have any other choice? Take cover over there." Dad points to a boulder.

Cory pulls at my hand.

I run to keep up with his pace as we race toward the large rock. Beyond it, a forest in front of us.

I feel the rushing vibrations of the ground beneath my feet, and the roaring giant brandishing a spiked hammer calls, "Found you!"

10
SHADOW VINE FOREST

WE TAKE COVER BEHIND a rock, watching Dad and Fran stop to face the giant. The creature leaps forward, cracking the ground beneath his feet, like the other one before him. The force thrusts Dad and Aunt Fran backward, and they both lose their footing.

The sword in Dad's hand goes flying, stabbing the ground a few feet away. Eyeing it, I wonder if I dare retrieve Dad's weapon.

"Don't even contemplate it," Cory warns in my ear.

"What?" I protest, annoyed that he again is slipping into my head.

Another rumbling thud from the giant distracts me from grabbing the blade, and the beast leaps into the air, trying to dive at Dad and Fran.

"Dad!" I scream, and the giant diverts attention in my direction. He pounds the ground a couple of steps when suddenly mud binds his ankles, causing him to trip and tumble face-first to the ground, like a towering tree falling in a forest. Cory and I scamper out of the way, giving us time to regroup.

"What now?" Dad asks Aunt Fran.

"We run. The spell may give us enough time to reach the forest."

"I don't understand. Shouldn't we finish him?" I ask. "I mean, he's just going to come after us again."

"She's right," Dad says. "He's a tracker. He won't stop until he catches us."

"And if you remember, Jeff," Fran counters, "trackers also have the summoning ability if we get too close, he will have a chance to bring us within his reach."

"What do you suggest we do then?" Cory asks.

"Let's get that big lug as close to the forest as possible, perhaps he'll give up when he sees where we're headed."

"I highly doubt that," Dad says. "Following your lead, My Lady Fran."

I can tell Fran didn't like Dad's teasing, and she chose to ignore him. "Come on. This way."

Following her direction, we run toward the forest. The giant roars behind us, followed by rumbling thuds of a running rhythm.

"He's going to catch us!" I shout.

Something whizzes by my ear and I whip my head around, witnessing an arrow hit the giant behind me, but it doesn't seem to bother the beast as he continues to pursue us.

"Not today," Fran says, smiling. A second arrow flashes through the air and bounces off one of the giant's biceps. I look around and don't see anyone else but us. A third shot flies and hits the beast in the shoulder, and it bellows in pain, but it still doesn't slow him down.

"Fran, can you recast to give us more time?" Dad shouts.

"Of course," she shouts back, "but you need to keep running. I'll catch up."

I stop to watch as she extends her fingers outward toward the giant, pinning him with more mud that wraps around his ankles.

She turns to look at us. "Go, go! You need to get away as far as you can."

"Why don't we kill him?" I protest.

"Because it will drain our energy, and we need to save it to get past Shadow Vine Forest. I've got this, now go!" she shouts.

I turn around to look back at the giant's feet rooted to the ground. He has something shiny in his grasp. It all happens so fast that I don't have time to warn anyone. The beast throws what looks like a weapon. It takes me a second and I realize it's my Dad's sword. It comes flying so fast that there isn't any time to react, and it pierces Aunt Fran in the back. She drops to the ground, lifeless. Even my massive, newfound speed doesn't get to her in time.

"No! Aunt Fran!" Another arrow whisks by, scoring a direct hit between the eyes of the giant, killing him instantly. His fall shakes the whole ground, knocking me down in the process.

I stumble to Aunt Fran's side and hold her limp body. "Why can't she heal herself?" I sob. "She's a healer, she can't die!"

Dad bends down to embrace me, staying quiet as he too begins to tear up. I don't think he knows what to say. He hugs me tight. "Shh, my sweet girl, it will be okay," he says, His tears are a little ironic, considering the animosity between them.

"How can you say that? She's dead!" I sob. "If I'd taken the chance and grabbed the sword, none of this would have happened."

After a long pause, Dad finally says, "When a Deagon is struck in the heart, they are killed instantly. No powers can save them. The giant must have known that. Aiming for her heart was intentional."

I sit here, bawling. The woman who raised me, the one who played the mother role in my life, is gone. This time, it isn't a car accident that takes her, and she miraculously comes back from the dead, no, this time it's real. The pain hurts so bad, I don't want to move. I know there is a rage inside me that is festering, and I also know Cory is keeping it at bay. The last time I lost her I didn't have a moment to grieve with being so busy figuring out how to save myself, but this time... this time I'm hit with so much pain I don't know how I'll get through it. It's not the same rage and sadness I felt when Moyer killed all those innocents in the dining hall, either. This pain is the loss of a parent. Someone who unconditionally loved me. One who accepted me for all my faults and forgave me, no matter the cost it would bring. I have a mother who loves me, but Fran was the mother who raised me, even if she didn't allow me to call her that. She will always have a place in my heart as Mom. I can't control the tears pouring down my cheeks. I lie upon her body and sob.

Dad bends down to Aunt Fran's ear, and he whispers something in a language I can't understand.

"Come on. We must get out of this clearing and under the protection of the woods. It's time to go," Dad urges, trying to pull me to my feet.

"I'm not leaving her!" I shout. "And what did you say in Aunt Fran's ear?"

"A prayer."

"You mean a spell?" I retort. "I'm sick of hearing about magic and spells and what they can do. If they can't bring back my aunt, I don't care to be any part of it."

Dad doesn't answer my question but instead points behind him to a stretcher lying on the ground a couple of feet away. "There is no saving Fran, with magic or spells, but if her heart grows cold, then there is no saving her spirit, either."

At first, I'm confused about the cot and his comment and realize Cory must have conjured it. I don't argue with him and both he and Cory lift Aunt Fran to the bed. Dad pulls the sword from her chest wiping the blade with a cloth, saying, "We must hurry to Geneviève's Ranch as soon as possible."

I'm reminded of the gift I have. "I can heal her. She can come back to us." I run up to her dead body with my hands glowing.

"No," Cory says, grabbing my arm, "you can't bring her back from the dead. Nobody can. And if you try, you will open a path of evil so powerful it will consume you. Don't make the same mistake Moyer did."

"What do you mean?" I ask.

"It's how the whole process started with Moyer. It's how that portrait of a sweet girl you saw in the foyer at the manor changed her life forever. She overstepped her boundaries. Selling her soul to Vothule," Cory answers.

"I've heard that name before."

"Yes. He's Lord of the Underworld and the leader of the House of Zhir."

"You never did tell me about how Moyer turned evil. What happened to her?"

"Love," Dad interrupts, picking up the front end of Fran's bed. "We need to keep quiet. We're entering the Shadow Vine Forest. Now is not the time for chatter. Stay on the path, and do not veer off under any circumstances."

CORY TAKES THE BACK end of the cot, as we proceed forward to the dark woods of Shadow Vine Forest. The caws of crows mingle with the wind whistles through the tree limbs, reminding me of a scary Halloween movie. Rustling footsteps that are not our own can be heard in the short distance through the trees. Some branches to the right of us move abruptly like there is a large animal on the limb. I begin to speak, but Cory shakes his head as though to indicate not to make a sound.

More footsteps run to one side, but I can't see a thing. I know something else is out there watching us. "Stay on the path," Dad mumbles, as I walk beside the cot.

The forest doesn't appear to be very long, and there is light ahead of us sprouting among the trees. It's such a short distance between the clearing where we defeated the giant to the other side of these woods.

"We will be out of this area soon," Dad adds. Without warning, the front end of Fran's cot drops, and Dad is yanked up in the trees.

"Dad!" I look around. There is no one but us.

"They are indeed tricky little buggers, aren't they?" Dad growls. "And we stepped right into one of their traps." Ropes in the shape of a net encase his body. The more he struggles the tighter the cords become.

"The Dryads," Cory warns. "The keepers of the forest. They see us as strangers. A threat." Cory turns in a half circle. "Keep quiet and don't make any sudden movements."

Dad hangs upside down. He's fumbling with something in his hands. My keen eyes zero in on a pocketknife, and he works on cutting the rope caging him.

The forest begins to move. The leaves rustle upon the ground and tree-like creatures come to life, circling us. Faces emerge from the bark and tree limbs that become arms and extended fingers, with the roots as their feet. They have faces like a human, oval-shaped eyes, and their ears are pointed with leaves sprouting from the sides. I watch in amazement as these creatures change before my eyes becoming more human by the second, revealing their flesh and bone bodies. It's like looking at a human trapped inside a tree.

They observe us with curiosity and apprehension. A flurry of leaves kicks up around us, sending a chill rushing through my spine.

One of the Dryads steps forward. It glides gracefully above the ground, as though barely touching it. Large roots sprout out, and he stops, attaching himself to the surface.

Another cold chill brushes across my cheeks, and more leaves graze the dirt beneath our feet.

"We mean you no harm. I'm Cory. We're on our way to Geneviève's Ranch." He points. "This here is Wynter Storm and that man up there you have is Lord Jeoffrey. The queen will not be pleased that you have him roped up."

Winds rush through the path, more forceful this time. A fog blows in, and the forest becomes dark. We are surrounded with nowhere to go. Some of the tree creatures hang back in the trees above. Their faces blend like chameleons among the whispering leaves.

"They see your aunt lying on the cot and are not happy," Cory whispers. He adds aloud, "A giant killed Lady Fran. We must race to the ranch to save her heart. We need to seek out Priestess Nyta as soon as possible."

Wind gusts kick up, brushing my skin and giving me goosebumps.

"Again, I assure you we mean no harm," Cory pleads.

Dad is nearly free from the ropes entangling him.

The wind stirs again, and some of the branches behind the leader that is speaking grow into vines, and slowly travel toward us.

Dad frees himself and crashes down to the ground, startling the beings around us. They appear to become agitated and angry, which prompts a huge dust storm. I shield my eyes.

Something touches my arm and I'm pulled away from the group. Whatever grabbed me has my hands bound behind my back and my feet rooted to the ground. Vines crawl up my legs, restraining my movement. After the dust settles, Dad and Cory are pinned like me.

A voice shouts, "Let them go!" Someone in a hooded cloak with their face hidden falls inside the circle of Dryad creatures and repeats the words. Her red ringlets fall against her cheek that's hidden beneath her cowl.

She sounds familiar, but I can't quite put my finger on it. "Her, too," the stranger says, pointing in my direction. A few of them step backward and the vines loosen, freeing my hands but not my legs.

There's something oddly familiar about this person defending us. A draft passes through again, but not as forceful as before.

"They're with me," she says. "I'm the one who killed the giant and it's true—the beast pierced the lady's heart." She pauses, "Now, please, let. Them. Go."

Another breeze kicks up, and the vines release Cory and my dad, and then me.

"Give my regards to your queen," the voice behind the hood says.

Before I have a chance to say thank you, the stranger flashes out of sight.

"You two okay?" Dad asks. He massages his wrists.

I nod, and Cory gives a side smirk. "Just another moment of adventure," he says.

"Who was that?" I ask.

Dad picks up the end of Fran's cot. "A friend. Come on, let's get out of here before they change their minds about releasing us."

Cory follows up with the back end. "Gladly, sir."

I glance around. The creatures are gone with only the natural forest trees remaining. Branches waver in the breeze and the leaves rustle as a waft of air brushes against my skin, reminding me that they are still there watching. Trees move backward, blending back into the woods. "I can see why this place has the name Shadow Vine Forest."

"They're the protectors of Geneviève's Ranch and Pine Willow Valley. No one can ride or walk without going through here first. Unless you fly," Cory says.

"Fly?"

"Cut the chatter," Dad snaps.

We follow Dad, down the path from which we came, not looking back. I don't know where we are, but all that matters is I want out of this creepy place as soon as possible.

WE REACH THE END of the Shadow Vine Forest to a clearing of a meadow that resembles the nightmare I had when Moyer put me in a dream stamp.

The sounds of horses to the left grab our attention and the same hooded stranger from moments ago rides toward us, along with a team of men behind her.

Dad nods his head. “Thank you for coming to assist when you did. I’m not sure the Dryads were pleased we trespassed through their home.”

“It’s a pleasure, my Lord, and my duty to protect, Sire,” she says, sliding off the animal. “Shall we tie the cot to the back of a horse? It will be faster.”

“I suppose you’re right,” Dad agrees.

Her voice is clearer, but I still cannot figure out who she is. “Who are you?” I demand.

Ignoring my question, Cory and Dad strap the cot to the horse and secure Aunt Fran to the bed. Then the stranger turns, dropping her hood.

“Hello, Wynter,” she says, smiling. “It’s been a while, hasn’t it?”

I can’t believe my own eyes. I glance at Dad saying, “I don’t understand. Is this some kind of joke?”

Dad grunts.

I look at this hooded stranger that saved our lives. “Is that really you?” My eyes must be playing tricks on me. “Rory?”

11
UNEXPECTED SURPRISES

SHE SMILES WIDE, NODDING. "Yeah, it's me. I brought you horses."

"Rory, My Lady, we must make haste if we are to get your Lady Fran to Nyta in time," one of the riders on horseback says.

"Quite right, Thane. Take her away, I'll be right behind you."

The man she calls Thane takes Fran's cot and hitches it to his horse. "Good to see you, again, Lord Jeoffrey." He passes the reins to a spare horse.

Dad nods. "Thanks." Dad directs his attention toward Cory and me. "I'll meet you back at the ranch." He climbs on his steed and takes off with the rest of Rory's team.

"We can talk later," Rory says, getting up on her horse. "Grab your horses and follow me."

"We must be close to the ranch, I take it?"

"Just over that hill," she says, pointing. She clicks her tongue as she tugs the reins to her right. "Let's go." The horse takes off, leaving Cory and me behind.

I huff. "Well, that was an unusual welcome home, wasn't it?"

"Not every day a member of the court returns home dead."

My heart aches at the loss of my aunt. "Do you really think Nyta can help?" A part of me thinks she can still be saved.

Cory doesn't answer my question, saying, "This meadow is safer, unlike the one we experienced earlier, but it is still dangerous to be out here alone. We should catch up to them."

I glance to the hills on my right, spotting the gigantic boulders. "What about the rest of the giants?"

"These mountains to the side of us are too steep to cross. And to the left over there," Cory points. "Through the oak trees is a cliff, leading to the ocean. Trust me, they will not reach us from here."

"An ocean?" I listen to the sound of waves that didn't bring attention to my senses until now.

He smiles. "Would you like me to take you there sometime?"

"That would be nice. I haven't seen the sea since leaving Washington State."

Cory motions to one of the horses. "Here," he says, handing me the reins. "Perhaps I can show you once we settle into town a bit?"

I look at the leads and smile. *A horse? I don't know how to ride this animal.*

"What is it?" he asks.

I shake my head. "So, what do I do with these?" I ask, holding up the reins in my hands.

"You can remember how to ride, Wynter."

"I have no recollection of ever riding a horse." Without hesitation, I lightly wrap the reins in my left hand, stab my foot in the stirrup, and swing my right leg to the other side.

"Ah, see. You seem to know what to do already," he argues, pointing to the obvious way I mounted the animal.

"Weird." I look at my hands, observing how I naturally hold the reins.

Cory's face lights up, grinning. "Obviously your subconscious remembers something." He climbs on his horse. "Let's get out of here." He gallops ahead in the direction of the others across the meadow, and I follow his lead.

Memories come back to the forefront as I look around, noticing the familiarity of the landscape. It also brings back the fake dream Moyer tried to stamp on my mind. Are all my memories skewed?

I remember the anxiety I felt knowing I would have to make new friends coming to a strange new school and making a fresh start. Rory's the first person I befriended when I entered a new high school for the first time. We hit it off instantaneously. It's as though I'd known her my whole life. Perhaps I have? Seeing Rory has me wondering why she's on Ladorielle. It's all starting to make sense. The only way I will know for sure is to ask her. Maybe she can shed some light on my past.

It's not long before we come to a path etched out at the end of the meadow where a stable nestles among a few trees. An arched gate beyond it leads into a town a few distance away. The horses that Rory and her team rode are already corralled and eating hay.

A large, hot kiln burns next to the stable where a man is pounding on a horseshoe while a young boy mucks up a stall a few feet away. Both have cowboy hats and are dressed like they belong in a Western movie. Neither one seems to notice us approaching the hitching post.

Cory whispers, "You see that man hammering? His name is Max. The town's metalsmith. He forges items for the village here, and makes horseshoes, among other things." He nods to the boy in the stall. "Over there is his son Oliver." Dismounting from his horse, he adds, "We can tie the horses here." Following his lead, I do the same.

"Come with me. Let me introduce you." He walks over to the metalsmith. "Hey there, Max, I brought you a couple more horses to look after."

The man stops hitting the horseshoe and looks out from behind a bench. "Cory, is that you, lad?"

"Indeed, it is, sir."

"It's been a while. How's your mum?"

Cory pauses and looks over to me. "She's... good."

"And who is this lass, you've brought?" he asks, taking off his gloves as he approaches.

"Max," Cory says, "this is Wynter Storm, of House of Storm River Manor."

Bowing, he grasps my hand, kissing the back of it, like an old-world gentleman. "My Lady," he says, "it's a pleasure to finally meet you in person." His grip is strong, yet gentle, and his hand is a bit stubby. He's a tad shorter than most men, having a beard to hide most of his facial features, but his eyes speak of kindness.

Embarrassed by the introduction, I bow. "Sir, there is no need to do that."

"I disagree," he argues, "with a person of such stature like yourself, one can't ever be too informal in front of you."

Before I have time to quiz him, Cory says, "Where are Jeoffrey and the others?"

Max points to a cottage at the top of a small hill with a mossy roof. Smoke escapes the chimney top.

"Thank you, Max," Cory says, giving a slight bow.

We pace toward the little house. "Who's up there?" I ask.

Cory smiles, not answering my question.

A man outside tends to a garden on the side of the home. Our approach distracts him, and he looks up. His stare is dubious, giving me chills.

We reach the front door of the cottage and I notice a bench with shoes stacked on a rack underneath it. "The priestess prefers shoes to stay outside," Cory answers and unlaces his boots. Sitting next to him, I do the same.

"Still more mysteries. If only I could read your mind like you do mine, I wouldn't have to ask so many questions, Cory."

"It's good that you don't," he teases, "else you may not like me at all."

His smirk takes me by surprise. "Are you that dark and evil on the inside that you have to keep so many secrets from me? You make it sound as though I can't handle your past." A part of me feels hurt that Cory doesn't trust me.

"Oh, I'm sure you can. It's the changes you've shown recently that has us wondering if you have the power to restrain your emotions when you learn the truth. If I tell you everything now, perhaps you will change your mind, kill, and eat me for lunch. No. I'd rather not take my chances for now," he jokes.

His words sting as I relive the memory of when I felt the impulse to kill him and my family. It unsettles my soul, and a rush of panic floods my veins. My throat burns as I try to push the bile back to my stomach. It must have been so bad. My own family has come to the point that they no longer trust me. Those thoughts pang my soul.

"Don't dwell on it, my sweet. We will find a way for you to ease into your newfound power. For now, we have come to give that coffer you hide inside your pack to Nyta."

"Nyta, is she the priestess you talked about? The same person you mentioned that day when we were in the Hall of History when Moyer set a trap and I was captured? Is this her home?"

"Yes. She lives here in the village. The town's healer, or what you're familiar with as a... doctor. Some call her a seer while others call her a diviner. But to the royal court, she's the High Priestess of Ladorielle."

"So, she's the same priestess that fled during the great battle?"

Cory laughs, as though my comment is an ignorant one. "She's protected here. Vothule can't reach her as long as she's within the realm of Geneviève's Ranch." He pauses. "Her home was destroyed the day the Storms left."

"So, she's protected like we were at the cottage at Storm River Manor?"

"Much like that, yes." Cory gets up and raps on the front door.

Dad opens it, nodding his head while we pass through. "We're about to get started."

Rory stands near a window, peering out as though she's deep in thought. She still wears her cloak and her quiver set. Looking closer I notice her features are a bit different. Her ears are pointed, and her hair a brighter red than before. She's taller too. As though she notices me staring, she says, "Our physical appearance changes slightly when we're sent to Earth." She turns to look at me and smiles. "I'm glad you're home."

I huff. "Home sounds strangely comforting." I don't recognize the aromas inside the small cottage, yet my senses still feel a familiarity. A fireplace is lit in one corner with a pot of boiling liquid hanging near it. Aunt Fran lies on a table near the hearth, appearing to have her chest prepared for surgery. It looks like we've walked into a cave, rather than a small cottage. The walls are plastered in mud and the floors are made of dirt. It has me confused. Why would we take off our shoes if we walk on the soil beneath our feet?

A snarl comes from a dark corner of the room. As though my thoughts were read, a voice answers, "The ground grows all my fresh grimmroot needed to heal and preserve life."

Appearing from the shadows, a woman dressed in a purple robe with a large gold belt secured around her waist comes forward. Her irises are purple, matching her garment, and her face is thin and long. White hair cascades down over her shoulders and pointed ears poke through her long locks. She looks elegant, yet strong in stature.

"I'm the village healer and the seer of life. I can read thoughts too," she says, chortling. "I can see the look on your face, and it shows signs of confusion." Wobbling over, holding a staff, she continues, "The white hair is a genetic trait, much like yours."

Dad interjects, "Priestess Nyta, this is my—"

"No need for formal introductions, Lord Jeoffrey. I know who she is. The more important task at hand is getting Fran's heart out of her body and preserved before it grows cold."

"Preserved?" I ask.

She peers to Dad, as though irritated. "You have not told the child yet?"

"No..." Dad appears hesitant to answer her. "Wynter seems to be going through some... changes of her own. It caught all of us off guard, of course. We were hoping you might have some answers."

There he goes again, talking out loud as though I'm not in the room.

Rory pulls away from the window. "When did you begin the changes, Wynter?"

Startled by Rory's question, I say, "I—I don't know. It began small. Back at the manor, I suppose. As you can see, I have white hair now not the black hair you remember."

"Nyta, it's started, hasn't it?" Rory steps closer to the priestess, with a fearful expression on her face.

Nyta puts her hand up, stopping Rory from saying more, and hobbles over to Aunt Fran's lifeless body. I watch with fervor as she takes her hands and pierces through my aunt's chest without using so much as a scalpel. "I warned you, Jeff, this might happen." We stare as she takes the large red mass from Fran's torso. A gaping hole is in the center of the muscle. "When you and Isalora decided to remove Wynter's memories, it made her vulnerable to emotion. Now, you must wait it out and allow her to sort it through on her own."

Nyta takes the organ, places it in a cloth, and sets it on a small table beside her. There, the priestess works her magic as her hands glow with light, much like the way mine did when I healed Cory that day in the classroom from his broken ribs. She massages the heart in her palms and mumbles a chant before a jolt of electricity passes through her fingers. Seconds later, the heart begins to move like it's beating on its own. "Please understand," she continues, "Wynter is the one to stop *her*. You must allow her to follow the path of fate that she is destined to travel." The heart maintains a strong beat in Nyta's hands.

"You see," she adds, looking directly at me, "when a Deagon dies, their heart lives on. As long as the body is still warm when the heart is taken, life will remain preserved. In your aunt's case, a damaged heart must heal first."

She takes a small box, looking much like the coffer hiding inside my jacket, and places it inside. She chants again, then closes the lid, locking it with a key hanging around her neck.

There's a long pause before the shock wears off from what I've witnessed. Remembering the box I still have hidden in my coat, I interrupt Nyta's channeling, "My mother wanted me to give you this."

Nyta turns to face us and watches me pull out the box.

"Ah, yes. I do believe that has fallen into the wrong hands at one point in time." Setting my aunt's coffer down, she retrieves the other one that's in my hands. "Did she tell you what is inside?"

"No, but Fran did."

Many more locked boxes lined the shelves behind her.

"Indeed, you're correct, my child," she says, taking the key hanging around her neck. We wait with anticipation to find Nyta fails to open the coffer. "It appears the magic holding this chest shut is stronger than I anticipated."

"Who is keeping it from opening?" I ask, curious.

"Sarmira. Her magic is strong. It's going to take me some time to manipulate the spell that has been placed upon this case." She glowers, as though her whole plan is defeated, and lifts the box in her hands to the shelf behind her.

There is optimism in my father's eyes. "Can you bring her back?" he asks.

"Dear boy, no. Have I taught you nothing?" She sounds surprised by his question.

His silence speaks volumes and gives more mystery for me to file away in the already large pile stacking in the back of my brain.

"Cory, I thought you said nobody can be brought back from the dead?"

Nyta turns to me, giving a firm smile. "He's right, dear." Then she sternly glances at my dad. "Past lessons should be a strong indication you mustn't even think of going down that path, Jeoffrey Storm."

That's the first time I have ever heard my dad be called by his middle name. Nyta speaks to him as though she's his elder. One with authority over him and he takes her chastisement without argument. Who is she to him?

As she places Fran's coffer on the shelf next to my mother's, Nyta says, "You all must be very tired from your long journey. Perhaps it's wise to go see Geneviève. She'll be expecting you." She turns to Rory. "Will you give this to her please?" Nyta pulls from her pocket a small scroll.

"What's this?" Rory asks.

"A little something Geneviève has requested. Who am I to question her?"

Rory nods, taking the parchment and tucking it into her pocket.

"What about Aunt Fran?"

"She will be buried along with the rest of the Deagons that have fallen," Nyta explains.

"I don't understand. Why the theatrics of taking my aunt's heart?" Anger and sorrow mix with my emotions. I feel that all this new information needs to be explained. I'm tired of unanswered questions.

"All in due time, Wynter. We must allow fate to take its course. It will all turn out right in the end." She grabs some bottles from the table below the shelf, handing one of them to me. "Here, this will help you on your journey." She hands Cory and Dad a bottle as well.

"What is this?" I ask, briefly glancing at Rory, noticing she clearly didn't get such a gift.

"Invisibility potions. It may come in handy when you go back to Storm River Manor," Nyta says with a grin.

Rory slips out the door, as though she, too, is hiding something. That scroll she carries has some significance, and I'm determined to find out what it is.

"It's time to say your farewells now," Nyta says, interrupting my thoughts.

Cory takes my hand, and I push it away, stepping toward Aunt Fran's lifeless body, trying to shove away tears of loss. Saying goodbye to her isn't going to be easy.

"Do not cry for me, my dear niece. For I'm with you. I may not have a physical body, but I'm here," a voice whispers in my ear.

"Did you hear that?" I say, turning around to look at everyone in the room.

"Hear what?" Cory asks, confused. He attempts to grab my hand a second time, looking concerned. This time, I held his palm tight.

I look directly at Nyta, and she stares, nodding her head, as though she heard it, too. "She's still considered a new death. It will take time before she can appear as Isalora can... but she can speak to you. As long as the heart beats, one can still live in the spirit form... Now go, I have work to do."

Cory steps up to Nyta. "Your Priestess, may I have a few words first?"

She gives a slight glare. "Cory, is it?"

"Yes." He nods. "I have one request, please." And he lifts the hem of his pant leg, showing the valiancium steel cuff still attached to his ankle. "Can you remove it? Jeff told me you might know of a way."

"I know of one," she says, moving from the shelved coffers back to the table where Fran's body lies. "But it isn't going to be an easy task for my magic can't dispel it. And there is nothing here strong enough to cut it off."

"Then how do I remove it?" he asks.

"With keys," she states. "In the mines, down where the goblins pick for treasure, there is a dungeon. If you're lucky, you may come across one of the jailers. You must find a set of keys if you wish to be free of the cuff you wear."

"Is that the only way?" I press.

"I'm afraid it is, my dear." She pauses as though she remembered something. "Years ago, when Sarmira's army came to pillage the lands of Ladorielle, and when she came to attack the Storm Castle, the war left the palace vulnerable to looters like goblins. They stole much more than the keys to free people from valiancium steel chains."

She takes a needle, threads it, and begins to suture up Fran's chest. "If you can find the emerald dagger hiding within the mines, it will be an added bonus to you. It, too, can slice through that metal like butter, but it hasn't been seen for centuries."

Stunned by her words, she adds, "Now if you will excuse me, my dear lovelies, I have work to do."

"Thank you, Priestess Nyta." I kiss my aunt's forehead, and we turn for the door.

12
GENEVIÈVE'S RANCH

A LOT OF QUESTIONS weigh on my mind and some of it is beginning to make sense. The mystery of what is in the coffer that hid in the floorboard at the cottage is now solved, but like always, a new mystery seems to appear. The thought of Cory and the others being weakened by the valiancium steel has me yearning to find those keys and that dagger. They need to be at their full strength if we are to beat Madame Moyer.

"Dad, what do you know about the goblin mines? And what's this heart preservation thing all about?" I ask as I put on my boots. Cory nudges me with his elbow, as though to imply I shouldn't ask right now.

Dad firms his lips. "The goblins are sneaky and dangerous. Let's save that tale for another day, shall we?" he says and laces up his second boot.

Avoiding the question.

Not expecting a reply, Fran says, *"They're trying to protect you."*

Dad interrupts, "The preservation spell Nyta did in there, well, it's a way to preserve the life of a soul. As long as the heart beats, like Nyta said, the spirit lives in the real world. Otherwise, it goes onto the afterlife." He pauses with a smile. "What many might call heaven."

"So, in other words, it's entrapment for the spirit?"

"I wouldn't call it entrapment," Dad argues. "More like a form of immortality."

"This destiny is much greater than you or me, Wynter," Aunt Fran interrupts. *"Leave it alone for now. Trust me, you will learn the truth soon enough. Perhaps we should seek to find the keys and dagger, though. It may come in handy later."*

"It would free those trapped in doing Moyer's bidding." Out loud, I say, "There were a lot of coffers on the shelf in there."

"Yes, and I imagine you will see spirits soon, too, walking among the living, if you haven't already," Dad says as we head down the path.

"Cory, you have been quiet through all of this. Why?" I ask.

"I'm sure the more your memories come back naturally, the less confused you will be," Cory says. "Nyta is right. You have to regain your memory on your own without anyone interfering."

"It's all so frustrating. The continuous deflecting annoys me."

As we walk to Geneviève's, I scout the area. It looks more like a village or town than a ranch. I'd pictured a barn with many horses and a farmhouse stuck somewhere, but on the contrary, people are out and about everywhere. Some are on horses and some appear on flying creatures I haven't seen before.

People are dressed in odd attire, wearing bracers, helmets, gauntlets, and chest armor, while others wear tunics and leather bindings, with still others having plain clothing. It all gives me the impression I've stepped into a medieval world or a Renaissance Faire. Some women wear hoop skirt dresses and others colorful robes wrapped in decorative print. A select few women wear plain clothes like jeans and T-shirts. Did I walk onto a movie set? Although déja vu has kicked in, certain things, such as the flying creatures above have me thinking I've been here in the past.

"I see you're remembering more forgotten memories," Fran remarks.

"What are they?"

"It's a Lyongriff," Fran states.

"A what?"

"Lyongriff. A flying hybrid of a vulture and a lion. If you will notice to your left, that tower next to the horses' stable..."

I stop where Fran is directing me to look. *"Such strange looking creatures."*

Dad and Cory stop along with me. “Ah, yes. The transporter,” Dad says. “We will be riding that to Storm Castle.”

“I seem to have a faint memory of being on one. It’s not clear yet, though,” I say.

Dad replies, “Sounds like your memory is improving.”

As we travel to Geneviève’s house, I notice up in the trees, catwalk bridges made of wood planks are held in place by ropes. Some of the larger trees have houses attached to the trunks.

“Strange,” I say.

Cory veers in my direction, looking upward. “Many, if not most of the Pine Willow Elves, live among the trees.” Cory motions with his hand outward and gestures to keep up with my dad.

It isn’t long before we come to a house that looks like a horse ranch, with white fencing around the perimeter. A barn sets a few distances away to the left. Horses graze along the hillside above and behind the outbuilding. “This is Geneviève’s home. She owns the Inn in town, but Nyta told me she didn’t come in to work today,” Dad says as we round the wooden gate entrance.

A woman comes to greet us with a smile on her face, hugging Dad like they’re old friends. “Jeoffrey, it’s been a long time. Rory said you were coming up.”

“Where is she?” I blurt, forgetting my manners.

“She’s in the stable tending to the horses,” the woman answers with a surprised expression. “Who’s this you have brought with you, Jeff?”

“This is my daughter Wynter. Geneviève, I’m surprised. Has she changed that much with her white hair?”

“Oh, My Lady, you will have to excuse me,” she says. “I didn’t recognize you.”

Geneviève’s red curls dangle downward as she bows immediately before me. She has soft features and pointed ears like many of the folk we passed through town.

Feeling completely confused, I touch her shoulder, ignoring the pleasant fragrance coming from her hair. “Ma’am, no, you don’t need to do that, please. I’ve barely accepted it myself that my family is a member of a royal court, let alone having you bow before me. Besides, I’m a knight’s daughter, not a princess.”

Cory smirks.

She looks up. "Such modesty from a young lady." Genevieve pauses a few minutes, as though searching for someone. "Jeoffrey, where's Mae? Didn't you bring her back with you?"

Silence accrues for a minute. I swear Dad doesn't know what to say, and I glance at Cory, as though to ask for a telepathic explanation, knowing he can't tell me. Instead, he shrugs his shoulders as an answer.

"She's still there," Dad says, in a low tone.

"Jeff," she says, stepping forward, "you promised me she would come back with you. Why did you leave her... there with that... monster?"

Dad looks around to see all eyes on him. He hesitates to respond. "Geneviève, she's been turned. We can't bring her back right now. At least not until we find a cure."

"Turned, but how? That shouldn't make a difference, anyway. They're all over on Ladorielle." Her cheeks flush and for the first time, I hear a different heartbeat pound, and it's not coming from our little group. It becomes faster and stronger, like the sounds of adrenaline pumping to fuel a heart.

"She's an excellent marksman," Geneviève argues.

The strange heartbeat becomes heavier, and the thought of blood pumping gives me a thirst I have never felt before.

Geneviève presses, "There's no way Sarmira would have gotten to her; she would have pierced an arrow through that witch's heart before the speed of any vampire got her."

"It wasn't a vampire that turned her," Dad says.

Vampire? No, it can't be. I refuse to believe the monster inside me is that.

"If not a vampire, then what?" she says, having a confused look in her eyes.

Realizing it's Geneviève's heartbeat I hear, I glance to Cory to see if he notices my sudden change in feelings. And when I do, his look confirms my fear. I know he feels the same thing. Yet he seems to be controlling the urge to strike Geneviève down, unlike me.

Dad ducks his head. "Geneviève, shall we go inside? Perhaps... a more private place... to talk," he coaxes. Dad turns and glares at the both of us.

Does he know what just happened? The urge I feel again to kill, to taste the blood of another.

She bows and gestures with her hand. "Sure."

I follow them when I feel a hand on my shoulder pulling me back. "Wynter, wait. Can I speak to you for a minute?" Cory asks.

At first, I think he wants the chance to steal a kiss, but there's urgency in his body language. "I saw your thoughts, Wynter. Do you think you can hide it?"

Trying to brush off his remark, I ask, "What do you mean, Cory?"

"Don't play coy with me. It isn't going to work, you know that. Tell me what's going on with you? It's getting stronger, isn't it?"

I can't lie to him. Besides, when you're smitten with a person that can read your mind, it's kind of hard to keep it a secret.

"When Geneviève's heartbeat became fast and strong, I could hear it. And it was loud. It rang out louder than anything I've heard before. I don't understand it, Cory." We walk a couple of paces toward the barn, and Cory takes my hand.

"I mean, sure, heartbeats are nothing unusual since I turned eighteen. You all taught me to learn to drown it out, the white noise... but this?" Shaking my head, I look at my feet. "No, this is something different happening. There is rage I feel in my own heart. Like it's waiting to come out and destroy anyone who comes in my path... I fear I may hurt someone. Someone like you."

"You won't hurt me."

"How do you know that, Cory? Don't you remember what happened on the cliffs? Did you not hear what Aunt Fran said? As I become stronger, you will not be able to help me."

"Which is why you must learn to constrain your emotions. This isn't anything new, Wynter. I've told you from the very beginning this is something you need to overcome. I've been trying to wean you from my interference in settling down your emotions." He leans in, as though he's going to kiss me, whispering, "If what you're implying is true, that something dark and sinister is festering inside you, I know you well enough to know you will fight this evil to the bitter end."

"Bitter end? Is that what you think? That I will die?" I step away from him.

"That's not what I mean," he counters. "You will not let evil take hold of you like it did with your grandmother, Moyer."

"Yeah, about that, what do you know? How did she become the way she is?"

"I don't know the whole story. That tale is best told by Jeoffrey."

"My father? What does he know of it?"

"Only heard rumors of course, but it's said that when he was young he hid in the attic from Maura Moyer-Storm. She came looking for him and noticed the door to the upper level was open. Thinking she caught on to his hide-and-seek, she ventured inside the room to look for him. Instead of finding your father, she found a covered mirror instead."

"Why was it covered?"

"Nobody knows. Your father saw it all happen before his very eyes." Cory takes both my hands. "You're not *her,* Wynter. Moyer's evil comes from Sarmira's possession. Remember that."

"Then what is it inside me that is so strong that it wants to take possession of myself?"

"I don't know, but we will find the answer." He takes my chin, holding it still, and kisses me. "I won't let anything happen to you."

"Now, I understand why Moyer wants you so badly," I hear a familiar voice cut in behind us.

WE BOTH TURN AT the same time, not expecting an audience. "How long have you been standing there, Rory?" I ask, a little annoyed at the thought that she's eavesdropping.

"I heard enough," she says. "So, does Jeoffrey know about you two?"

"I think he suspects," I say. "We haven't officially announced it to the world, Rory. Geez, what did you hear?"

She shakes her head, giving a grin. "Don't worry, your secret is safe with me. Besides, I always did love a little spice of gossip."

"We need time. Wynter needs to learn to rein in her power."

"Oh, is that all?"

"Rory, don't. Not now." Cory appears worried like he's trying to keep a big secret and doesn't want me to know.

"What's going on?" I ask.

She glances at Cory, as though she is reveling in the mystery. "It's nothing, Wynter," she begins, "just a couple of old friends reminiscing about the past."

Her attitude takes me by surprise; she's not at all the same person I knew back in Washington. Or is this the real her and the Rory I knew a fake?

"I can tell you two must have some history." Then it hit me. "Wait a minute." My blood begins to boil again in my veins. I'll consider this my first test learning to control my emotions. "The day we were walking home from school... you already knew, didn't you?"

Smirking, she gives the same mocking look she had that day in the bathroom when I fetched the necklace out of the pool, except this time her demeanor is different. "My, she catches on quick, doesn't she, Cory?"

"What's your problem?" I snap.

"There's no problem." She sneers, as she passes me but not before nudging my shoulder. Putting up her hands, she says, "Sorry, my mistake. I lost my footing."

"Yeah, sure you did." I reach out to deck her, and Cory catches my fist.

"This is not the way to solve a misunderstanding," he implores, turning around to face her. "Hey, Rory, if you have a problem with me, don't take it out on Wynter."

"I have no problem with you or her," she bounces back. "How else are you going to learn to tame the beast if first you don't teach her how to master it?" She laughs, before turning up the walk to the front door of Geneviève's house.

"Are you okay?" he asks.

"Fine. I don't understand what's gotten into her. Why did she say those things?"

He sighs. "Rory blames me for her sister's fate."

"Her sister?"

The door to the cottage opens and Dad calls, "Hey, are you two coming in here or what? Geneviève cooked a fabulous lunch."

"I'll tell you later," Cory murmurs.

So, the mysteries continue.

We cross the grounds and into the house to see an average-looking suburban home. To the right, stairs are decorated with fresh-smelling garland, and the banister is strung with lights. In the corner, a Christmas tree stands next to a warm crackling fire, the windows are coated in fake painted-on snowflakes, and the kitchen island is covered with decadent sweets.

I look at Geneviève in amazement. "What's wrong?" she asks. "You look surprised."

"I am. I mean, I feel like I stepped into a house at the North Pole."

She giggles, grabbing a plate of cookies to offer me. "Chocolate chip?"

"Thank you," I say, grabbing two.

Geneviève adds, "We celebrate Christmas like people on Earth. Long ago, we discovered Earth's lovely tradition and liked it so much that we, too, celebrate it in December."

"So, it's December here, too?"

"Oh, yes. We don't get the snow on this side of the mountains, of course. Too close to the ocean and it doesn't even stick. I mean it snows, but most of the time it rains instead. I can remember it snowed once when I was a little girl." Geneviève seems to get lost in a memory. "But that is for another time. Please, come sit," she says, pulling up a chair.

We huddle around an old wooden table where Geneviève brings us mugs of steaming hot beverages. On the stove something cooks, but it has a different smell than what I'm used to.

"I was in the middle of cooking lunch when the dogs alerted me of your arrival. Are any of you hungry?"

"Yes, please. Thank you," Dad says.

"Dogs?" My question is quickly answered with two German Shepherds sniffing my legs. "Wow, they just came out of nowhere."

"Here on Ladorielle, they're invisible to strangers," Geneviève answers. "It isn't until they assert you're no longer a threat do they become visible."

"I see." I reach down and pet them both until they're satisfied, then they wander over to their dog beds.

"We came in from Songbird Meadow. Took us longer than expected." Dad peers toward me and then quickly looks down at his mug.

"Oh, I see," she says, bringing out the plates from the cupboard and placing them in front of us.

"I noticed Fran isn't with you. How is she?" Geneviève asks, setting down a plate full of sandwiches. "Hope you like tomato basil soup and grilled cheese." She places a large pot in the center of the table along with bowls.

Silence from the table is deafening as we all look down at our drinks, not saying a word.

After a long pause, Dad confesses, "It was a giant. Fran trapped him with her vine spell, and he somehow retrieved my sword, throwing it when her back was turned."

"And it hit her?" She sets down a pitcher of milk next to the pot of soup.

"Through the heart," Dad mumbles.

"I do hope you were able to save it. We need her if we are ever to defeat Sarmira," Geneviève says.

"Wait, what?" I know Fran is listening, but will she answer me?

"Of course, I will, and no, I won't tell what Geneviève means. At least not yet."

"Right because I need to find out on my own."

"No, because you will be upset with me if you know the truth, and I need you to focus."

"Yes," he says. "It's safe with Nyta."

"Excuse me," I interrupt, "but what is so important about preserving one's heart?"

"Jeff, have you not told her yet?" Geneviève probes.

"Tell me what?" I ask, looking at them both. "What other secrets are there? When is it all going to stop? What are you talking about?"

Dad shrugs, glancing at me. "No, I haven't told her. She has a lot more to discover." He takes a quick sip of his warm beverage. "Besides, we've seen what Wynter is capable of doing. We can't take any chances right now."

"Hello, guys, I'm right here. Tell me what?"

Rory is the one to answer. "Sarmira must be defeated in the spirit form. The prophecy states there will be a child born of dragon blood, and a descendant of the Kingdom of Ladorielle, who will come into her power at the age of eighteen with the ability to see the undead. This child will be the one to end the suffering of Ladorielle, granting peace to the land."

"Rory, stop! You have said too much," Dad snaps.

"You're all implying I'm that child?" I look at Rory in disbelief. My cheeks flush and my anger builds as I try to block out the rage. I give a quick glance to Cory. "I mean yes, it's been hinted here and there. People suspected. But it sounds like you all are believers of this, too?"

Dad shifts in his chair, appearing uncomfortable.

"You all knew about this all along, didn't you?" I ask, looking at Rory. "That day at the school when I mentioned I saw someone watching me, you knew who they were already, didn't you?" I stay calm. I'm not going to be the monster they all expect I'll become.

"Yes. And I knew about your Dad's plan, too," Rory adds.

"But you were compelled, that night. You had to be," I argue. "I saw the way your body language was unaffected by the events that played out."

"Yes, I was compelled. I don't remember what happened that night you left. The last thing I remember is your dad telling me to forget you." A tear rolls down Rory's cheek. "It wasn't until time passed a few days later that my memory returned. You were gone, along with Jeff and Fran. It's then I knew my mission was complete."

"Mission? I was a mission to you?" I clench my fists but remain calm. "I thought you were my friend?"

"No, Wynter, it wasn't like that," she protests. "We were friends... I mean *are* friends."

I feel calmness flow throughout my body, and I know Cory is at it again. *He doesn't think I can restrain it.* "Stop that!" I yell at him.

He gives a lopsided grin. "Okay, but only if you settle down first."

"You do realize the anger within her is in her nature, right?" Geneviève says. "It comes from the Deagon side. She will soon be stronger than you, Jeff. If you don't allow her to manage it, she will become more dangerous as that power in her veins grows."

"I know," Dad says. "But she's not ready to know the whole truth. Now is not the time for her to lose control."

"This is why we do things in baby steps, sir," Cory says.

Dad glares at Geneviève.

Her eyes grow big. "Oh no, don't go pinning this on me, Jeff. She should have found this out when she turned eighteen, the day she saw Isalora for the first time. When her power was in its infancy. The longer you two wait in hiding the secrets, the angrier she will become." She pauses, looking directly at Cory. "And the harder it will be for you to calm her down when she really does need help."

"Would everyone please stop arguing and tell me what the hell is going on?" I yell.

13
HIDDEN TALES

"LONG AGO, THERE WAS a great battle," Rory starts.

"Yes, I know," I say, impatiently. "I've heard this story before. The knight kills who he thought was Sarmira."

"No," she counters. "This goes further back than that. Where legends are only tales; however, this story is every bit true, passed down from generation to generation. What you don't know about me, Wynter, is I'm a Druid. Much like my mother here."

I look at Geneviève. "Your mother?"

She smiles with a nod, adding, "And Redmae is my other daughter."

Stunned, I say, "Redmae used to be human?" On the inside, I'm reeling with questions.

"Patience, my niece, you will soon know the whole truth, as we all do. But they are right; you must learn to control your anger. These secrets hidden from you are attempts to keep you safe," Fran says.

"So, is what they are telling me true? Your heart must beat for you to walk in spirit form?" I ask.

"Yes, also true. But we can talk later. For now, you must listen to the legend's past. Catch up on lost time. There is still much to learn before the Super Blue Blood Moon rises."

Solemn nods surround the table, and I lean back in my chair. "All right, I'm all ears. I promise to listen and not get angry. I understand there is much to discover and much you have been forced to keep hidden. What story will I hear first?"

"You know what," Dad replies. "Geneviève and I have business to attend to. Rory, why don't you and Cory show Wynter around?"

"Yeah, sure. Okay." Rory gets up from the table. "Come with me, I'll show you two to your rooms."

"Dad, no, tell me. You always do this. 'I'll tell you later,' and then keep me hanging." My anger flares again. Dad interrupted Rory's tale on purpose. To distract me from more secrets he's managing to keep hidden from me.

The calming of Cory's aura swoops in again, soothing my emotions. Even that makes me want to lash out, but like before, my body melts into coolness.

Rory ignores my theatrics as she walks away toward the back of the house.

"I promise it will all come to light, soon, my dear niece."

A tinge of resistance lingers but I grab my pack and follow Rory upstairs.

Rory gestures to the first door on the right. "We don't have many spare rooms but seeing how Mae won't be using hers right now, Cory, you and Jeff can sleep in here," she says, turning the knob as we walk in. "I know it's not exactly the neutral type of room, and I'm sure she won't mind."

"She has a bunk bed?" I snicker. "Didn't expect that."

"Yeah, well, she says it's perfect for storage. As you can see, she collects a ton of stuff up there. My mom hasn't changed this room since she left. Should be simple enough, just toss any extra bedding on the sofa over there," Rory says, pointing to a ragged old couch that clearly has seen better days.

I giggle on the inside, envisioning Dad and Cory both sharing a bunk bed with pink comforters. Her room is painted with multiple flowers covering one wall in colors of oranges, yellows, and reds. A small cottage sits in the distance with trees shadowing it.

"This mural is beautiful," I say.

"Mae did it a long time ago," Rory says. "She loves to paint."

I can tell the subject of her sister still hurts. "She's so talented."

Rory gives a slight smile and clears her throat. "Anyway, you can make yourself at home here," she says, looking at Cory. She points in the direction to the left of the couch. "There's a bathroom through there. Just lock the other side when you use it. It connects to my room."

"Thanks," Cory says. "I could use a good shower about now."

"Towels are in the cupboard behind you," Rory states.

"We all could," I say.

"There is another one in my mom's room," Rory suggests.

"That would be nice, thank you."

I glance at Cory, and he smiles. "I'll meet up with you two in a little bit."

"Come on," Rory says, pulling on my arm. "I'll show you to my room, where you can prepare to clean up, too."

We walk through the Jack and Jill bath to Rory's bedroom.

"Oh, and... Rory, I see through walls, remember?" Cory reminds me.

"Right. Like I'm going to do anything to hurt her." She shuts the door behind us, not waiting for a reply from Cory.

I gulp. *"Sees through walls?"*

"He was teasing. He doesn't really see through them, but he has exceptional hearing," Aunt Fran answers.

"What's that all about?" I ask Rory.

She shrugs her shoulder and shakes her head. "I don't know." She pauses, as though she wants to say more. "Cory and I have a long history together. Our families don't exactly get along. But that's for another time." She grabs towels from her closet and hands them to me. "My mother's room is across the hall." She points. "Through those doors and to the right is the other bathroom."

I KNOCK ON RORY'S door and open it with my hair still wrapped in a towel.

Rory has headphones on, reading. She looks up. "Hey." Setting her book down, she takes off the earpieces. "All freshened up?"

I smile. "Yeah, Thank you." I glance at Rory's bathroom. "He's still—"

Rory huffs, rolling her eyes. "Yes."

I sit at the edge of her bed, using the towel to dry my hair more. The silence is a bit awkward.

"Hey, Wyn, I want to say I'm sorry."

"For what?"

"About earlier. You know, in the stable. I was upset that—"

"That what?"

She moves to the end of her bed and sits with me. "I was trying to provoke you. To bring out your rage."

"But why?"

"I was hoping—never mind, it was wrong and I'm sorry. Sorry I haven't been there for you. A part of me wishes..." She stops, as though her tongue is tied.

"Wishes what? Rory, you had no idea how this would've turned out. How could you have possibly known?"

"That's just it." She hesitates and turns to look out the window.

"What aren't you telling me, Rory?"

"I knew this day would come should you succeed." She stands to part the curtains to let in more light, then turns to face me.

"What do you mean should I succeed?"

"Your father told me what he saw. The options we all had in defeating Sarmira. This path we are on now is the strongest choice."

"What are you saying? That you knew I would be kidnapped, and my family would be on the run again?" I stiffen and work on remaining as calm as possible.

I had already gone into a fitful rage before when Dad let it slip that he knew I would face the wrath of Moyer. His allowing me to go through such torture and pain still festers in my gut. I don't want the beast inside me to come out again. It needs to stay dormant as long as possible. That much I know.

"No, see, Wynter, you don't understand. It's my fault you were put into that position in the first place," she confesses.

"What do you mean, your fault?" I sense her heart quicken. In the short time I've had my new abilities I've learned to decode the language of a heartbeat. Rory's tells of panic and guilt. Perhaps now is my chance to ask Rory what happened in Washington State. I pull the pack from my shoulder. "So..."

"So," she counters, looking down at her hands.

It's an awkward moment for us both. "How long have you known?"

"Known what, exactly?"

"You know what I mean, Rory. How long have you been playing this double life? Pretending to be my friend and Dad's employee?"

"It isn't a double life, Wynter, and I'm not pretending to be your friend." She looks as though there's a real pain in her eyes, and her heartbeat falls to a sorrowful pace.

"Is this what you and Cory meant by learning to drown out the white noise from different heartbeats?"

"Yes," my aunt replies.

"We were raised together... sort of. You haven't come to that memory yet, and I can't offer you more. Else you will—"

"Yes, Cory told me. It may never come back." I pause, and I try hard to stifle the anger building inside me. "So, why confess at all?"

"If you ask the questions, I can answer them without harming your memory." She sits down on a chair in front of a desk and touches the surface. Her fingers hover over what looks like a mouse, and clicks, prompting a monitor hanging above her head on the wall to turn on. It's as large as a big-screen TV.

"Is that a computer?" I ask in shock.

She huffs. "Yes. Why so surprised? Wynter, it's not like you haven't seen one of these before."

"Yes, but here? I mean, in a place such as this?"

"You think your world, rather other worlds such as Earth, is the only place with similar items?"

She clicks the mouse again, and the tabletop lights up with keys. "No clunky keyboard?" I ask, stunned, wondering how the entire desk has been turned into a console panel. Rory hits a few keys, and the next thing I know we are on a sandy beach with seagulls flying above our heads.

"The computers here can turn a whole room into a hologram. We can go anywhere you like. Name the place and we're there."

"What? You mean now?" I ask, astounded by what I'm seeing.

"Sure, where would you like to go? I can change the beach scene if you like. It's on my default."

"It's as though I'm really walking along the beach. I feel like I'm stepping on real sand."

"You are. Take your shoes off," she suggests.

I do as she instructs. "Unbelievable. I can feel the warm sand underneath my feet."

She giggles. "And if you were to venture into the water, you would get wet, too." Rory's face lights up, and I'm sure it's because of the expression on my face.

I reach down to grab the sand and watch it fall between my fingers. "This is freakish, Rory. Almost makes my head spin." I feel dizzy and sit on the ground.

"Yeah, careful, it's a definite mind-bending experience."

Rory turns off the computer, and we are back in the walls of her room—the only difference is there are still flecks of sand lingering in the crevices of my fingers and toes. Looking at my hands, I say, "This is truly amazing."

"You haven't seen the half of it. So much to explore in this world, so much you have not observed, or rather have not remembered. There are devices some carry where one doesn't need a Druid anymore to jump from realm to realm."

I brush the sand out from between my toes. "You mean that beach we saw is real?"

"Yes. And anyone you see on the beach can end up here if I were to suddenly turn off the hologram. There are settings, of course, to allow the computer to control the outputs. I have mine on minimum reality. Which means only natural items can be brought back. Like empty seashells, sand, plants, you get the idea." She gives a spirited grin. "The best analogy I can provide is it's like what humans have their internet set to public or private."

I remember back to the car accident. Did someone in Moyer's group have one of these hologram devices with them that day?

"Tell me, Rory, the day we left when I heard my dad tell you to forget about me, was it all an act?"

"No. That much is true. True as you know it." She takes a long pause as though my words stung. "Your dad really did compel me that day. It's exactly like I told you downstairs: it had to be done to keep you safe from Moyer. He knew that Moyer's people were closing in, and I shouldn't get caught in it, or else it would compromise everything, including my sister. We all believed if your mind was swept clean of memories, you'd be safe, and that necklace would keep you shielded."

"Yes, I remember." The memory of that night brings me back to the awful events that occurred shortly afterward.

"My sister and I were raised as archers, and as you can see, this family is all Elven."

"Even you?" I ask, looking at her in shock.

"Yes, even me." And she turns her head to the side revealing her pointed ears. "I taped them back when we were in high school. It's not every day humans see people with pointed ears," she says, laughing.

The shower in the bathroom stops. "Guess Cory's done," I say.

Rory gets up from her computer chair and goes to her closet. "Might as well pull these out for later tonight." She tosses blankets on her bed.

"So, what do we have planned for today?"

"I don't know. Ask Cory, he seems to have it all figured out."

"I heard that," a muffled voice calls from behind the bathroom door.

"I counted on it," Rory shouts.

"What's with you two, by the way?" I ask as I put my socks, and boots back on. "It's like you hate each other."

She avoids my eyes, folding her arms. "We don't exactly get along. That confrontation earlier, down at the stable... yeah, it wasn't so much me antagonizing you, as it was me trying to provoke Cory."

"But why? Cory is one of the gentlest and kindest people I have ever met."

"He wasn't always that way."

"Maybe you're confusing him with Cole."

She huffs. "Well, isn't that rich. Cole is portrayed as the evil twin. Fascinating how the table quickly turns."

"What do you mean by that?"

The bathroom door swings open before Rory has a chance to answer.

"Filling my love's head with false information, are we now, Rory?"

"I wouldn't think anything of the sort, Cory." Her sly reply tells me she has more to say.

"I should hope not. You wouldn't want Wynter to trigger a false memory, now, would you?"

Her cocky posture changes, and by my newfound ability to measure heartbeats, Cory's is calm and cool, while Rory's beats like a drum at a football rally.

"You ready, Wynter?" he asks, with a smile.

"Ready for what?"

"There's something I want you to see." He glares at Rory as he hooks his arm around my elbow moving me toward the door.

14
HOUSES DIVIDED

"WHAT'S THAT ALL ABOUT?" I ask once we leave the house.

"That's what you call a rivaled history between Houses."

"You mean like the clans that visited Storm River Manor during the party Moyer threw?"

"Yes, something like that. Except Moyer deals with the dark side, and those were clans of vampires, necromancers, and werewolves."

"Werewolves? I didn't see any of the sort there at the party."

"Trust me. They were there. There's only one group that can stand to be in the same room as the other vampires, and that's the hybrid Moyer created—her vampire-werewolf species."

"More Nytemires?"

"No. Nytemires are of Storm blood. The sorcery of a necromancer mixed with the vampire, remember?"

"And Redmae, is she one of these creatures?"

"Not exactly. Unlike the typical werewolves, she's a dire wolf. But that's not what makes her unique. Moyer didn't make very many like her. Too dangerous and they're hard to control. You see, similar to the changes that we vampires go through, we can stay fairly human looking." Cory grabs my hand, guiding me down a path through some trees.

"Where are you taking me?" I ask.

"I promised to show you the sea, remember?"

I smile. "Right." I follow alongside him as he continues his story.

"As I was saying... unlike most of the creatures Moyer has concocted, there's something in the gene of the dire wolf that mutated, and instead of having human features, the wolf remains a wolf."

"Except her size is magnificent," I say.

"Yes... well, she does stand nearly as large as a horse," he adds.

"So, you're saying Redmae will always look like a wolf?"

"Except," he says, "her true form only comes out on a full moon night."

"Does she know she's been turned?"

"I don't know. We vampires don't exactly get along with her, kind."

"What about you and Redmae?"

He huffs. "Redmae despises my brother Cole."

"Seems Redmae and I have something in common already," I say.

"And so, you can see where I might be going with this, can't you?"

"Maybe but tell me more."

"Before Redmae was kidnapped by Moyer's men, she and Cole would always challenge each other. Not exactly sure what started it. It was their pride, really. Mae felt as though she was better than Cole at archery. Cole, I think, didn't like being beaten by a girl. So, he would always try to prove himself better than her."

We come to a small clearing, and I hear the ocean's waves crash. "The water is beyond that cliff," Cory says, pointing.

I look to where the sky meets the water and birds fly above squawking like seagulls would. They're a different-looking kind of bird though, bigger, having a turquoise tint.

"They get their color from the sea and the green algae from the lower rocks. They're not freshwater birds, and most of them don't go past the beach." He smiles. "I haven't been down here in years. Follow me, I know of a cave down below off the shore. I wonder if it's still there."

Curious, I ask, "And what's in this cave?"

"I don't know, exactly. I never went inside. Blair was always one step ahead of me. I remember once, as I entered the mouth of the cavern she appeared in front of my brother and me, warning us not to go any farther, and if she ever caught us there again she would take away all our electronics."

"And did you go back?"

"Are you kidding me? A boy that age wouldn't risk losing his toys."

We wind down a trail leading to the beach below.

"Oh, come on, Cory, where's your sense of adventure? Weren't you the least bit curious why Blair ordered you away?"

"Of course. Why do you think we're going there now?"

"Cory, I'm joking. It could be dangerous. I mean, if Blair said to stay away from this cave, there has to be a reason why."

"Now look who's claiming not to be adventurous?" He smirks.

We hit the bottom of the cliff's edge, and I notice the sand is mixed with small gravel rocks. Not sandy like the beaches I'm familiar with, but layered with coral, orange, and cream pebbles.

"My brother and I used to come here all the time. It's the one place we could go to think. I remember we could always communicate with our minds here, not having to say a word. Our conversations were protected that way, but my brother and I can't communicate like that anymore, and it frustrates me."

As we approach the cave, an arrow whizzes by my ear, hitting a large piece of driftwood. "That's far enough," I hear a familiar voice say.

We both turn around to see Rory with a bow in her hand and a quiver set around her back. "Do you honestly think I'm stupid, Cory?"

"What's the big deal? I want to know what's in that cave."

"Something you don't want to find out."

"Now, you see," he persists, "that's exactly why I do want to know. What are you and the Pine Willow Elves hiding, Rory, that is so secret you cannot tell me?" His voice rises. "I'm a Storm and Wynter is, too. We have the right to know. As descendants of this kingdom, I command you to stand down."

And as though this is all a big joke, Rory begins to laugh. "You command me?" She steps closer. "I do not serve you." She takes another arrow from her quiver set and prepares to aim. "Now, kindly back away and go about your business. I won't miss a second time."

"Seriously? You're going to shoot me? In front of Wynter?"

"Rory, what's going on?" I ask.

"Stay out of it," Rory yells. "You have no idea what you're getting yourself into here."

"Oh, I think I do. You have that arrow aimed at Cory's heart. What's gotten into you?"

"Why don't you ask your boyfriend? Perhaps he can shed some light." She stretches the bowstring. "I don't see you two moving yet."

"Come on," Cory says, taking my hand. "I'll show you another time. It's not worth it right now."

"Over my dead body, you will," Rory retorts.

"That can be arranged," he snaps. "I'll find out what you're hiding in there."

After we are a few distance away and I feel it safe to speak, I say, "Cory, what are you not telling me about her? Why do you two hold such animosity toward each other?"

"Remember Drena?"

"I think so. She's Blair's mother, right?"

"Yes, well Drena's father was a Pine Willow Elf. One day while fetching water from a nearby stream, Drena saw smoke. It was then that she found her family's house burning with her sisters and mother inside. The Underworld's men claimed them to be witches, panicking the town. The men took her father hostage. Drena got away. He later met Geneviève's mother Laveena, and the town was renamed Geneviève's Ranch. Pine Willow Village was brought back to stability from the chaos. This valley is very much hidden from the rest of the realm. The mountains divide this section of the world. Either portal or flying is the only way in."

"How do you know this?"

"My mother," he says with a grim smile.

"So, does that mean Rory is your cousin?"

"Yes, I suppose you can say that. Distant cousins that is."

"But if she's family, why would she turn on you like that? I saw the hate in her eyes, Cory."

"Long ago, according to the stories told by Blair, a vampire turned Drena, and the Pine Willow Elves have never forgotten."

"Who told her that?"

"Geneviève." He glances at me. "The animosity you see coming from Rory isn't toward me personally; it's about what I am. She and Geneviève both know. They know Jeoffrey is, too, and they suspect you might be as well." Cory grabs my hand, and we stop at the edge of the shore, listening to the waves crash around us.

"But I wasn't ever bitten." In the far distance, Rory is keeping a watch on us both. "Can she hear us?"

"No, she doesn't have the listening skills you and I have."

"How is it I can have the same symptoms as you and Cole, yet the beast within me never appears?"

"You have the essence in your blood. You're a Storm. Neither Cole nor I were bitten, either. Rather it developed later after we turned eighteen. Why that age is the magical number, I do not know."

"Tell me something, Cory. How is it that I have this fire ability? If I'm a Nytemire like you, why do the flames not burn me alive? You said so yourself, only fire can kill a vampire and the like."

"That's the mystery, isn't it?" he counters.

"So, you don't know either?"

"Fran had a similar ability. Perhaps it's the Deagon side of you?"

We walk farther down the beach and find a place to sit down. I reach to pick up an odd-looking shell lying on the sand. It's coiled in shape, with black spikes protruding out, with the color of mother of pearl.

Cory grabs my hand. "Don't touch that."

"What is it?"

"It's a Sea Spike. Once you touch it, the poison will travel through your veins until it reaches your eyes and blinds you permanently. No magic cure after that."

I retract my hand. "I really do need to ask you before touching something so exquisitely unique." The Perpalily comes to mind.

"Or remember who you are," he adds.

"Right. Do you know why Drena's father was kidnapped by the Underlord's men?"

"He was a Druid. The most valued porter next to Geneviève. I suspect that cave has a portal, and perhaps that's how the Underlord came through to grab Drena's father."

"So, Druids seem to be very valued."

"Indeed, they are. Each Druid is unique in that not every Druid can teleport to the same location. Here on Ladorielle, we call them porters for short."

"Rory showed me a hologram in her bedroom. Why have a Druid if you have a computer with a hologram that can take you to wherever you want?"

"Because it has its limits. And what Rory may not have explained to you earlier, it has its own glitches, too. While you can go anywhere you like through a hologram, you can also be abandoned."

"Meaning?"

"Meaning, if one ventures to a destination, they can be left behind should the hologram shut off. It was developed long ago, and it's how Ladorielle banishes those who have done crimes and gone against the crown."

"How barbaric."

"Not as barbaric as Earth. At least here, the prisoners are free to roam the world where they have been banned, instead of jail or the dungeons, like it used to be."

"Tell me more about these Druids."

"They must require a rune first. Some are simple quests to achieve this mastery, other times you're awarded the honor from The Counsel, and on rare occasions, a Druid may find one hiding throughout Ladorielle."

"That's extremely fascinating."

"Perhaps, it does sound intriguing, but I hear it's quite a painful process, once they obtain a rune."

"What do you mean?"

"When a Druid acquires a new portal rune, once they grab it in their hand, the rune absorbs into their palm, then travels to a certain part of their body, tattooing itself underneath the skin."

"I haven't seen any tattoos on Geneviève."

"That's because you can't see them unless you're under a special light."

"Like a blue light?"

"Yes, something like that. You know the blue light that flows through the dining room at Storm River Manor?"

As though a lightbulb comes on in my mind, I remember when all the orphans became pacified while eating their food. "So, that's how Moyer can find the Druids?"

"Yes. That's her most effective way of locating them. And the other scary part is her eyes can filter them out. Remember that time when I told you the family from our world came to Scotland?"

"You're talking about when she had her men kidnap that boy, right?"

"Yes."

"Are you saying she has this... this blue light built into her eyes?"

"She does, as do I. And every other Nytemire."

"My father, too?"

"We all do. The only difference is she's not a Nytemire. Nobody has been able to figure out how she's able to have such skills. The closest conclusion we all can render is that she acquired the magic along the way through the centuries stealing others' gifts."

"And what about me, Cory? I can't compel. I don't have the glowing blue eyes like every other Storm, either."

"Not yet, anyway."

"What do you mean by that?"

"Well, aside from everything else, your ability to use fire and your inability to compel, it has me rather perplexed, too." He pauses to pick up a few rocks, throwing them into the crashing waves. "It also may have something to do with the necklace you wear," he says, glancing at my neck.

I grab it, looping my fingers in the chain. "It does keep me from being compelled, so perhaps that means I can't do the same to others." I glance down at the locket, and the amulet begins to glow bright. "Cory, what's going on?"

"I don't know," he replies, as he, too, looks at the illumination emitting from my locket.

Out of the corner of my eye, I see in the sky a flock of birds coming at us. "Those seagulls appear to be flying in a hurry."

"Those aren't birds." Cory backs up, appearing concerned. "They're dragons, and someone appears to be riding one. We need to take cover. Now!"

"Get down!" Rory screams from a few yards away, as she prepares an arrow while running. "Take cover!" She takes aim and fires. "Move to the rocks."

"Wynter, use your fire magic," Fran interrupts.

"How long have you been here?"

"Long enough, now do it."

I do as Aunt Fran says, and grab hold of the energy within me, but nothing comes to the surface. *"It's not working."*

"Because you're not concentrating."

Before I have a chance to muster up a fireball, one of the dragons unleashes his own. We make a run for some rocks set into the side of the cliff and dive behind a large boulder. "It appears that there is only one rider, the rest are following his lead," Rory says.

"What do you suppose they are after?"

"If I had to guess?" She stares at me.

My eyes get big. "Right."

Rory shakes her head and steps out into the open, firing another shot, and landing a direct hit on one of the dragons. Ducking back behind the rock for cover, she boasts, "Got one." A screech of pain comes from the beast.

"It appears so," Cory says. Flames of fire shoot past us, as the rock we're behind builds heat. "You managed to provoke him more, though."

"We can't let them reach the town. They'll destroy it," Rory calls, preparing another shot.

"Wynter, listen, when Rory makes this next round, I want you to join her and make fireballs. Think you can do that?" Cory asks.

"Yes, but what are you going to do?"

"Conjure a distraction." He grins. "Don't worry, you got this. Look at it as a part of working on controlling your gift. A test. Rory needs your help. Use your anger, allow it to build. Take this opportunity to take that rage and turn it to your advantage."

My necklace glows brighter, its blue hue taking hold. A cool sensation runs through my veins this time, rather than the boiling heat I'm used to.

"What's happening Aunt Fran?"

"You're allowing fear to control you right now. This is good. Better, actually. What I want you to do, when the dragon breathes fire, use your abilities and fire back."

Rory again steps out, aiming at one of the beasts. The leader comes straight for her, and I move out, too. I think I surprised the rider of the dragon, and he pulls up on the reins right as the creature sets fire to the shoreline. Rory shoots, and I release every ounce of energy I have consumed, but instead of fire, water emerges from my hands, directly hitting the dragon's mouth. The power is so strong the rider falls into the ocean.

The dragon tries to retaliate with anger of his own and opens its mouth, but nothing comes out. It wails out loud, screeching in frustration and the rest of the fleet retreats. The large dragon grabs his rider from the water with its talons and they fly away, but not before the rider gives one last shot with his arrow.

"You did it!" Cory shouts. He comes up to hug me. "I knew you had it in you."

Out of the corner of my eye, I see Rory fall to the ground. She's hit in the shoulder.

"Rory!" I race to her aid, and I see a lot of blood. My first reaction is to pull out the arrow.

Cory holds me back. "Wait. This arrow may be poisoned. We can't take a chance touching it.

"I'm fine, guys. It's just a scratch."

"Yeah," I say, "a fine scratch. Hang on, let me heal you."

"Don't touch the arrow," Cory reminds me.

Nodding, I concentrate on trying to heal Rory. My hands glow a bright yellow. "Look away, this might hurt your eyes." I hover over her wound, sealing the flesh around the arrow, hoping that will suffice until we can get her back to Nyta.

Can you walk?" I ask.

“I think so,” she says.

“It won’t last long, though,” Cory says. “If it’s the poison I think it is, your healing is only temporary as long as the arrow is embedded in her shoulder. Let’s get her back to town where we can ask Nyta for help.

15
OLD HISTORY

NYTA BREAKS THE ARROW shaft. “This will hurt,” she warns and pushes the arrowhead through to the other side.

Rory screams in agony.

“Isn’t there something you can give her?” I ask.

“Like what? I have nothing to ease the pain. Unless you have a better idea?” Nyta answers.

I look around her cave-like house. “You have nothing in this... this place?” I turn glancing in all directions. “There must be something?”

Nyta stops. “There is.” She glances at Cory.

I stare in her direction. “You?”

“You know it may not work, Nyta,” he answers, as though he knows exactly what she’s implying.

“Right, the mind thing,” I say.

Cory approaches, and Rory exclaims, “I’d rather die than have that monstrosity lay his eyes upon me.”

“Rory, don’t be so stubborn. It will help you forget the pain,” Cory hisses.

“No! I’ll deal with it. Nyta, go, I’m ready.”

“On three,” she replies. “Ready... one... two.” Nyta doesn’t finish counting, pushing the arrow through Rory’s shoulder as she screams.

“There, it’s done.” Nyta smiles as she throws the arrowhead into the fire. “Quick and unexpected, just the way I like it.”

The pain must have been too much for Rory to bear, and she lays there, unconscious.

"Will she be okay?"

"She'll be fine," Nyta assures, "for now, but the healing you did on her will not last. Eventually, the poison will travel through her body if we do not find an antidote soon.

"What will it do?" I ask.

"Blind her."

"Sea Spike poison," Cory blurts. "I had my suspicions."

"Yes, it appears so. Wynter managed to slow the poison." Nyta takes a jar from one of her many shelves, removing what looks to be leaves. She drops them into a mortar bowl and begins grinding them with the pestle.

"What are you doing now?" I ask.

"You are a nosey one, aren't you?"

"Just curious is all."

Nyta snorts. "Is that all? Seems you're quite intrigued about everything. I'm not surprised, though, you do have your reasons." She continues to grind, adding more leaves, but from a different jar this time. "I'm making an ancient herbal tea. It will help slow down the poison."

She stops grinding to prepare a kettle of water and places it on the hearth. "This tea is used on many poisons to slow the process," she says and moves back to the table continuing to grind the leaves with the pestle.

"Why do you think someone poisoned the arrow tip with Sea Spike?" Cory asks. "Why not something deadlier?"

"Perhaps they didn't intend to kill anyone. Just blind the ones around their intended target. Easier that way than starting a war against another House." Nyta diverts her attention, adding, "Something tells me Vothule knows you're here, my child." She glances at my necklace. "Did that amulet glow by chance?"

I look down at my chain. "Yes, blue."

"Seems your powers are getting stronger, Wynter." She turns back, taking the mortar bowl over to the kettle of boiling water and dumping the leaves in, saying, "And the amulet didn't glow before today?"

"Not that I can remember, no. I've only known it to protect me from Madame Moyer, although Aunt Fran did say it would shield my location, too."

"Ah see, now that's where you're mistaken. It's much, much, more than just an amulet." She turns and smiles at us both. "My dear Wynter, you hold around your neck The Amulet of Protection. When your great-grandfather made that locket, he had it enchanted before giving it to your great-grandmother Sara."

Nyta gestures with her hands to a sofa at the other end of the cottage near the kitchen. "Please, sit. Let me fix you both some tea as well."

Taking a box out of a kitchen cupboard, along with three mugs, she fills them with water and sticks them in a microwave. She must have heard my huff of astonishment because she chuckles, saying, "This village is not all barbaric. We still indulge in some earthly modern technology." She shuts the door and presses the buttons on the appliance.

"This is black tea. I have green if you prefer?" she asks, pulling out three bags from the box.

"No, this is fine, thank you," I say.

"Tell us more about this necklace Wynter wears." Cory seems more intrigued than me at this point.

"Yes, well, the legend of the Storm family's tale is told among the many Houses, each having its own version. I'll tell you the side I know to be true," Nyta begins.

"At first, we didn't know what to do when Sarmira came for the kingdom the first time. Most of us couldn't defeat her magic, and the only one close enough during that time was Dragonscale. I sought shelter here among the Pine Willow Elves. I had some magic, but I'm no match for Sarmira's power. She tried to claim the lands for herself. The only way to do that was to weasel her way in."

The microwave sounds off, letting us all know the mugs inside are ready. She takes them out and places the tea bags in each cup. "Cream or sugar for your tea?" Nyta asks, pulling out sugar cubes, along with a container of milk from the fridge.

"Straight up for me, thanks," Cory answers.

"Two lumps please," I say. She fixes all three teas and adds milk to hers.

Setting the cups down at the coffee table in front of us, she sits in a recliner and takes her first sip. "To a new king, if Sarmira could claim the heart of the ruler, perhaps she would have the advantage to gain control. Our only choice many years ago was to flee the lands the people called home. So many came here because it is well hidden to most predators. Others fled to the world you remember, with no magic at all."

She sets down her cup, then folds her hands in her lap. "At first, it worked perfectly, but Vothule and his crystal ball, found where many escaped. He sent Sarmira to rake the land, sparing nobody.

"She had strict instructions, kill the queen of all the realms, and force the king to marry her. She knew she had to plan it just right, too. Trick the king into thinking there would be a truce. The kingdom planned a gathering of feasts between the houses of the realm. There, it is suspected, Sarmira slipped a poison in the queen's drink." Nyta stares at her teacup, adding, "It was the poison of an Iknes Shaw."

"Isn't that what Nora became?" I ask, looking at Cory.

"Who's Nora?" Nyta asks.

Cory chuckles. "Wynter's lady's maid back at the manor. They seem to have a difference of opinion."

"I see, well, I don't know of this... lady's maid you speak of, but I can assure you, the poison they carry is very deadly."

"Yes, that's what we're told," Cory concurs. "So, what you're saying is this queen—"

"Laurawyn was her name," Nyta cut in. "And yes, she was poisoned. Died when her girls were still young, leaving Greyson a widower. Sarmira moved right in. The whole kingdom was outraged that he would marry her so quickly after the death of his beloved queen. What we didn't know then was he was compelled by her magic."

"The glowing blue eyes," I say.

"Yes." Nyta picks up her cup, takes another sip, then gets up, placing it on the kitchen counter. She walks to the kettle boiling on the fire. "Looks like this herbal tea is about done. Wynter, will you grab me a mug from the kitchen cupboard please?"

Bringing the cup over to her, I ask, "What happened next?"

"She started a war." Nyta takes a strainer, filters the liquid into the mug, then takes a cloth and dips it.

"What is that anyway?" I turn away and plug my nose. "And that smell is gawd awful."

She snickers, as she twists out the rag. "Grimmroot, basilore, and lily dust. It will help with Rory's pain and slow the poison." Placing the cloth on her shoulder, Nyta adds, "Would you mind helping me lift her head? We need to get some of this liquid in her."

I do as she instructs. Rory stirs slightly, saying something under her breath, which allows Nyta to give her some fluid. "There, that should do it."

"Now what?" I ask.

"Now we wait."

"Please tell us more about this war."

"Has your father not told you of the last battle of Ladorielle?"

"No, I'm the one who told her," Cory answers. "My version, that is, or the story as it was told to me."

"Ah, I see. Well, let me tell the story about the hand which laid the deciding blow."

"Wait," Cory says, "you knew Sir Bryce?"

"Aye, back then, I was the priestess of the royal court. Also, the one who did confessions for the kingdom," she boasts as she refreshes the cloth with warm liquid. "Bryce came to me with his admissions. He had slain the evil queen of her madness but hadn't suspected what would have come next. When he pierced Sarmira with the Sword of Valor, shattering her in a million pieces, he had no idea that it would in turn also sacrifice his life."

Nyta pauses, appearing to gather her thoughts.

"He told me when he lay near lifeless on the ground he was within arms-length from his beloved Petra. That's when she touched him; healing his injuries, and in doing so, sacrificed her own life. He never forgave himself for that. During the years Petra and he were married she never revealed her powers and kept them well hidden from everyone. Of course, it wasn't until the eldest boy Gavin turned eighteen did Bryce realize his children held the necromancer gene. Knowing the price he paid all those years ago, he sought out the wizard of magic to see if he could find a way to bind all three of his boys from ever obtaining such sorcery."

"The three necklaces," I blurt.

Nyta stops what she's doing and looks up at me. "Yes, those were some items, but not the ones Bryce had made."

I touch the chain around my neck, thinking of the story Dad told me in my room, remembering how the jewelry had come about.

"Ailbert your great-grandfather had become an apprentice for the wizard a year before Gavin, Ailbert's older brother, turned eighteen. So, it was only fitting for Bryce to ask if such jewelry could be made. The watches and rings among other things. The Storm family wears all such items made by this wizard to this day."

Nyta wraps Rory's shoulder, leaving the medicated dressing pressed against her upper chest. She talks as she cleans Rory up. "In reference to your necklace, Ailbert had one made for his betrothed. This is where the story tends to get shifted, but the true story is this: It's tradition to give the wedding party trinkets. So, as gifts on Sara and Ailbert's wedding day, he gave the two other necklaces to his brothers to be given to their betrothed should their time arrive."

"But Dad said the chains were enchanted."

"Aye, and indeed they are, but the brothers had them charmed after the Storm family discovered Sarmira was alive."

"The rings Jeoffrey, Chad, and Derek wear are spellbound by magic. They cannot wield their gifts like they are able to. They are shielded by wearing the ring. You see, the rings are like a double-edged sword. Wearing them will protect your mind from Sarmira, but if you take them off, you have to quickly learn your born skill in a matter of hours before the matriarch finds you."

"Are you saying the rest of the Storm family possesses powerful magic, too?" I ask in disbelief.

"Indeed, they all do, but they are powerless, so long as they wear the valiancium cuffs about their ankles. And your dad Jeoffrey keeps the ring on for one thing only. To protect you. He knows as soon as it is taken off, your location will be like a beacon. Your father is very powerful, my dear."

"That's it, isn't it?" Cory questions. "This confirms that we must find the keys."

"And now, the Waxlily," Nyta says. She gets up and wobbles to the kitchen.

"Waxlily?"

"You must seek the goblin mine but be very careful. Some of them will see you whether you are invisible or not. The potion I gave you earlier will not work." She hands us both a small trinket resembling charms. "Attach them to your enchanted items. As long as they are on you, you will see anyone that is invisible. But the caveat is they, too, can see you. You will notice them by their aura. Those unseen by the physical realm will have a gray glow surrounding their body. You two will now have the same gray aura. Tread lightly, for most of those invisible are so for a reason."

Thunder rumbles outside, and rain pelts the windows. "Looks like we're getting a rainstorm," Nyta says.

Distracted by the swishes of water and wind, I pause a moment before asking, "Where do we find this mine?"

"I know," Cory answers. "It's the cave I tried to show you today. Remember when I told you Blair would take Cole and me to the beach?"

I nod.

"Sometimes, I would see strange beings come in and out of that cave. When I asked her, she ignored me, and said to not speak of it or go near it."

"But why there?"

"Because it is where you will find the Waxlily," Nyta answers. "I need its roots to cleanse Rory's veins, and you need the keys to free your family before the war of the Underworld begins, again. I see this as a win, win."

"If it's so dangerous, should we be going alone?"

"You're not, my dear." And as though the door has ears, a knock comes from the other side.

16
THE CELLAR

Cory opens the door to Geneviève and Dad standing drenched from the downpour of rain. Crossing the threshold to Rory's side, Geneviève asks, "What happened?"

Dad follows behind, but not before taking his wet hat and hanging it outside. "It appears the rains have come early this year," he says.

I begin to speak, but Nyta beats me to it. "She was shot by a poisoned arrow. I examined the tip. It has the markings of a Trek."

"You mean the ogres? What are they doing this far south?" Geneviève asks. The concern in her eyes gives me a sense of fear. "They have no business in this part of the world. That's impossible; they would never risk such a treaty." She pauses, looking at me. "Unless..." Getting up from where she soothes her daughter, she paces toward me, but not before my dad puts out his arm, holding her back.

"Now hold on a minute. We don't know all the facts yet. Besides, do you think I'm going to stand here and allow you to harm my own daughter?"

I swear I see a glimpse of color change in Geneviève's eyes, giving me a sense that something is not quite right with her either, along with the rest of this supernatural world I'm in.

She pushes Dad's grip away. "What do they want with you? What... have... you... done?"

I take a step back. "Me? I have no idea what you're talking about."

"The only time the House of Trek would ever step foot into our territory is if something drastic has happened. They would never break the treaty binding them."

"I assure you I haven't done anything, and if I had, I wouldn't know what it was."

"Lay off, Gen," Dad says. "Trust me, we will get to the bottom of this."

Rory stirs, waking from her slumber. "What's going on?"

Geneviève's body relaxes, and she turns to her daughter. "It's all right, sweetie. You had an accident."

"Yes, I remember. I was shot by a Trek, riding a dragon with Ashengale markings."

"No, that can't be," Geneviève argues.

"I saw what I saw, Mother," Rory asserts. "They were after Wynter, shooting Sea Spike poison arrows."

Her mother turns to face us. "I—I don't understand."

"I do," Nyta says. "Wynter is the only one of her kind. Every House in the land is after her head." She changes her direction toward me, saying, "My dear, I don't think you realize how much power you have inside that little body of yours, nor know how valuable you truly are."

"You know they will come looking for her as long as she stays here," Geneviève challenges.

"Yes, which is why I have put her and Cory on a mission," Nyta says. "To wear off their scent. When they discover she is no longer here, the outsiders that venture into this town will leave." She again stares at both Cory and me. "You two will depart at dawn."

"Not alone." Dad steps in.

"Of course not," Nyta says, coming from around her kitchen island. "Here, take this." She hands him a charm like the ones she gave Cory and me. "It's enchanted with an invisibility spell and will help you on your journey."

The rain outside pounds down upon the roof, making it hard to hear. "Come with me," she adds. "I have more to show you in the cellar." Nyta diverts her attention to Rory. "You may go home with your mother. There is nothing more that can be done for now, except rest."

Geneviève's eyes glint a hint of glow, like Dad's, only green. It's as though something else has possession of her body. I feel I'm the only one that notices.

"That's it?" Geneviève asks, appearing annoyed.

"My dear friend, what else will you have me do?" Nyta asserts. She tilts her head to the side and folds her fingers. "Go home."

"Mother, she's right. I should rest in my own bed," Rory says as she gets off the examination table.

Both women go to leave. "Thank you, Priestess Nyta, for all you have done," Rory adds, before shutting the front door.

"What's with Geneviève?" I whisper to Cory.

But Dad answers, "She's half Dryad.

"Wait, but I thought... I'm confused. Isn't she Drena's sister?" Then my eyes bug out, realizing the stretch of age span.

"Try not to think about it too much," Cory interjects.

"Okay, I won't. But we're going to talk about this later," I say. "But that still doesn't answer my question."

"No, I don't have Dryad blood in me if that's what you're wondering," Cory answers. "Drena and Geneviève had different mothers. Long after the death of Drena's family, her father Gage met Geneviève's mother."

"Laveena I think I remember you saying."

"Yes, she's the Dryad Queen of Shadow Vine Forest. When you saw Rory speaking to one of them, it was the royal guard of their court. Queen Laveena stood off in the distance. You may not have noticed, but I saw her observing through the trees," Cory says.

"So, Drena's father escaped capture?"

"Yes, but that's for a different time to discuss," Nyta says. "We have more pressing matters to deal with right now."

We come to the bottom step of the cellar to a combination door where she dials a code, then presses her hand upon the markings that appear on the door and it unlocks. Inside the chamber is much like the Hall of Secrets at the manor, only this time it's housed with an armory, in addition to a pedestal book. It, too, has many doors.

"Welcome to the Hall of Protection," Nyta says. "You might be familiar with similar rooms scattered throughout the universe."

"I've seen one at Storm River Manor."

"Yes, indeed. The council voted that it would be advantageous to build one there," Nyta says.

"So, the council decides where to place these rooms?" I ask, wondering what other areas have such portals.

She turns and smiles. "The council decides most things, but I brought you here for this." She walks to the area holding stocked items of weapons. "If you're going to venture out into the dangerous goblin mines of House of Grengore, you need to be prepared."

The anxiety grows as she speaks of this awful place we're all about to venture to. "What about seeking out Dragonscale or the Sword of Valor?"

"Rory can't hold off on the poison traveling her system," Cory says. "For now, this is the more important task at hand. Besides, Nyta is right, if we can somehow acquire the keys that will remove the cuffs and free the House of Storm from Moyer, it will put her at a disadvantage. And we need all the help we can get to defeat Sarmira at her own game."

"I know this is all new to you, and I know you're scared of all the changes. It will be fine," Aunt Fran says.

I huff aloud, and everyone turns their attention in my direction. "Don't be so disappointed," Nyta judges. "These armor pieces you see are much more powerful than you think."

On the inside, I'm reeling with frustration. *"Sometimes I forget you're still hiding within my mind."*

"Not in your mind, my dear. I'm right next to you if you would stop and look."

To my right, Fran gives a little wave. I know Cory sees her, too, through my eyes. He tilts his head and smiles, putting a finger to his lips.

"Why did Cory do that?"

"I'm thinking Cory suspects I'm your secret weapon, and if nobody knows I'm around, they cannot see me. It's brilliant. I concur with the idea."

"What do you mean by that?"

"In case you're captured." A grin forms on her face.

"Oh, you're reveling in this, aren't you?"

"I don't revel. Excited maybe, but no reveling. I'm thrilled to finally go back to the House of Grengore. It's been a long time. Perhaps I'll have a chance to play with the old chap."

"Old chap?"

"The goblin king. He thinks he's so clever." Aunt Fran appears lost in thought. *"No matter. I'll tell you about the adventure another time, I suppose. Pay attention to Nyta,"* she orders.

"Here is the perfect tunic for you, Wynter," Nyta says, waking me from the mindful conversation with my aunt.

She hands me a black, hooded robe-like garment that is shortened in the front. From the back, it resembles a long cape. Accompanying the outfit is leather pants. "It doesn't look very comfortable."

"I assure you it is, dear." Nyta smiles. "Now, along with this, I'll hand you these boots. They will help guide you in the direction of what you're looking for. Wear them, and you will never lose your way," she says and hands them over.

"As for you two." She directs her attention to Dad and Cory. "I have something different for you over here."

"I'm to wear this?"

A snicker comes from Aunt Fran. *"My dear, you're not in New York anymore."* She pauses to admire what I'm currently wearing. *"Besides, you'll stand out like a sore thumb if you continue to wear what you have on now. Can you imagine if the garments you're holding were worn on Earth—"*

"I get it."

"What would people think?" She looks directly at me. *"It's not any different here. You must dress appropriately. Might as well have a target on your back otherwise."*

"Okay, okay I get it," I say again, and this time, aloud.

Nyta diverts her attention to me. "My child, whoever are you talking to?" She stops and looks around. "Very odd, there's someone else in here. A ghost perhaps?" she asks.

Trying to think of a quick response, I say, "No one. I tend to have outbursts when I don't particularly like something."

"Lying, I see. No matter." She peers into my eyes as though trying to penetrate my mind. "Odd indeed. I can't hear your thoughts anymore." She diverts her stare to my neck. "Perhaps it's that amulet. You did say it glows now." She takes a deep breath and steps closer. "Are you saying the clothing isn't to your liking?"

I give a hesitant shrug.

"I assure you they are of the finest quality. Besides, you cannot go around this world in the same attire you're wearing now, drawing attention to yourself."

"I know, I get it. I don't have to like it. But I get it."

"Oh my." Nyta appears alarmed. "You do seem to have a mismanagement of your emotions indeed. Jeoffrey, I do hope you help this poor girl find her way. I see she needs a little boost of training."

"Agreed," Dad says. "We were hoping you might have some insight as to what to do."

For no apparent reason, my anger builds, and I can't control the rage evolving. It's like Nyta's words have sparked an uncontrollable fury.

"That's it," Nyta taunts, "bring it to the forefront. The only way to overcome it is to face it."

That's the wrong thing to say, and I throw the items down. Advancing toward Nyta with antagonism festering inside me, I grow a fireball in my palms.

"What's happening?" I ask my aunt. *"I'm so angry."*

"You're allowing the beast to take control. Will it away. You cannot win a battle with Nyta. At least not now, you have no idea how to curb your power."

I don't feel Cory stopping my feelings, either. I want to oppress it, but whatever it is, is gnawing inside, and has the upper hand.

"I'm not emotional. Take that back." I hiss, and my skin turns gray. Black veins appear once more and I feel my teeth extend, as I let out a growl.

Nyta smiles, giving me a cool and collected look. Dad and Cory approach, but she puts a hand up in the air, stopping them. "Gentlemen, I have this. It's no different from taming the others before her or you two long ago. Besides, whatever it is you boys are currently doing isn't proving fruitful for her, now, is it?"

I snarl as we circle in the middle of the room. My nails grow, and my muscles burn like fire.

"You want to challenge me, Wynter?" She smiles. "Go ahead, give it your best shot."

I want her to suffer and pay for thinking I'm this *poor little girl that doesn't know any better.* I'll show her. The ball in my hand grows bigger, heating the whole room.

"What are you waiting for? Throw it," Nyta taunts more. "Let's see how truly powerful you really are, shall we?"

The Wynter part of me lingers, pulling back, trying to fight the urge to kill but the beast is stronger, and without hesitation, I launch the ball of fire toward Nyta.

Nyta freezes the flame in midair. "That, my dear, was a mistake. Let me show you how it's really done." She flings my flaring ball back at me, knocking me against a wall. My eyes blur, and I lose focus, then it goes dark.

17
REDMAE'S STORY

It's dark and I wake in an unfamiliar place. Looking around, it hits me that I'm in Rory's room. I roll over to see her asleep. Reflecting on earlier events, it's clear the monster inside me is changing fast, and I'm not sure how to contain it. Cory's absent attempts to bandage my emotions has me concerned.

Not able to sleep anymore, I sit up. That's when I see Cory laying on a cot, with his elbow propped. "Good morning, sunshine. Sleep well?"

I glance over to Rory for a second, then whisper to Cory, "What happened?"

"Nyta sent you sailing on your ass is what happened."

Reaching for the back of my head, I notice a large lump. Touching it is painful. "How long have I been out?"

"Only a few hours."

"I guess you were right. I'm turning into the beast you and your brother are."

"I'm sorry. I was hoping it would have skipped you. With time, like everything else, you will learn to manage it. The difference between my brother and I, though, is he hasn't mastered control yet."

"Then, how did you?"

"Your dad… and Geneviève."

"What?"

"Remember when I told you I would sneak down to the cottage and fish along the river at Storm River Manor?"

"Yes, go on."

"Well, I didn't tell you everything. Your dad, with the help of Geneviève, would port me back and forth from the manor to Ladorielle for training." He pauses for a second and sits up against the nightstand.

"You mean to tell me you've been traveling back and forth? And Moyer never caught you? I mean, why come back to the manor at all, in that case?"

"I'm not going to leave my mother and brothers behind. When Moyer would leave on her 'business trips,' I would sneak out. No one would be the wiser. We didn't have the strict confinement nearly as much when she went away on excursions."

"So, that's how you have been able to hone your powers like conjuring tents and wands?" I feel a bit enlightened.

"Something like that, yes." He smiles. "Besides, your father likes the element of surprise. If Moyer caught on to our plans, she would have the upper hand. There's something else you must know."

"What's that?"

"I think Rory blames me for her sister's accident."

"I do not, you big brute," a voice comes from the other side of me and a pillow slams into Cory's face.

"Good morning to you, too, Rory," he says.

"Seriously, what's up with you two," I blast, raising my hands at the both of them. "And besides, shouldn't you be resting, Rory?"

"Can't rest with all your babbling," she huffs. "Besides, I feel fine."

"You say that now, but you won't later when the poison reaches your eyes," I reply.

"Well, regardless of what you two say, I'm going with you to the House of Grengore."

"How do you know about that?" I ask, surprised she's so intuitive. "And you're doing nothing of the sort."

"Hey, I'm not broken. I can see just fine, and Nyta gave me this medicine that I'm to take twice a day until you two find the Waxlily. Don't treat me like a child."

"Since when are you so eager to join in on the adventures?" Cory asks.

"Since it's my sworn duty as a Guardian of the Court."

"Guardian of the what?" I look at them, stunned. *More surprises.*

"Don't be so astonished, Wynter. It wasn't an accident that you and I spent the last couple of years together in high school."

I glance at Cory. "You knew about this, didn't you? I don't like being kept in the dark."

"Wynter, before you go off on your boyfriend, perhaps we should back up to when our little feud started."

"Sure, I'm all ears," I say in a sarcastic tone. "So, tell me more about this place and all the secrets you two have been hiding from me."

Rory takes an extra pillow, sits up, and stuffs it behind her back. "I don't know where to begin."

"How about the beginning? Now, there's a logical thought," I say.

Rory grabs one of her pillows and hits me. "Smart ass."

I giggle in spite of it all. "Seriously, I'll stop. Please, I'm truly intrigued."

She takes in a deep breath, grabbing back her pillow. "There are many Houses in this world. You're in Pine Willow Valley, and Geneviève's Ranch is the village, as I'm sure you're aware. You may have noticed earlier that throughout the tree-tops, many of us Pine Willow Elves live among them."

It's odd hearing Rory call herself an elf. When I think of elves, I think of fantasy books or online video games. The people here look like any other race, all shapes and sizes. In fact, not a single feature looks different except maybe the ears. They do have a slight point to them at the top. But it isn't noticeable, at least not to me.

"This is where I was raised, along with my sister Redmae, and Cole and Cory, for a time. We all used to be close." She glances at Cory.

"It's strange to think Redmae used to be human," I say.

"She still is... when the full moon is out." Rory smiles. "It all started one summer's day when we were all down by the river, having fun." She glances at Cory again. "Your mother Blair went up to the house to grab refreshments."

He smiles. "I remember."

"And where was I in all this summer fun?"

Rory turns to face me. "You were living somewhere on Ladorielle, safe, and away from Sarmira's detection."

"In Ladorielle years we were around ten years old," Cory says.

"Except Redmae. She's much older," Rory says. "Anyway, it was a lovely day, and the glow from our sun was nice and bright. It was very hot, and as I said before, Blair went to grab refreshments. Cole and Cory were down by the river, along with Redmae and me. We all were fencing, getting in good practice."

She pauses to look at me. "Your father thought it imperative that all young people should know how to defend themselves should a sword fight break out. He didn't care about who had what talent."

"Good ol' Dad," I say, flashing back to the time he, too, had me train at the cottage.

Rory presses on with her story. "Casey observed from the sidelines. He wasn't as nimble as the rest of us, but he did enjoy watching." Rory was deep in thought. "You see, something you may not be aware of is Casey is Blair's older son, and she didn't like the fact that Redmae and Casey had become close. Not exactly sure why Blair didn't like their unique bonding, but nevertheless the two grew quite fond of each other. Redmae would do anything for him. They were best friends."

I glance over to Cory as he nods, validating what Rory is divulging. I stop and think about what Rory said. "It makes sense why Redmae and Casey seem to have an understanding when she stood down the day she tried to eat me for dinner."

"Yes… and that is a whole other story. Basically, one of Moyer's attempted experiments went terribly wrong," Cory admits. "I guess you can say Moyer made them both who they are today."

"How long were you on Ladorielle before Moyer found you?"

"A while," Cory says.

"Getting off-topic," Rory reminds.

"Sorry," I say. "Please continue."

"Well, Blair and my mom Geneviève come down the hill, bringing lunch and refreshments, when a portal opens up over the river. Coming through the gate are a few of Moyer's Shadow Walkers. I didn't recognize any of them, except Chad."

"Chad? You mean my dad's brother?"

"Yes, but this happened before Jeoffrey gave him the protection ring he wears now. We all scatter. My mother reaches for me because I happen to be closest. Blair stares them all down, but her mind control isn't working. One of the shadows grabs Casey first. Blair freezes, watching. I mean not literally frozen, but it's like she didn't know what to do. Seconds later, she reaches for Casey's hand, as he calls out for help. Then the twins were grabbed. My sister Redmae managed to nail a couple of Shadow Walkers with her arrows. You see what we didn't know at the time—"

"Piercing them in the heart stops them dead in their tracks," I interject.

"Hmm," Rory remarks, "speaking from experience, are we?"

"Just a little." Cole being stabbed by Cory comes to mind.

She chortles. "Well, as you probably know then, pulling out the arrow on one of them was not a wise decision on our part. The beast reached for my sister's throat."

Rory grins. "Thankfully, all those stubborn days of insisting I learn archery paid off, and I slammed a second arrow into the Shadow Walker's chest. Of course, we also knew they were not officially dead, either. And we didn't know at the time how to kill them for good."

"So, what happened next? I mean, at this point Redmae hadn't been bitten yet. How did she turn into a wolf?" Knowing that Redmae was a human once has me hoping perhaps we can bring her to her old self once again.

Rory turns to me. "Not long after the kidnapping of Blair and the boys, Redmae and I went to Storm River Manor to see if we could get them back."

She pauses, fumbling with the blanket between her fingers. "It was stupid. I think the real reason Redmae wanted to go to Storm River Manor so badly was to bring Casey home. She wasn't afraid to venture outside our realm. She heard about the stories that Blair and Jeoffrey told. We used to all hide on these very stairs outside my room listening to all their tales." She laughs, and Cory makes a slight smile. Rory adds, "If our parents knew, I'm sure we would have been in deep trouble. Thankfully, they never found out."

"Or perhaps they did, hoping it would scare us to never venture to Madame Moyer's world," Cory cuts in.

"Perhaps you're right, but it didn't seem to work." She smirks. "Wynter, if you ever have the chance to meet my sister again, you will find she can be very persuasive."

Memories of meeting Redmae in the barn come to mind. "I remember her as a vicious animal."

"Yes, I do suppose that was an unexpected moment for you." She glances at Cory and smiles. "At any rate, my sister and I had never been to Storm River Manor. Looking back on it now, we should have gotten ahold of a map. We had hoped Cole and Cory would help and didn't expect that Moyer already had her hooks in them."

Cory stays quiet, letting Rory continue. His eyes look sad and his facial feature filled with regret.

"We were so careful, too," she went on. "Redmae was an excellent marksman. Father raised her to be the top archer of the family. I wanted to be like her, but he said I was to be a Druid like my mother. At that time, I only acquired one rune. A stone that would always take me home no matter where I was, and I would never be adrift. I can take up to three people with me. On that day, when we went to rescue Casey and the boys the first time—"

"You could only take three with you," I interrupt.

"Yes. Redmae insisted I get Cory and Cole, while she went to look for Casey. I protested the idea, but she wouldn't have it any other way. When I went back for her, after failing to find the twins, it was too late. I found her in the barn."

Rory's voice softens, "That's when I saw her lying on a stack of hay in one of the stalls. She looked cold and was sweating severely. At that point, she hadn't been changed... to a wolf, but what I didn't know was she had already been bitten."

Tears welled up in Rory's eyes, but she manages to stay composed. "Casey caught me and said not to go near her, or I would catch what she had. That's when he told me his side of the story."

"What happened?"

"According to Casey, Mae found him feeding the horses. He knew something was up because the animals were restless. When he turned around he saw my sister and a beast sneaking up behind her. When she turned around, the animal attacked her. She hadn't time to react before it gouged its teeth into her neck."

Rory fumbles more with the edging of her blanket and pulls her knees up, as though the memory haunts her every thought.

"Redmae gathered her composure and ripped a dagger from her waist, slashing the beast, which allowed her to take aim with her arrow. She managed to get a shot off but missed, which enraged him more. It howled, and soon a pack formed around her in the barn. She readied another arrow, hitting the creature in the right eye. The large dire wolf howled again, in pain, allowing her to get off another shot, which landed a direct hit to the heart, killing the beast instantly."

"No silver tips?"

She snickers at my ignorant comment. "This isn't a werewolf, at least not the kind told in storybooks. No. No silver anything, just her usual poison arrows... dipped in Iknes Shaw venom. After witnessing their leader die, the pack of wolves submitted to Redmae. It left her confused. That's when Casey told her the news that she was one of them now from the bite the leader had inflicted and that there is no known cure." Rory wipes her wet cheeks. "I have lived with the guilt ever since."

"When I came back that evening and told Jeoffrey what happened, we both agreed to leave out the part to Geneviève about Redmae being bitten. He convinced my mother he would get Redmae back, but for now, it was too dangerous to return. These unexpected events seemed to alter Jeoffrey's perception of the future."

"It's my understanding that my dad can see the future far in advance. How is it he was surprised?" I ask and reflect on when Dad explained at the kitchen table his gift of seeing the future; that it's subjective and not always concrete.

"He can control his own future actions with those close to him but he can't see the futures of most others. It's out of his control," she says.

"So, what you're saying is my dad's clairvoyance is subject to what is directly influencing his own life's path?"

"Yes. I suppose it's possible he can see others' future, but it's not as reliable."

"Or," Cory interjects, "he may have weighed in all the possibilities and chose the least of the damaged outcomes."

"Which was why he probably risked running with Fran and me, jeopardizing his own death, hoping if it played out as planned I would escape in the end." The feeling of rage inside me from my earlier tantrum comes to light, and I realize he probably thought the choices he made were best for me.

Cory reaches up to touch my hand. He smiles. "We will all get through this."

Rory stares at the opposite wall, as though she's dazed. "When I returned home alone, your dad was not pleased."

"Because you went out on your own to bring them back?" I ask.

"Yes. He said it would be his life's mission to keep you safe, and that I was never to leave your side from that day forward."

"I guess this explains why you claim to be my guardian."

Rory glances at me. "Anyway, Jeoffrey ordered a memory stamp be placed on us all. That day, we left Pine Willow Valley and remained absent until we were safe to return."

"Tell me how we ended up in Washington."

"It was yet another attempt for Moyer's men to grab you, of course," she says.

"What about Mr. and Mrs. Jenkins? Who were they?" I ask.

"An illusion placed on our minds," she confesses. "After about a year, mine wore off and I started to gain my memory back. Realizing I was caught up in a strange place with no clue how to get back to my home, I played their game until the right time came along to confront Jeoffrey and Fran. I regained my full memory, and the fake one stayed with me, too, so I didn't have to wonder why. I already had all my questions answered for the most part."

"What did you discover?" I ask.

"The side they knew, and why it's important to protect you." She rolls her eyes. "Other than the obvious, of course."

"What do you mean by that?"

"Nothing. You've been sheltered from the truth your whole life, memory stamp or no memory stamp. The end goal was to keep you out of the loop until the time arrived. It was easier to hide it from you while you were a child. But the closer you reached eighteen, the harder it became, and the more vulnerable you would be to everyone. Your dad said it was only a matter of time before *they* would find us all. We were already planning an escape to the cottage in the Cascade Mountains that same day you saw the hooded figures at school."

"So, you admit you knew who they were?"

"I knew they were Cory and Cole, yes. But I had to make you believe I was just as surprised as you."

"This all makes me feel like my dad and Chad were right. I can't trust anyone."

"It will all make sense soon," Aunt Fran says.

"Everyone keeps telling me that, but I keep seeing more mysteries and lies adding to the ones already existing."

"If it wasn't for Cory warning Jeoffrey that Moyer's men were on the way, you wouldn't have had the head start you did in the first place," Rory says, bringing me out of my thoughts.

I look at Cory. "I thought Cole was already a lost cause. Why was he with you? Cole has been under Moyer's thumb for years, according to you."

"They both have," Rory says. She glances at Cory, and he lifts his arm to point at the watch.

"Right after Rory tried to bring Redmae back and failed, Jeoffrey managed to have these watches made, hoping the second one would get to Cole in time," Cory says.

"I see. It's all starting to make sense now. And that's when my dad told you about the letters that would be hidden?" I ask.

"Yes, Isalora told Jeoffrey that the prophecy had begun and to prepare. We have to win this battle, Wynter, or we all will die."

"It will be the end of us all," Rory agrees. "What I don't think you quite understand, Wynter, is that once the Super Blue Blood Moon occurs in the Earth's universe, it will also mirror our own. We, too, will have an identical eclipse, giving a conduit of the Underworld to pass through both our realms freely. If that happens, life as we know it will no longer exist."

"How long will the eclipse be active? Ten minutes?"

"More like six hours over a span of several time zones in both universes."

The thought that all this happening in a matter of weeks gives me anxiety. I know Cory can feel it, too, because I feel a sensation of warmth come over me, and although I don't particularly like him doing this, I welcome it this time.

"This is why Isalora sent us on a quest to find the Sword of Valor, only then can we have a chance to stop her," Cory says.

"Only a chance?" I ask, worried. "This Sword of Valor, if it's so desirable, then why hasn't anyone found it and stopped Sarmira yet?"

"That's a question for Dragonscale," Rory says.

There's a knock at the door and we all jump to it swinging open. "Oh, you're all awake. Good. You two," Dad says, pointing at Cory and me, "downstairs in thirty. We need to go." He shuts the door.

"Guess that ends the stories for now," Rory snaps. "You go get your shower in first. I can wait."

I tilt my head at her but keep my thoughts to myself. I know exactly what she meant.

18
AN UNPREDICTABLE EVENT

CORY AND I WERE down in thirty minutes like Dad instructed. In the living room, we find another person with him and Geneviève. This new guest is dressed in unusual attire, wearing a fitted leather crop top, revealing a rippled torso, and tight leather pants. Her dark hair, with one silver stripe, is braided, falling over her shoulder and leading to her waist.

She notices us first. "We have company."

Dad and Geneviève stand and turn to face us.

"Hello, you two," Dad says. He gestures for us both to come forward. "I would like you to meet Lira. She is going to help us retrieve the Waxlily."

Cory and I both shake her hand. "Pleased to meet you," she says.

I nod. *"Another new face."*

"She's a shapeshifter," Fran answers. *"One that can change into anything. The way you can tell is by the stripe in their hair. They are quite dangerous and valuable at the same time."*

"Can we trust her?"

"I don't know yet. I've seen others like her before, but I don't know Lira."

"Interesting."

"This is an old friend. I met her long ago." Dad smiles. "Lira here saved my life once."

"Really, dear brother-in-law. Funny you never told me about her before?" Aunt Fran mutters.

"So, you're indebted to her?" I ask, not at all afraid to speak my mind.

Lira sneers. Her eyes give a spark of blue like Dad's does when he's contemplating a move. Although I can hear her unusual heartbeat and it is calm at the moment, my guard is up. Cory sneaks a glance my way. It's a look of suspicion, giving the impression he and I are on the same page.

"Shall we move to the dining room?" Geneviève proposes.

We gather around the table where she has already prepared a big meal to start our day. "I've packed each of you the appropriate meal sacks, too, for your journey," she adds.

Fran's ghost-like form walks over to Lira, getting up close and personal. She touches Lira's shoulders and blows a breath of cold air on her neck. Cory follows with his eyes, confirming he, too, sees Fran, through my visions.

Lira grabs her elbows, as though she's catching a chill. "My gawd, Gen, turn up the heat in here, will you?"

Cory grins, and I snicker under my breath. Geneviève turns to glance at the fire that is wildly throwing out flames. "Are you feeling okay, Lira?"

Lira turns in the direction of the hearth and covers her biceps, moving her hands back and forth quickly. "I see, yes. Well, perhaps I should put on my cape."

"I can see why you're cold," I burst out. "Dressed like that, anyone would be." This woman gives me a sinking feeling something is not quite right.

"Wynter Storm," Dad scolds. "That's no way to talk to a guest."

"She's not my guest, Dad. She's Geneviève's. Forgive me if I'm suspicious, but I don't trust her." I glare at the stranger. There's something about her that doesn't sit well with me. "It's funny, why have you never mentioned her before?"

"I see," Lira hisses. "Well, if you will excuse me, Gen, Jeff. I'll be going now. I won't stand here and help you on this dangerous journey if my own party won't give me a chance." She gets up from her seat and heads for the door. Dad rushes after her.

Why does he care whether this person leaves or stays? Is he blinded by what I see?

The one cool thing about having exceptional hearing is my listening skills have improved.

"Wait, please, Lira, don't go. We need you on this mission," Dad says. "We must stick to the plan."

"If she can't trust me, Jeff, we will never get past the gates."

I know Dad knows we can hear them both.

"What do they mean 'get past the gates,' Aunt Fran?"

"I don't know," she answers. *"I will find out. Won't be gone long."*

"Where are you going?"

"To find someone who might know what Lira is talking about." Fran pauses for a split second. *"Or what she's up to."*

Her presence disappears and I suddenly feel alone and unprotected now.

I glance at Cory and he whispers, "Something's off, I feel it. What did she say to you?"

"I'll tell you later. I don't feel safe talking out loud." I take a bite of food.

Geneviève is staring at us. "Is there something you want to say?"

"No, just that I don't understand why she has to tag along." I point toward Lira.

Geneviève's eyes narrow. "She's a shifter, and the only one who can get you past the guards to the gate of Grengore."

That must be what Lira meant by *gate*. Too late to warn Fran, she's already gone.

"So, when do we leave?" Cory asks.

I can tell he's not thrilled with the task at hand either.

"In an hour," Dad cuts in, bringing Lira with him from the hall.

Ignoring my instincts not to trust this new ally, I ask. "So, what now?"

"We travel to the cave portal. The gate to the Underworld, which will lead us directly to the Grengore mines," Lira explains. "There I will mask myself as another sentinel. I'll be able to distract the other guards, allowing you all to enter. I must warn you, though, the mines are a very tricky place to be, and it's like a maze. You can get lost in an instant."

"Lira knows that area like the back of her hand," Dad adds.

I look at her, then to Dad. "How long have you two known each other?"

Lira answers. "We met long ago during one of your dad's quests." She looks down at her hands, pausing. "We ah... both landed in the same cell, captured by ogres."

"Let's not talk about the past. Right now, we need to figure out a plan to get in," Dad says, trying to divert the subject.

"Right, well, first we need to get to the mouth of Grengore's gate," Lira says. "That's when the invisibility cloaking spell is used. Follow my lead, and you will be safe. Don't veer off the path. We must go through the mines to the other side. The Waxlily grows around the lake that is surrounded by mountains. It's the only place this flower flourishes."

"And the keys?" Cory asks.

She sighs. "Yes. Well... finding the keys is an entirely different challenge altogether. They're deep in the mines near the goblin quarters. It will be next to impossible to get those."

"Sound's exciting. I'm in," Rory announces, standing behind us under the archway in the dining room.

She is dressed in attire fitted for an adventure.

"You're not going anywhere," Geneviève declares. "You should be in bed resting."

"What, and miss all the fun? I don't think so. I'm going!"

"Over my dead body."

"That can be arranged," Rory snaps.

"Rory Elizabeth, what has gotten into you?"

"Me? You're not my mother." She takes an arrow and points it at her. "Who are you?"

"I-I don't know what you're talking about. Put that away."

Rory stretches the bowstring. "Start talking or I start shooting."

"Rory, what are you doing?" I cry. Cory gets up from the table and pulls me to his side. Dad tries to intervene.

"Nuh-uh, Jeff, not another step. Don't try to stop me. You're all being fooled. This is not Geneviève Fernshadow. Don't you think I know my own mother?"

She releases a warning shot with precision, nicking the side of Geneviève's cheek before the arrow embeds in the wall behind her.

Geneviève smiles and wipes the blood. "I had all of you fooled for a while, didn't I?"

The smell of her blood is intoxicating, and I feel Cory's hand tighten within my grip. Blood oozes down the side of her face, and it takes every bit of will in me not to pounce. The hunger deepens, and I want so badly to devour Geneviève as the monster within me takes hold. Cory pulls me back as a low growl sounds from behind my throat. How is it he has more control than me?

Rory snickers. "Seems my best friend is yearning for a good, warm meal. You better start talking. None of us have the strength to hold her back. That blood is music to a Nytemire's senses, and you very well may be her first meal." She pulls her bow for a second shot. "Start talking."

Geneviève cackles like she's fearless. "You have no clue what you're all up against."

"Who are you working for?" Dad demands.

She turns her head to Dad. "Why, you of all people should know that, Jeff." She gives a wicked smile and darts toward him, but before she can attack, an arrow stabs her, and she falls backward, hitting the floor.

The beast within me implodes as I dash to Geneviève's body, devouring her flesh. The animal part of me takes over, and Cory yells, "Wynter, no!" but it's too late. I've tasted the blood, and I am consumed with satisfaction.

The imposter pretending to be Geneviève takes her last breath and changes into her true form.

"Trek!" Cory confirms. "And a shifter."

It takes a few minutes before I gather my composure, and I see the dead body on the floor. "Eww, what is that?"

"You don't remember?" Rory grins.

"That," Cory states, "was your breakfast, my love. Please tell me you remember?"

"Umm, eww... no." Looking at all of the people in the room appearing dumbfounded, I say, "The last thing I remember is leaping for Geneviève's throat. I was so angry that she put us all in danger."

Cory gives me a grin. "Well, it appears the Nytemire side of you has come out. That is indeed the first sign of your changes."

"That explains the urges I felt yesterday when I first met Geneviève."

"Nytemires find the ogres especially delectable," Cory says. "At first I thought it was your initial changes with emotions but seeing this, I now understand. I had them, too, but not like you did. I should have known. I can smell a Trek a mile away. I chalked it up to faux senses because I've been so wrapped up trying to protect you."

"Cory, I'm sorry."

"Don't be. However, we have more pressing matters now." He looks at each of us in the room. "How did a Trek get past our mountains?"

"Like any other intruder, through the cave of course," Lira states.

"Better question," Rory begins. "Where's my mother?"

19
THE BRIDGE

"DID YOU GET IT?" I ask as we walk down the path from Nyta's house.

"Yes," Rory replies, "but it wasn't easy."

"Did Nyta know?"

"No, she had no idea. The Trek impersonating my mother, fooled even her."

"So, what now?"

"We meet the others down by the cave, as planned." Rory flinches, and she stops to take the bottle of medicine Nyta gave her out of her pocket.

"Rory, are you sure you're okay to travel? I mean, what if something happens?"

"I'm not going to allow you to go on your own." She takes a swig. "Especially since I'm the only one that can evacuate all of you if trouble erupts. I'm fine. Besides, I don't need my vision to teleport us out."

"Hey." I stop, pulling her sleeve. "Are we straight? I mean, earlier. What you saw... What I did..."

"It doesn't bother me, Wynter. I've seen Cory do the same thing many times."

"What?"

She snickers. "Come on, I'll tell you on the way. When we were younger growing up in this valley, Blair would take the boys hunting. Except for Casey, of course. He didn't particularly like killing animals.

"How does he eat?"

"What does he eat should be the better question, Wynter."

"You mean, he's not a Nytemire?"

"Ironically, he doesn't eat meat of any kind."

"You mean he eats plants?"

"Yes. Anyway, Blair taught Cole and Cory to track prey. They didn't have their gifts, of course, but they still had the innate abilities they were born with."

"Vampire."

"Yes. She taught them to hunt animals and fish in the ocean. One day when they were on the beach, the boys caught sight of a Trek passing through to the cave."

"Ah, it all makes sense now why Blair didn't allow them near it, and why you were so protective."

"None of us have been inside, which is probably why Cory is still intrigued."

"I bet he's just itching to go on this quest, then."

Rory giggles. "I am, too, for that matter. I was always sworn to protect the mouth of the cave."

"Do you think we will find your mother where we are going?"

"I hope so. Since it was reported to the townsfolk that a Trek was found in our home, the guards and watchmen have scouted every inch of the village. Nyta went so far as to find her locator recipe. Geneviève's not within a hundred-mile radius of here. It only leaves one other logical place."

"Grengore," I answer.

"Yes, or the ogre camp. Either way, she's not here."

"When did you realize that the Trek was an imposter pretending to be your mom?"

"I had my suspicions yesterday when you came into town, and Geneviève asked who you were. At first, I brushed it off, but then I began to notice other things."

We come to the edge of the cliff leading to the ocean and the rest of our group is waiting by the big boulder that protected us from the fiery flames of the dragon yesterday.

"Like what other things?" I ask, stepping down the trail with her toward the beach below.

"Just the little things, ya know? Like for example, she would never have come to Nyta's house. In the past, she's had someone come get me. Usually, she's too busy. As long as I'm not dying, apparently."

"That's awful, Rory. I had no idea you and your mother didn't have a close relationship."

"We did, once, but that was before I left my sister at Storm River. Deep down, I think she resents me for leaving Redmae."

"You had no choice, though."

"Hey, there you two are. Did you get it?" Dad calls.

Rory smirks. "Duty awaits." We both approach the others. "Yes, we got it," she says, holding up the item.

"What do we do with it?" I ask.

Dad seizes the flask from Rory. "This." He takes a swallow and then hands the small bottle to Cory. "Just drink a sip," Dad says. "It will give the creatures in the mines and anyone we come across in that cave the illusion we're goblins."

He passes the container around to the others until it reaches me, and I do as the rest.

It tastes bitter, like the rind of an orange. "This is crazy, Dad," I say, but when I turn and glance at everybody looking like goblins, I see exactly what he predicted. I look at my hands and they change before my eyes. "How did you... never mind, not going to go there, or my head will hurt." I march my way toward the cave while they snicker under their breath. But I stay calm. I don't even flinch. *Huh, that's astounding.* Not too long ago I would have gotten nail-spitting angry.

I feel the presence of Cory catching up to me. At least I hope it's him looking all ghoulish. "That was great composure back there, Wynter. I didn't even have to butt in and calm your nerves."

"Yeah, odd, huh?" I answer. "Why do you suppose that is?"

"Well, I have a theory."

"Do share, Cory. Don't hold back," I say, still annoyed.

His attention seems diverted. "I smell something odd. Nothing like I have sensed before. A rotten, awful odor."

I stop, focusing on the scent. "Now that you've pointed it out, so do I. What is it?"

"I don't know," he says, perplexed.

"You're smelling the death coming from that cave, my lovelies," Dad interjects, passing us in the process. "The illusion also gives you the senses a goblin experiences. So, play along, and you might live through this."

Dad's behavior strikes me as odd. Perhaps similar to when Rory explained she knew something was off about Geneviève. *Don't overthink it, Wynter.*

We get to the edge of the cave as a couple of ogres come out, sneaking up the side of a large rock.

I pull the side of Cory's sleeve. "They'll see us."

"Not your true form," Dad answers. "You have the lovely skin of a goblin, remember? We do however want to stay out of sight. If they see us, they may wonder why we are out of the caves."

"I'll handle this," Lira announces. "You all go ahead." She walks off toward the rocks where the ogres are perched. "Good afternoon, boys," she coos. "Know where I can find some big, strong muscles that can help me?"

"Wow she's laying it on thick, isn't she?" I whisper.

Rory pulls at my arm. "Come on, let's sneak in while Lira has them occupied." She points at the ogres. "Notice the gray haze around them?"

"They're invisible to the naked eye," I say.

"Yes."

It gives me a chill, realizing these creatures have been going around Pine Willow Valley undetected.

"Most of the people here don't have the magical 'see invisible' capability," Rory adds.

"That means your village is in much more danger than we first thought," Cory says.

She nods. "Agreed. Thankfully, Nyta is aware now. Something darker than we know is coming to this land. She thinks it's all tied into the coming of the Super Blue Blood Moon."

We approach the outer mouth of the cave. It's dark, and I can't see past the opening.

"Stay close," Dad says.

Once I walk past the threshold, my eyes seem to automatically adjust to the darkness. There are tree roots growing through the cave's ceiling, and water trickles down the side walls. We walk a little ways when we hear two voices arguing.

"One thing I forgot to mention," Rory explains, "while we wear this goblin illusion, we, too, can understand their language. But once it wears off... it won't be easy to comprehend them."

"I don't understand you!" the first goblin says in a loud whisper.

"Well, do something then," the second one replies, "before the ogres come and have our heads."

One fumbles with a pouch in their hand. It appears a few knapsacks are lying on the ground. "Are you done looking, Crue?"

"No, now shut up, and give me a hand," the one called Crue says.

I feel a tug on my sleeve, pulling me back against the wall as our group sneaks around the arguing imps. They are so wrapped up in themselves that they don't notice us passing. Dad doesn't seem to care that we left Lira in the dust, but something tells me she can hold her own.

Once we round the corner at the rear of the cave, I feel like we can breathe again, until I hear, "You there! Stop!"

Do I dare look behind me? It wasn't the sound of the two goblins arguing earlier, but a huskier voice ordering us to halt.

Dad turns around.

"You, there!" the ogre yells again, sounding authoritative. "Why do you dare cross the gate? Who has instructed you to do so? I'm in command here," the ogre approaching us says.

"I'm taking these thieves to our king. I caught them rummaging through the bags back there." Dad points in the direction we came.

The ogre comes closer and smells us. "Stinking goblins. I've never trusted any of you, always thinking you can steal from a Trek."

"I didn't get them all, sir," Dad says. "There were more, rummaging through the bags. When I approached them, they scattered. These are the ones I caught."

"Is that so," the ogre roars. "Begone," he says, and runs the other way toward Crue and his accomplice.

"Quick," Dad presses, "we better get through the gates before he finds out we're intruders."

We come to a ledge, near what sounds like a waterfall. A bridge reaches across a deep crevasse and Dad points. "Just beyond that bridge is the gated portal. Be careful, one slip and you're a goner," he cautions as we follow him.

Small beetles scurry across our path, clacking. "Gawd, I hate bugs." More roots poke through the upper ceiling of the cave and water drips from its stems. Creatures hang in the cracks above, too.

"Bats," Cory blurts, as though he reads the pictures in my head.

"I see that," I say, glaring at him.

He grins. "Sorry. I'm in your thoughts again."

"Yes, too often, I might add."

"We don't want to wake them," Cory says. "One loud noise and we can forget destiny."

"Right." The bats do give me an uneasy feeling. Not sure which I would prefer seeing, beetles crawling across my boots or the bats above swinging upside down.

We approach the start of the stone bridge, and it's so narrow that it looks like a tightrope. "We cross that?"

Turning to look at Cory I take a huge gulp. "Did I ever tell you I'm afraid of heights?"

Rory laughs. "Well, it's nice to know one thing hasn't changed in that memory stamp muck you acquired." She looks at Jeff. "Couldn't you have at least taken that memory from her?"

Dad huffs and looks at me. "Okay, Wynter, you have to do this. It's the only way." He pauses to look down into the deep cavern below. "Just take my hand."

"I'm not taking your hand!"

"Okay," Dad soothes me, trying to calm me down. "I'll go first." He begins to cross with ease, and like an acrobat in a circus, finishes to the end in less than thirty seconds. "Now your turn," he says.

I shake my head, backing away from the ledge a bit.

"Oh, come on, Wynter," Cory urges. "You didn't think twice when you rescued the backpack at the mountain valley where we encountered the giants."

"That was different," I lie. "My mother's heart was in the coffer."

"You can do it again," Cory coaxes. "Think of it this way—we're saving Rory this time."

"I'll go," Rory interjects and she steps onto the bridge with ease. A couple of stones come loose and drop to the floor below.

"Says the Druid that can port her way out of anything," I retort, still seeing the images of the small rocks falling.

"Come on, Wynter, you have to do this. It's the only way."

"Give me a minute," I snap. I concentrate on my center. I think back on all the yoga teachings Fran instilled in me after I came into my power. A feeling of tranquility enters my veins instead of the burning of fire. Cool sensations I've come to learn usually mean calmness. I turn to Cory. "Stop that!"

"Stop what? I'm not doing anything."

"You're trying to calm me again."

"I'm not doing anything of the sort. You're doing that all on your own," he says.

His confession surprises me and makes me wonder if I do have my own calming ability. But how can I remain cool when I'm faced with such danger as crossing a bridge hanging over a deadly precipice? I take a few deep breaths before attempting my first step.

"That's it, Wynter, you can do it," Rory calls from the other side.

I glare at her. "Would you shush and let me concentrate?"

I ease my way farther on the bridge. *I can do this. Oh, Fran, where are you?*

As I take another step, small rocks scatter to the depths below. Breathing in deep, I shut my eyes. *What if I fall? No! You can't think like that.* I take another large breath and step one more time. Again, I think of my center. Inhaling again,

I stretch my hands up over my head and exhale, then pull them back to my center. *Okay, Wynter, you can do this.*

I open my eyes and scoot my way to the opposite side, keeping in rhythm, and focusing on my core being. Rory reaches for my hand, grabs it, and pulls me to her. I scream at first but realize I've made it to the other side.

"Such theatrics, Wynter." Rory laughs. "I told you, I'll always have your back, girl."

I heave a few breaths, putting my head between my knees. "Please tell me we don't have to do that again anytime soon?"

We look at Cory. It's his turn now, and he skips across like he's done this for years.

"Show off," I mumble.

He smirks, bowing his head. "All in the wrist my sweet, but in this case the ankles."

We come to the portal, and it glistens much like the one at the cottage, but this time I can't see through to the other side.

20
DOUBLE CROSSED

THIS PORTAL GIVES THE same sensation as before when I passed through to Songbird Meadow. Once we reach the other side, I witness much of the cave-like features of the tunnel we just traveled through. Many goblins hit the side of the cavern with a pickaxe, railroad ties are fixated to the ground, and carts are filled with what looks like coal. More beetles crawl across my boots, and I almost scream but catch myself.

"How are we going to get past them?" I whisper to Cory.

"We are all goblins like them, remember? They can't see who we are, but I will remind you they can hear us, so we need to step cautiously."

"Well, that's reassuring."

Cory grabs my hand, and we follow the others through the tunnel.

You there!" one ogre yells. "Get back to work." It was a goblin that had stopped to bend down and grab something off the ground.

The farther we go, the more uneasy I feel. A spirit crosses our path, and it looks directly at us. I know he sees right through our protective spells. Nudging Cory, I veer him in the direction of the ghost.

"Now that's something we did not want to find roaming around in here," Cory says.

Cory's comment grabs Dad's attention. "A goblin spirit spotted us. He will be bringing others soon. We need to find our way out of here and fast."

Rory takes out the scroll resembling the same one she was to give to Geneviève earlier. "Wasn't that intended for your mother?"

"Yes, but I didn't give it to her." She smiles. "I'm not the only one in Pine Willow Valley that suspected my mother as being a little off. Nyta intended it for me and at the time didn't know who could be trusted. It's a map of these caverns. I didn't understand what it meant until now."

She pauses to look where we are. "Jeff, go right," she instructs. "There will be a door, about five hundred feet to the left according to the map, then we turn right, again."

He nods. "Someone count to five hundred as we take each step. We don't want to get lost."

"I'll do it," Cory says.

After a few minutes, we come to a turn and are stopped by ogres with auras.

"What do we do now?" I whisper.

And as though someone had been listening, I hear, "You there, stop!"

An ogre dressed in silver armor with a sword strapped to his hip charges toward us.

Without warning, steel cuffs wrap around all our hands and ankles, as though they had a mind of their own. Chains attach to each binding, and all of us find ourselves shackled to each other.

"What the—" Cory cries out.

We all turn around to see Lira, in model-like fashion, catwalking forward, with confidence." There's my prisoners," she says, sneering.

A witch. I know Cory can see images in my head, and nods, as though he agrees.

"Mistress Lira, I had no idea they were with you," the ogre says. "If you will excuse me, please carry on." The ogre bows and leaves.

"Where did she come from?" I murmur to Cory.

Cory shakes his head, but Lira answers, as though she heard me. "I've been hiding out, keeping a distance."

She has better hearing than I thought.

"Come this way."

Dad clears his throat, indicating we still are bound in steel chains.

"Oh, yes that..." She grins. "Be patient, we are going into dangerous territory. If we are to ever get past the royal guards, you may want to rethink those chains. If they think you're my prisoners, we'll be able to sneak by them."

I don't trust her. We're running straight into a trap. I feel it in my gut.

Rory takes the map we have and tucks it into her palm. Her skin folds open like the pocket of a kangaroo's pouch. I'm in awe, not believing what I'm witnessing. Rory sees my face and winks. Aside from having a hiding spot pocketed under her skin, I can tell she, too, doesn't trust Lira.

We reach a door that's locked, but Lira has a key and opens it.

She pulls on our chains. "Let's go. Down this way." We trail down spiral steps built into the cave.

Once we reach the bottom, Lira leads us straight into a large, circular dome-like room. In the center, a derrick sits lodged in a pit with walls emitting orange and red light. The rig doesn't appear to be pumping any oil. Instead, a conveyor belt that's chained with buckets of black coal is being hiked up to the upper mines. The containers pour out at the top onto a conveyor belt that directs into another passageway.

"This way," Lira says.

We turn down a long corridor where the cave begins to resemble the entrance to an underground palace. Two guards stand watch before a drawbridge that precedes to a grand castle carved from the rock on the opposite side.

The guards cross their swords at our approach. A tall figure dressed in black wearing a hooded cowl flows across the bridge effortlessly. Gnarled green fingers poke through the ends of its sleeves. Its thin face is green and grotesque.

"Lira, what brings you this far north in the tunnels?" the strange creature asks.

"I bring prisoners." She bows slightly and glances at Dad, giving him a side grin.

Somehow I get the feeling we are Lira's bait. Who's to say she's not playing both sides? In the books I've read, most witches are not to be trusted, but that is fiction. Fiction, I've come to realize, plays a very real role in my life right now.

"I see. Well, they look like ordinary goblins, to me, Lira. What did they do that provides such a warming presence from you, Mistress?"

She lifts her head, frowning. "They were caught snooping in the royal trinket bags that King Zeelx had instructed the ogres to bring to the Trek Commander."

"And these goblins couldn't be thrown to the whipping chamber instead?" he queries, looking as though he's a little suspicious.

"No. One of them holds great value to the king."

Cory and I look at each other. I worry that my first assessment is correct. *"Oh, Aunt Fran, where are you?"*

No reply comes from the voice in my head. Instead, the cloaked figure answers, "And what value might that be?"

"That is for the king to decide," Lira says.

"You dare challenge the grand master?" he coos. "Might I remind you what happened the last time you crossed the king? This better be legitimate, else it will be your last crossing... with anyone."

Lira stiffens. "I assure you, he will not be disappointed."

So, they have a history.

The cuffs around my wrists and ankles seem to calm the rage I feel building. I sense something but I can't quite figure out what it is. This must be what Cory meant by being bound in valiancium steel. Is that what binds us now? Is Lira on our side, or her own? My sudden urge to get to the keys increases.

"Yes, well... we'll see about that. Follow me if you dare." His words slither out, bringing chills down my spine, and I'm no longer feeling like a force to be reckoned with, but a timid girl who no longer has the powers to defend herself.

Once we cross the threshold, the drawbridge abruptly closes behind us. *Peachy, locked in.*

We're led down a rock path through the castle. This place appears like the rest of the cavern except more refined. There are gold sparkle flecks in the stone on the walls that gleam and shine from the lights above. The ceiling is sunk in, with can lighting like you would see in a modern house and the floors glitter like polished granite. It's as though a craftsman took in every detail and turned this place into his own working canvas.

Cory is chained behind me while Rory is in front. By her body language, it's clear she's up to something. Is she bound by the power of these chains like Dad,

Cory, and me? Will she be able to port us out of this mess at the last second? If she does, our cover will be blown.

At the end of the corridor, guards stand in front of closed french doors.

"Wait here," the grand master says.

Lira glances at my father and smiles. "It will all be over soon." She glares at the rest of us. "Our plan is working out perfectly, don't you think?"

Who's plan, Lira's? Where's Fran? She's been gone too long.

The french doors whisk open and the hooded man who calls himself the grand master, gestures for us to enter. The room is magnificent, with pews set to the sides against the walls. A throne in the distance is in front of us with a man sitting, and not at all looking like I had envisioned. He isn't green like his protégé. The cloaked grand master pushes forward and whispers in the king's ear, prompting him to stand.

"You dare interrupt me, Lira. This better be good." His face looks human, not like the goblins in the mines. He's quite a bit larger than the green gnarled creature standing next to him, too. In fact, his physique looks more like a Trek. He wears a green robe with armor woven into the fabric. A scar cascades down the side of his cheek, and his long black hair is tightened in a braid.

The man paces forward, towering over all of us. He's almost the size of Casey. "They smell of goblins and their stench burns my nostrils, Lira. Do you play me for a fool?"

"Wait, Your Majesty. I can prove to you they are not who they appear to be," she pleads.

I knew it! Dad says always listen to your gut. Why didn't I? Why didn't Dad see through her? My mind reels with all the possibilities.

With the snap of her fingers, Lira reveals our true forms.

The anger in me stews, but I'm powerless to do anything. I look to see Cory back to his gorgeous self and Rory, too. But when I look at Dad, it isn't him, but someone I had never seen before, having similar features as Lira. We've been duped.

"Here, darling," Lira purrs, and she releases the shackles from the man who posed as my father.

"I thought you forgot, my love," he whispers. His black hair is spiked in a mohawk, having one silver stripe trailing through it. A nose ring hangs from one nostril, and he has a scar on his chin.

"Well, you've definitely outdone yourself this time, Lira, haven't you?" the king says. "How did you pull off such a charade?"

"It wasn't without great difficulty, Your Majesty," she purrs.

"Yes, I imagine so." He smiles wickedly.

"Be careful though." She points to me. "That one is very powerful. Those chains she wears suppress her energies. She's the one you seek in the prophecy."

"Yes, Lira. You indeed have done well. You shall be rewarded for your efforts." He smiles, pacing forward. "And who are the others?"

"Tagalongs, I think?" She smiles at Cory. "Although he's pretty cute. I see why she keeps him around."

I move my arm to strike at her, but the chains pull me back.

"Oh, a real firecracker, aren't you?" She cackles.

"Grimwald," the king calls, "would you please show our two guests to their quarters." He turns to speak to Lira. "You shall have your money first thing in the morning. I would be honored if you would attend our feast this evening in celebration of your accomplishments."

"Sire, there's no need," she protests. "My coven waits for me back home."

"I insist," he says, taking her hand and kissing the back of it. "Either that or be thrown in with the rest of these prisoners. You wouldn't dare embarrass me like that, now, would you?"

"No, of course not, My King," she says and bows. "If you put it that way, Miles and I would be honored."

So, Miles is his name. I file it away for later. I wonder what Cory is thinking. Better yet, what's Rory's opinion? She always has a plan. If there's one thing I know about her, she's never stuck on plan A.

"Looking forward to seeing you later this evening," the king says, and Lira and Miles leave the room with the grand master, the king called Grimwald.

"As for you three... what shall we do with you?" He circles us again, pacing as though in thought. "I don't think you quite realize how valuable you are, Wynter."

The king calling me by my name focuses all our attention.

"I do say it's remarkable that the two of you haven't sold the princess out, yet?" He circles us again. "Interesting, indeed."

Rory says, "Some don't comprehend what it means to be loyal, but then again, I guess you wouldn't identify with that, would you?"

"Ah, is that so?" he sneers. "You're much like your mother Geneviève, I see."

Rory moves toward him and is stopped by the chains.

"And full of spite, too. Tell me, Rory, what did you hope to accomplish by coming here? Steal my treasures, perhaps?"

"We didn't come here for your riches," Cory says. "We wish to travel peacefully through your tunnel to the Lake of No Return."

"And why would that be? There's no escape from there, unless..." He peers at Rory. "Unless you're a Druid like your mother. I see now. How convenient."

"Let us go, by order of the queen," I roar, hoping to sound authoritative. *Even though I haven't met the queen, yet.*

The king laughs. "You? Ordering me? You have no authority here."

"If you know who I am, then you know when Dragonscale finds out you have captured me, he will kill you." *At least I assume he will.* "Yet you dare cross him?"

"Oh, my dear, I think not." He laughs more, as though my warning is hilarious. "I would like to see him try."

By this time, Grimwald has returned. "Sire, what would you like me to do with the others?"

"Take them all to the dungeon until I have figured out what to do with her." He pierces me with a malevolent glance. "Better yet, bring her to my chambers. Have the maids get her ready."

"As you wish, Your Majesty," Grimwald says and leads all of us out of the throne chamber.

What did he mean by that? His chambers? If he thinks I'm going to bow down to him as his slave, he's got another thing coming. He will not get away with this, and I will get my revenge.

21
THE KING'S BRIDE

GRIMWALD DOESN'T SPEAK THE entire time as he leads the three of us through to the dungeon. We aren't led to a spiral staircase like Madame Moyer's pit of horror, but I can smell death just the same. A crater smolders in the center of the cavern with its edges glowing bright orange and yellow, looking much like the previous derrick we saw earlier. The difference this time is cages are hanging above. I notice people are in them. My keen eyes concentrate on who they are, but I can't get a clear vision of their features.

Great, they're sending us up there. As we draw closer, I notice one appears to be a man and the other a woman.

I'm yanked by the chains binding all three of us together. "Keep the pace!" one of the guards next to Grimwald yells.

Thoughts race through my mind as I'm suddenly reminded of the past when Moyer locked me in the cell of her dungeon chamber. This isn't happening again, is it? I try to bring the thoughts of fire to my fingertips, but nothing surfaces. No matter how much I think about what's happening in the present, the blood within my veins doesn't heat beneath my skin.

My mind wanders, wondering if Dad is somewhere around in this horrible place. Is he one of those poor souls caged above the pit? How are we to escape this hell hole? And Rory, she needs to get to the Waxlily.

We all stop before a cage, like the ones that hang above the pit.

"Put them in here for now," Grimwald says. He glides off, and the guards shove us all into one cage.

Once the sentinels march off, I say, "So, what now? We need to devise a plan for escape. The double-crossing witch and her creepy accomplice will wish they never set eyes on us once I get done with them." I know the anger is building, but I don't understand why my strength doesn't show. "Why won't these gawd awful chains break already," I spat. I try with every bone in my body to split the bindings apart, but they don't budge.

Cory answers, "You're in valiancium steel chains. It holds in your power. You may have noticed the magic diminish as soon as Lira placed them."

I nod. "So my first assumption was true. I didn't know for sure, but I didn't want to say anything out loud."

"It keeps my power in, too," Rory says. "I cannot port us out of here."

"You're not a Nytemire, Rory. How is that possible?" I look at Cory. "Do these chains restrain my powers, like the necklace?"

"Similar, yes. The labradorite helps to bind your magic, which is why it can still protect you — your true power. If you took off that necklace, here in this world, your magic would come back in full force, and the beast within you, waiting to come out... will. But you forget one thing. The cuffs around your ankles and wrists will keep you from doing it, and we are all back to square one. At least that's the theory, anyway."

"So, you don't know for sure?"

"No. On the other hand, Moyer will know where you are." He winks as though his joke is humorous.

"Well, that's not an option, now, is it?" I look around through the cell door. Guards are everywhere. "They all know who I am, don't they?"

"Probably," Rory answers, "but I have this." She reveals under her kangaroo pouch a loop of jail keys.

"Are those—" Cory raises a brow.

"Shh," she cuts him off, putting her mouth to her lips. "I managed to pick-pocket them from Lira."

I smile. "You clever little Dru—"

She cuts me off too, saying, "We have to plan this out carefully." Rory narrows her gaze and smiles back as though she has the perfect strategy.

Thinking about the magical necklace I wear, and the danger at hand, I hope for some form of memory to surface, but all I remember is the past, like living in Washington State, being an average teenager, or recent ones such as the Trek attacking us on the beach. I know deep down these are not my true memories. "Cory, do you remember my necklace glowing blue yesterday when the Trek approached? What do you know about that?"

"My guess is it doesn't sense danger. The glow must mean something else, otherwise, it would have warned us of the situation we're in now."

"You're probably right."

The cell bars rattle, pulling us from our scheming plans. "Okay, Princess, here we go," the guard says, opening the door. He unlocks my chains from both Rory and Cory. "It's time."

"Leave her alone!" Cory yells.

The guard punches him in the jaw, and he tumbles backward against the back of the cage bars.

I move to Cory in protest, but the guard quickly yanks me back. "Don't worry," he says, "they will be of no use to you any longer." He calls another Trek guard. "Take the other two and hang their crates above the volcano pit. They die now, with the others. I don't want to take any chances."

"No! You can't do this!" I scream.

"Sorry, lass, by order of the king." He laughs at my distress. "Come now, he wishes you to prepare."

"Prepare for what?"

"Why marriage, of course."

"I will never marry him."

"Aye, he kind of figured that," the guard snarls. "It doesn't matter, though. Females don't have to agree. The sacrifice of a loved one seals the deal anyway." He points to the cage hanging above the pit. I notice that the familiar people inside are Geneviève and Dad.

"No, I won't marry him, and you will not get away with this. I will kill you, and your king if it's with my last dying breath."

"Such warrior words for a princess."

"I'm not a princess."

"Oh, my dear... do you not know? Has no one offered you the insight of who you truly are?" He pulls the chains, forcing me to follow behind him.

How are you going to get out of this one Wynter Storm? Cory said if I take this necklace off, it would be worse than if I found another way. What other way is there? Maybe Rory can think of a way to get us all out. I remember in high school once when she somehow slithered her way into class without the teacher noticing. I'm hoping she can again perform the impossible by getting us all out of this mess.

We come to a chamber where there are two women filling a tub with water. There's a bed and dresser. A gown hangs on a corner post.

"Here is your room. You will prepare for His Majesty."

"I won't marry him!"

The guard unlocks the chains around my hands and feet, but leaves the cuffs in place, laughing as he goes. "I would like to see you try to go against the king."

"He's not my king."

"Okay, Princess, whatever you say." He leaves, locking the door behind him.

Realizing I'm free from the valiancium chains but not the cuffs, I process my next step. I glance around the room for any escape route. I won't give up so easily, and if this Trek thinks so, then it'll be his worst mistake.

One of the two women preparing a bath comes over, encouraging me to take off my clothes.

"No," I say, and put my hand up. "Leave."

"But, My Lady, we can't," the woman says. "We have orders. Going against them would be our death."

"Then you shall die because I will not stand here and allow you to coddle me."

She takes a step backward as though she's shocked by my remark. "What do you think you can do? You can't possibly suggest going against our king's orders, can you?"

"He may be your king, but he's not mine. I would rather die than be forced to bow down to him."

They both gasp in surprise, as though what I said will curse us all.

"What does he have on you both?" I ask.

"We're Dryads. Our magic was taken when these were placed on us," the other woman says, and they both lift the hems of their skirts revealing valiancium cuffs about their ankles.

The woman dressed in yellow says, "My name is Kyla." She has blonde hair with ringlets cascading down over her shoulders. "This is my sister Gretta." She points to the other woman still running the bath. She wears a green dress that complements her red hair and emerald eyes. "We're your chambermaids."

Thinking of the story Rory told earlier, I'm reminded that many Dryads are porters. It has me wondering if they are, too.

"You're not my chambermaids. I won't be sticking around if I can help it," I snap. "How long have you two been held captive here?"

"Longer than we both care to count," Kyla answers. "But My Lady, if we don't give you the bath he requires, and fulfill the instructions, he will kill us."

"Such a benevolent king," I say. "Well, as much as I want to be rid of the stench on my skin, I must decline his offer." I give an optimistic smile. "What is the chance of us all getting out of here alive?"

Gretta laughs. "Are we to believe the 'princess' is to be our savior and rescue us?"

"Oh, Gretta, stop. You always do this."

She sneers. "Do what?"

"You know what," Kyla argues. "So quick to judge before hearing what anyone has to say." Kyla looks at me. "What's the plan?"

"I don't know yet. But I'll think of something."

"See, I told you. She hasn't a clue how to get past those Treks," Gretta says with a snark.

I ignore Gretta's remark, saying, "What can you tell me about these cuffs?"

"They hold in the magic, keeping anyone who has such enchantments from using their gifts," Gretta answers.

"How do we get them off?"

She laughs. "You don't. If there's a way, don't you think we would have done it already?"

"I'm told that someone holds the keys to unlocking them. We can get them off that way, right?"

"Believe me, we've tried that route already," Kyla says. "It nearly got us both killed."

"Only because you couldn't find the right key to fit in the hole," Gretta blurts.

"So, you're saying that there is a key?"

"Oh, I'm sure there is, but the guards don't have them. At least the ones we have come across anyway. The keys they hold are for the doors and chains only." She pauses a few seconds, as though she's reminded of something. "At least the ring of keys we acquired. I went through all of them, and not one released our cuffs."

"Fantastic," I sigh.

"So, what's your next plan, genius?"

"Shh... let me think."

Gretta gives another smirk, but Kyla appears to look optimistic.

"I got it," I say, seeing a letter opener laying on the dresser. "One of you call for the guard while the other lures him to the side of the bed. I'll pretend to be doubled in pain, holding this." I grab the opener. "I'll stab him, and one of you hit him over the head with that poker stick over there." I point to the fireplace. Both girls are hesitant. I can feel it. "Look, do you want out of here or not?"

"Yes, but how will we be able to get past everyone else?"

"Very carefully. We must find those keys. If we can get these cuffs off me, I'll have enough magic to get us out of here." If there's one thing I do know I have, it's the rage that's built itself inside me over the years.

We get in position, and Gretta calls for the guard. "Something's wrong — she's convulsing!" Gretta cries. She shrugs a look like she didn't know what else to say.

Kyla giggles. "Guess you're having a spasm," she whispers.

I hide the letter opener in my hands and the guard opens the door. "What's the meaning of this nonsense?"

"Sir, over here," Gretta says.

Kyla is bent over, too, pretending to soothe me. The guard approaches as I wait for the perfect moment.

"Okay, now," I whisper to Kyla, and she moves out of the way.

The guard bends down, and I stab him in the neck with the blade and twist it. Before I have a chance to tell Gretta to make her move, she's smacked him over the head with the fire poker. It doesn't make him go down completely, but Kyla grabs a shovel from the fireplace, adding a final blow to his head. Blood oozes from his neck, and he stops moving. I take the keys from his waist and wrap them up inside my jacket.

"C'mon, let's get out of here," I press, as we all head to the door.

22
THE PIT

TWO GOBLIN GHOSTS PASS by our room, prompting me to push back against the wall behind the cell door, and I motion the other two women to do the same.

"I'm assuming you have special *eyes* to see the invisible, like us?" Kyla asks.

Her comment reminds me that Lira's magic valiancium cuffs canceled the enchantments of Nyta's charm. Which means I can no longer see those that are invisible to the naked eye. I still have my invisibility potion tucked in my back pocket, though. It will be a temporary fix. I remember the downfall of drinking this potion is it has a time limit. I pull it out, saying, "No, but I can see ghosts, and this elixir will allow me to see what is not there as well." I smile and down the liquid.

Gretta nudges Kyla, whispering, "I bet that's what alarmed the guards last time we tried to escape—the goblin ghosts."

"I'm guessing you two don't need invisibility potions?" I ask.

"No, not at all," Gretta says. "Just like you're able to hear and see exceptionally well, we can—" Kyla nudges Gretta's arm.

"How do you know I can see and hear well?"

Gretta sneers. "Haven't you figured it out already? Dryads know when vampires are near."

"Oh, Gretta stop. Now is not the time," Kyla scolds. "She obviously isn't dangerous at the moment, or she would have eaten us already." Kyla stares at me, and I hear her gulp.

"I don't know what I am, but I can assure you neither of you appeal to my appetite." It still boggles my mind that I find ogres to have a pleasing smell, however. "Don't worry, your secret is safe with me. My best friend is Elven and a porter. If we can find her, she can get us all out of here."

"So, you know we can see invisible people?" Gretta remarks.

"Yes, I can see your gray aura now that I've drunk the potion I had in my back pocket. Let's get out of here before the ghostly pair comes back this way." I open the door to our cell. "Stay behind me."

"Perhaps escape isn't a lost cause after all," Gretta whispers.

As we round the corner, I see hidden in the shadows an invisible goblin. His glowing green eyes concentrate on the working goblin miners picking away the side of one cavern wall. Lucky for us, a cart filled with coal sets in our path, allowing us to hide behind it.

"Now what?" Kyla whispers.

Gretta sees them right away like me and nudges Kyla. She glares, but it quickly fades when Gretta points to the goblin surrounded by a gray aura.

Kyla mouths the word, "Oh."

I put a finger to my lips and then point to my ears, gesturing that they can hear.

We wait until the invisible goblin moves away before taking our chances to go back the way I came earlier.

It seems like hours rather than minutes when we reach the cage that Cory, Rory, and I all had been in. *Where are they? They're gone.*

I know Cory can see my thoughts, but can he hear me? I try to project my body, so I can fly above and scout, but it doesn't work. These cuffs are preventing me from doing just about anything.

"What now, Princess?" Gretta murmurs.

"Please don't call me that." I realize the only way out is finding a set of keys that unlock the bindings subduing our magic. "We must find a way to remove these cuffs," I say.

"Good luck with that," Gretta says. "Like I said before, the guards don't have those keys."

Out of the corner of my eye, I see one of the cages hanging off the derrick, swaying back and forth. I realize it is Cory trying to draw my attention. Rory is in another one next to him.

If I can see him, then it means he can overhear me, too, if I drown out the white noise.

I whisper, "Cory?"

"Yes."

"Do you know how to find the keys to release these cuffs?"

"Yes, Rory has a set hidden in her pouch." He pauses. "I see a guard coming your way. Hide."

I motion to Gretta and Kyla to move with me to a large boulder that's a few feet away.

When it's clear, Cory adds, "We were contemplating when it would be a good moment to make a move. We won't have a lot of time, though."

"We?" I whisper.

"Hello, nugget," Dad says.

"Dad, are you okay? How's Geneviève?"

Kyla and Gretta give each other a look, and I'm not sure if it's a worried one or a deceitful one.

"She's fine," Dad says.

Rory unlatches the cage she's in, then delicately jumps to Cory's, unlocking it, too. She releases his shackles. I'm relieved to see Cory finally free from the cuff Moyer put on his ankle years ago. Rory, too, is free from the bindings.

A loud horn sounds, jolting my body, and for a split second, I think we are caught. A crowd begins forming around the pit as a figure pops up onto a large boulder.

"Gather around, my comrades, our people of Grengore. It's with great pleasure I announce to you our guests caged above, waiting to be sacrificed for favor to our Underworld Lord Vothule."

"Vothule?" I whisper to Kyla.

"Don't you know?" She looks at me as though puzzled. "He's the god they worship."

I remember when Moyer boasted to Casey in the basement, she was going to see Vothule after the power of my necklace sent her flying. It was the same day she showed me Blair hanging from chains, and Casey claimed I'm the lost princess.

The ritual becomes louder as the drums bang. Dad, Cory, Geneviève, and Rory are still in the cages. The crates rock back and forth while the rotator spins them around to the center of the pit. I watch with bated breath as the cages are released into the burning crater below. Cheers come from the gathering crowd.

It takes every ounce of energy not to cry out in agony. I know Cory sees my visions in my head, imagining them burning in lava. I want to scream, to save them, to use my superspeed and grab them all.

I feel a hand press on my shoulder. "No," Gretta whispers, "you can't move. They will kill you on sight."

Through the sounds of cheering, I hear a voice say, "We're out." Cory pops in behind me, tapping on my shoulder, and covering my mouth before I scream.

Rory is next to him, smiling. "See, one big happy family," she says.

"Lovely. You couldn't have warned me first before giving me a heart attack?" I say.

"You must not have heard me," Cory says. "We got out. There wasn't much time to react, so Rory tossed the keys to free Geneviève and your dad just in time."

"Okay, so, where are they?" I ask.

Rory isn't upset like me. "They ported out," she answers. "C'mon, we need to get out of here."

"How can you be so sure?" I protest.

"My mother is a Druid, like me. Remember?" She gives a confident smile.

"So, they left us here?" I ask, raising my voice slightly.

"Shh," Cory says. "We better get out of here before the people of Grengore notice something is awry."

"What?" Gretta murmurs. "You said we would be free of these cuffs. How are we to be free now?"

"Who's this?" Cory asks.

"I know these two," Rory interrupts, and she doesn't look pleased. "Gretta, Kyla. Nice to see you're... still alive." Her tone sounds disappointed and condescending.

"We can do small talk later. Shouldn't we figure a way out of here?" I urge.

"Wynter's right," Cory says, as he pulls my hand. "We need to go now while everyone is still fixated on the sacrifice."

Rory pulls out the map she tucked away earlier and looks at it. "It appears we are deep within the tunnels." She looks worried. "I can only jump three of you at a time. I haven't mastered the ability to carry more than that yet. So, who's first?"

"How far can you jump?" I ask.

"About three hundred and fifty feet. Comparable to a football field, almost. It comes in handy when I'm being chased."

"Take them first," Cory says. "Wynter and I will hide out behind this rock until you return. But make it quick. We don't have a lot of time before someone will see us."

Rory returns thirty seconds later, but it felt like thirty minutes.

It takes a few jumps before we reach the outskirts of the underground kingdom. "One last jump," Rory says, "and we're out of the caves."

We wait for Rory to come back one last time, hiding behind the pillar that opens the drawbridge. "We don't have the key to free me and the Dryads, Cory. We'll have to go back. You do know that, right?"

"Yeah, I know," he says.

"So, how do you feel? You're at least free," I say.

"Honestly, I don't know. I mean, I can conjure items, but I don't know what powers were truly hidden because I wore that cuff since before I turned eighteen."

"Well, I'm looking forward to seeing the new you. Not that the old you was bad, but it will be fun to grow together with our powers, right?"

"I suppose. I don't know what it will be, though, and it kind of worries me."

"Worries you?"

Rory pops in behind us.

"Geez, don't scare us like that!" I voice in a high whisper.

She giggles. "Sorry. So, what are you worried about?"

"Cory hasn't known what his gift will really do since he's always worn those steel cuffs," I say.

Rory smirks. "Probably like any other Storm. Are you ready or what?" Taking both our hands, we make a final jump out of King Zeelx castle dwelling.

As we make it through our last jump, we land in the same spot Rory left Gretta and Kyla. Only they are not waiting like the other times before. Unlocked cuffs are on the ground near a coal-filled cart.

"They had a key the whole time!" I'm furious that someone can be so selfish. "Great, I'm imprisoned within my own body. If they had a key, why didn't they leave earlier?"

"My guess," Cory suggests, "they came across someone who did have a key, right under our noses. I'm sure they knew who had them. Living in these tunnels, during their captivity, they probably learned to map the area."

"You know what," Rory cuts in, "it will be fine. They're Dryads, and I know where they live." She smiles. "Besides, my mom and Jeoffrey got out. I bet she still has the key I tossed to her in the pit."

"I'm guessing they were afraid of releasing you from your cuffs," Cory adds.

"Why? I already told them I didn't find them appetizing. They did manage to infuriate me though." I smile. "Although, King Zeelx will not be too happy when he discovers I killed his guard."

A shocked look from both of them makes me smirk. "No, I didn't eat him. I'm still full from devouring your mom," I say, looking at Rory.

Rory flinches. "Oh, Wynter, that is so wrong to say out loud. And she wasn't my mom."

Cory chuckles and I nudge his gut.

"Ow," he huffs.

"How did you manage to kill a Trek on your own with that cuff on? Cory asks.

"With strategic planning." I grin. "It's how I—we—escaped, Gretta and Kyla. I'm a little annoyed that they double-crossed us."

"Well, I hate to be the bearer of bad news, but when King Zeelx finds out you're gone, they will come looking for us. We don't have a lot of time to find that Waxlily. Let's get out of these tunnels," Rory says.

23
THE WAXLILY

WITH THE HELP OF Rory's map, we finally reach our destination at the mouth of the cave overlooking a lake. It feels too easy, and I sense something's afoul. A bright reflection of light bounces off the water making my eyes sting. It takes a moment for my eyes to adjust.

Hawks fly overhead, and my body flinches to its sounding call, remembering the singing birds in Songbird Meadow, as it echoes throughout the lake canyon.

"It's okay, Wynter," Cory says. "They're all over here. This is their territory. He's just warning other birds that they have guests."

"They're not like the birds of Songbird Meadow, are they?"

"I sure hope not. Although, I do feel a bit sleepy. I think I'll lie near this rock," Cory teases.

"Knock it off you two," Rory snaps. "No time for jokes, my eyes are not going to last much longer." She takes the bottle Nyta gave her earlier and drinks some of the medicine. "And I just drank the last of that," she adds, tucking it back into her coat pocket.

"Down that ravine should be the Waxlily." Cory points in its direction.

"Have you been here before?" I ask Cory.

"No, but Nyta showed me a picture in her mind when we were in her home."

"So, you know what the flower looks like?"

"Indeed, I do. Have you forgotten my talents already?"

I smile. "No."

"There isn't much time," Rory presses. "My vision is getting worse."

"Do you think you can make it down to the lake?" I ask.

"I'm not staying up here alone while you two go after it."

"Fair enough," I say.

"There isn't much of a trail," Cory adds as he hikes ahead of us.

I hold Rory steady as I hook my arm around her elbow. "Follow my lead and try not to stress your eyes. We'll be at the bottom in no time."

We hike for about fifteen minutes before Rory says, "I need to sit."

There is a boulder a couple feet in front of us. "Can you reach that rock?" I point.

Rory nods, and we make our way so she can rest.

"How much farther down do you think it will be, Cory?" I ask.

"Not far." He stops to look back. "Half hour maybe?"

Sweat beads across Rory's face. "We all lost our packs and have no food."

"We don't need the packed food," Cory says. "We're hunters, remember?"

"Not for my sake. For hers." I nod to Rory, who rests against the boulder.

"Oh, right," he remarks. "I forgot Elves have 'normal' appetites."

I glare at him as he begins to conjure something in his hands, creating a banana.

"Here you go, it's full of potassium. This should help for the short term." He hands me the fruit to give to Rory.

"Eat this," I encourage her, as I peel the skin away. "It will give a little strength. We haven't much more to go."

She takes the banana without questioning where it came from.

"Okay, I'm ready," Rory murmurs. "Let's get this done."

As we walk the rest of the trail, I keep my eyes on high alert. Mountains surround the massive lake. Cactus-like looking plants are scattered about. It's similar to a desert. We walk the trail slowly down a path leading to the lakeshore.

Nothing surprises me anymore. For once it would be nice to have no interruptions, get the flower, and get out.

Once we reach the edge of the water, we see an abundance of plants resembling ferns lying along the edge of the shore.

"I don't see any flowers at all. Where are they?"

“Right in front of you,” Cory says, conjures gloves, and put them on. He also creates a satchel and opens the flap of the pack.

“The Waxlily like the Perpalily needs to be handled with care,” he says. “Waxlily, too, is poisonous, but unlike the Perpalily, if you’re infected by the Sea Spike, the Waxlily will not kill you, but instead kill the intruding Sea Spike poison. The oils on the leaves will sting like a bee if one doesn’t wear gloves.”

“Well, that’s reassuring,” I say.

“Nyta needs the roots of this plant, but she told me all you need to do, Rory, is touch one of the leaves, and the stinging nettles will do the rest. It’s the antidote. I haven’t a clue what it would do to someone who hasn’t been infected with Sea Spike and touches it.”

“Hence the gloves,” I say.

Cory smiles, as he digs up the plant, revealing its long web of roots.

“Why does Nyta need the whole plant?” I ask.

“I’m assuming to transplant it, to keep a stockpile for future antidotes, so we don’t have to travel here again,” Rory answers.

“Precisely,” Cory confirms, “that’s what I would do.”

“Well, here goes nothing, I guess,” Rory says, reaching for a leaf.

“Wait, there is something you should know first,” Cory says. “Nyta said you might experience side effects.”

“Such as?”

“Your sight might change.”

“Meaning?”

“You will see the world differently.”

“If that’s the case, why isn’t everyone doing this?” she asks.

“Look around,” Cory says. “It wasn’t easy getting here. Plus, not too many know about the cure from the Sea Spike. As said before, back at Nyta’s place, I think the Trek were counting on the poison to blind anyone that crossed their path. When they came to shore, they didn’t count on us thwarting their plans. In most cases, the Sea Spike poison reaches the eyes within minutes. If it wasn’t for Wynter’s healing ability to slow the poison, curing you would not have been possible. Once the poison reaches your eyes, it’s too late. You’re blind indefinitely.”

"Alright, well," Rory says, "here it goes. I'll take the risk." She touches the plant. "Ow!"

"Stings like a bee?" Cory asks. He takes out a pad of paper from the inside pocket of his jacket, jotting down notes.

"Yes. And it feels like I have fire spreading throughout my veins. Gawd, it hurts." She tumbles to the ground, doubling over, and appearing to be in pain. "Cory, you didn't mention it would be so excruciating. A little warning next time, maybe?"

I worry, feeling helpless. It's hard to watch her go through so much agony. After a few minutes, the screaming stops, she stills, and appears lifeless.

I touch her neck, checking for a pulse. "No! Cory, you didn't say it would kill her. I can't find a heartbeat."

"If she truly has the poison Sea Spike in her system, it shouldn't have killed her, Wynter." He, too, begins to wear a look of worry.

Tears well in my eyes. "You said she would be okay!"

Rory's eyes are wide open, and her mouth is ajar.

"I don't see a spirit yet come from her body. Do you?" Cory asks.

"What?" I question.

"I can see what you see, remember? Rory hasn't released her spirit."

Cory's right. If she's truly dead, I would see her soul, and it hasn't shown up. "So, what are we supposed to do now?"

"We wait."

THE SUN FALLS BEHIND the mountains.

"We should set up camp before it gets dark," Cory says. He stands.

"Where are you going?

"To look for an ideal spot to pitch a tent." He points. "You stay with her and call out if you see any changes."

Worried, I look around the mountain ridgetops. "Make sure it's away from the giants, please," I joke.

"Ha ha, very funny," he says as he wanders off.

Sitting down next to Rory, I brush the red strands from her cheek. What if she doesn't wake up? My mind explores every possible option and I begin to accumulate some anxiety.

"There you are, Wynter. I have been looking all over for you."

"Aunt Fran?" I turn around and look behind me, and high up on the ledge is the translucent silhouette of her. *"Where have you been? Could have used you back in the mines, ya know."*

She glides down closer, much faster than one would do hiking down a hillside. *"Sorry, I needed to find out why Lira made me feel so suspicious."*

A look of worry sets upon Aunt Fran's face. *"What did I miss?"*

I scoff, irritated by her absence. *"A lot."*

She reaches me and sits. *"Wynter, I'm sorry—"*

"I'll fill you in later. So, what did you find out?" I ask, cutting her off.

She sighs. *"A whole mess of stuff."* Her translucent body begins to shift to a solid form. *"Which reminds me, I don't see your dad around."*

"Lira double-crossed us." I pick up a twig and toss it into the water. *"We got into an altercation with some ogres and goblins."*

"Really?"

I stand. *"Yes, really."*

Aunt Fran touches my shoulder. *"Wynter, what is it?"*

I flinch and she retracts her hand.

Facing her, I say, *"Dad turned out not to be Dad at all, but a shapeshifter in disguise, or a witch. Not exactly sure what that thing was, but he seemed to be Lira's lover. Does the name Miles mean anything to you?"*

"Ah, it makes sense now. Yes, that name does mean something."

"What can you tell me about them?"

Aunt Fran huffs. *"Miles and Lira are an item. Lira somehow made her appearance different."* She bows her head, picking at her lips. *I should have clued in that Miles was posing as your dad.*

"It's concerning, indeed. I thought ghosts were supposed to be able to see past the facades of the living?"

"You're right. Which has me concerned." She looks at me. *"But we have bigger worries than this."*

"Such as?"

"I found out that there is a price on your head, Wynter. I don't know why I didn't see this before. The entire realm must know you're here. And if they don't know now, they will soon."

"A price on my head? For what crime?"

"You're the heir, my dear. The one destined for peace, and the Underworld knows as long as you're alive, their kingdoms are threatened with extinction."

"I see. They assume I'm just as barbaric as them."

"Quite the opposite. Don't you understand? The Underworld lives for chaos and destruction. They will stop at nothing until both our planets are overrun with malevolent power. We need to get you back to Storm Castle where it's safe."

"Safe like my dream when Sarmira came after the Storm family, safe?"

"It was a different time then. Sarmira is stuck on Earth right now. She's banned from these lands. Why do you think she has others doing her dirty work?"

"The double-crossing witch and her accomplice never had any intention of helping us, did they?"

"All a ruse to get you down in the mines, it appears. I see they didn't keep you there. How did you escape?"

"Long story." I glance down at Rory lying on the ground. *"Can you tell me if Rory is... I mean, I don't see her spirit?"*

"She's not dead if that's what you're asking. Asleep, I would say. A very deep sleep. What did you do?" She looks around and sees the ferns. *"That's right, the Waxlily."*

"You know about this plant?"

"Indeed, I do. It's the same plant that healed me from the Iknes Shaw poison."

"But I thought it was because you had the healing ability."

"It only slowed it down. No, this plant is what cured me. Ever since then, I've had the gift of seeing the present. Even as a child. The healing ability comes from the

Deagon side of the family. We can heal ourselves, meditate through mind control, and are sensitive to fire. It's in our blood."

"Did Isalora, my mother, have it, too?"

"You mean the healing ability? Yes."

"So, that's how you acquired the gift of seeing the present? Not by turning eighteen, but because you were cured from this plant?"

"That's right, the theory anyway," she affirms.

"What was your gift then?"

"The same as yours. Throwing flames. Except I can burn people from the inside out. With the side effect of the healing Waxlily, I can see into their minds. It's quite fascinating. Although, when I was a child, the theory was I would adopt some sort of 'seeing' ability later. Seeing inside someone's mind happened after I turned eighteen. Like I told you earlier— when I was still alive, I couldn't project into a spirit to scout the lands or be in two places at once, that's all you." Fran kneels next to Rory's sleeping head. *"Not much is known about the mysteries of the Waxlily. Nyta keeps a record of the events of those who experience it though."*

"Can you see into my mind, too?" I ask, now realizing that my aunt had this gift all along.

She points. *"No, you always had that necklace on, remember?"*

"No wonder I'm so 'extra,'" I remark. *"all these innate abilities would make a normal person's head spin."*

Fran laughs. *"My dear, you will get used to it, I'm sure. It's one of the reasons you're so desired, and why we must protect you for the greater good of the kingdom. You're one of a kind, and nobody in this magical realm has ever experienced the likes of you before."*

"Wish I could remember."

"You will. Give it time."

"Hey, guys, I found a spot," Cory yells from a few yards away. He paces closer. "Hi, there, Fran. Nice to see you found us.

Fran nods in acknowledgment.

He comes to pick up Rory and drapes her over his shoulder. "It's not far. Follow me."

24
CORY'S DISCOVERED POWER

As before, the tent resembles a small cabin on the inside, while the exterior camouflages with the terrain. Cory lays Rory down on a cot. "Do you think you can possibly make a flame, Wynter? We should make a fire to keep Rory warm."

Concerned that my abilities won't work as well as before, since I still wear cuffs around my wrists and ankles, I say, "I can try."

I think of past incidents, hoping the anger won't let me down. It seems to be the foundation of my power. Perhaps that's the true fuel to my magical capabilities, so I work up thoughts of my past. Does that mean once I have control, the rage will go away? I think of when I was sent to the basement when Moyer forced me to see JC or Blair hang from the chains, or when she took that poor boy's soul, stealing his magic. I think of all the things that caused me to want to kill her, including the time when she used her sonic power, sending many children reeling on the floor.

That's it, Wynter. Remembering the lifeless child laying in my arms brings my skin to a boil, and I feel the rage race through my veins to my fingertips.

"Stand back," I say. "I don't know how big this fireball will be."

"Maybe we should go outside," Cory suggests.

I shake my head, as my hand burns. "I don't think we have time," I say, hissing in pain. The heaviness builds so intensely I can't stand the stress any longer, and the burden of force explodes into one single flame on my index finger, like a lighter. "What?" I heave. "Are you serious? All that anger built up, and I create a flicker?"

"It's all we need," Cory says, taking his conjured crumpled up paper and lighting it with my flaming finger. He tries not to snicker, but I know he's laughing on the inside.

"It has to do with those cuffs you're wearing. Hey, at least we can keep warm. And at least, we don't have to worry about your raging emotions for the time being, either," he teases.

Cory has a point, and I hadn't thought of it that way. No wonder Moyer has the entire Storm family bound by the ankles. I can imagine what we would all do if we finally had the full power of our abilities.

My mind races as we wait for the woodstove to warm. The stories Dad told at the cottage when I woke from my nightmare with Moyer come to the forefront. He shared some of the evil things witches and warlocks do with their dark magic. The light witches are rare and have mostly died off. I wish I knew who Lira was before she tried to slither her way into my life. I bet if I had my full memory back, I would know. Why did Gretta and Kyla leave? And what about King Zeelx? He's going to be looking for us. Lira and her accomplice, too.

The phony Geneviève must have been the spy who led Lira to Pine Willow Valley in the first place. Dad probably suspected, which is why they captured him. It explains why my nose was so sensitive to the scent of Geneviève. With him and Geneviève out of the way, I became an easy target. I don't think the Trek flying in on his dragon counted on Rory being there. The dragon didn't count on my water ability, either. I laugh out loud.

Cory clears his throat.

"What? Why are you both staring at me?" I ask. "I was having pleasant memories."

Cory veers away. I know that look. He's been inside my head, but why isn't he laughing, too, then? My thoughts should have played out like a silent movie.

Fran smiles. *"We both hear your thoughts."*

"Come again?" I look at Cory.

"I know what I can do now with the cuff off."

"What are you saying, Cory?"

He chortles in a teasing tone. "I guess I can say this now... might as well since you can't burn me to a flaming crisp at the moment."

"Cory, just spill it," I say.

"I can hear your thoughts. No longer just pictures. In fact, I can hear you and Fran, both speaking."

"So much for the necklace working to drown out 'your white noise,'" I say. "I'm not angry. At least I no longer have to repeat things to you." I take a few seconds to absorb the shock. "Down by the lake... you heard our conversation, didn't you?"

"Yes, every word."

"But how is that possible? You said so yourself, Aunt Fran, that you couldn't hear my thoughts when you were alive."

"Key word, my dear... alive. I can hear you all the time now that I'm a ghost. There are no boundaries."

"Says the ghost who couldn't find us in the mines," I say.

She nods. *"I'm still trying to think that one out, myself,"* she says. *"Although, you try weeding in and out of the white noise of ghosts. You want to talk about static—there's some for you."*

Her translucent figure comes closer to Rory. *"Can you imagine if everyone could see us? Probably why it's nature's way of not giving humans the ability to see ghosts in the first place."*

"And what about you," I say, as I look over at Cory. "Are you going to tell me it's because we're on Ladorielle? That the ability to invade my thoughts is because you no longer wear these cuffs?" I raise my arm, showing him my frustration.

"It's both," he says. "Before, it was the cuff I wore, yes, but you still have the extra protection of that necklace."

"And you have your watch."

"Think about it for a minute. Wynter, when we return to Storm River Manor, our enchanted items will still work like always. The only difference is I'll have my powers back and you will have your full memory."

"One would only hope I get it back, anyway," I say. "But unless we find a way to release me from these bindings, I have nothing to defend myself against Moyer."

"You will," Fran cuts in. *"Trust me."*

"Yeah, you keep saying that, but it hasn't reared its ugly head yet."

"Which reminds me, if Moyer's body is possessed with Sarmira's soul, where is the real Moyer?"

"I imagine caged inside her own frame. Her soul is in there, somewhere. The Moyer I know was Maura Moyer-Storm."

"Yes, I think I saw Maura once or twice when Moyer tried to compel me. It was like I could see right into Maura's soul. She was trapped in a room, behind the dark eyes of Moyer's pupils. Her hands banging on a window. I saw this woman mouth the words, *'Help me.'*"

"You must have seen the soul of the true Maura Moyer," Fran says. *"As a ghost, I can see many people possessed with their souls trapped."*

"What?" Cory gasps. His look of shock resonates with me.

"You mean there are more like Moyer out there?" I ask.

"Many, many, more, I'm afraid. It's a wonder Isalora never mentioned it to anybody," Fran says.

"She probably didn't want to alarm any of us, discourage our task at hand."

"This is more serious than first assumed," Cory says, and he takes a seat on the conjured couch in front of the stove. "If there are many soulless people walking around, we're doomed."

"We're not doomed," Fran says, *"there's still hope."*

"Hope?" He raises his voice. "What, like, fight all the undead that live inside the bodies of the living? How are we to defeat them? If any of us kill these possessed zombies—and yes, I'm calling them zombies because they are not people, we know them to be—then, when they are killed, they still roam, fighting among the living, killing us and helping Sarmira with her evil plan."

Cory's tenor worries me. For the first time, I hear his heart beating fast. It's always been a calming rhythm before; now it beats faster than anything I've heard since coming into my Storm powers.

Stopping to take a deep breath, I gather my emotions, putting all of what I've learned together, and it hits me like a freight train. Like a lost memory, I should have known all along.

"Cory, maybe this is what's supposed to happen?"

"What do you mean?" he questions.

"This telepathy we all have – you, Fran, me – don't you get it? This is how we are going to beat her."

They both stare, as though I have lost my mind.

"I wear this necklace, and you shouldn't be able to hear me, but you do. And Aunt Fran, you can read every thought of a living being's mind, right?"

She nods. *"Even animals."*

"Brilliant," I say. "Don't you see?"

"Are you saying that you and Cory are connected somehow?" Fran asks.

"That's exactly what I'm saying. And Cole is part of this. He's the third. I feel it with every fiber of my being. Aunt Fran, you and Dad always taught me to listen to my gut."

I see her smile, if it's possible to see the features of a smile on a ghost, anyway. *"Yes, we did."*

"Well, it's screaming at me right now." I grin. "Think about the letter in the coffer Isalora pulled out. Do you remember what it said, Cory?"

"Yes. 'The power comes from within, revealing all what's hidden. The final step, before three, can be one,'" he says.

"'Look to the west, under the sun,'" we both say out loud together.

"Don't you get it, Cory? The power will come from releasing the souls trapped in the bodies that the undead have taken over. When the host dies, their spirit will be released, and able to aid us in battle."

"Is it your theory that we're fighting a two-sided war? A war of flesh and soul?" he asks.

"Precisely. It's quite the advantage we'll have when we go to defeat Sarmira," I say. "There must be two souls trapped inside the people possessed. And the souls taken in possession are ones with magical powers."

"I get it now," Fran cuts in. *"I don't know why I didn't see this before."*

"What is it?" I ask.

"When you, Cory, and Cole combine your abilities, you three will be able to detect these undead souls possessing bodies. You can't see them right now because Cole is the missing link."

"Aunt Fran, you're a genius."

"Don't thank me yet. It's just a theory. We won't know for sure until we get Cole back from Madame Moyer's grasp."

"Fantastic," I say, sneering. "Another mystery."

"That still leaves one question," Cory adds. "The riddle said, *'look to the West, under the sun.'"*

"Oh, that's easy," Fran exclaims. *"Ashengale, of course."*

"How can you be sure?" I ask.

"Because Dragonscale Island is West under the eye of the planet, known as our sun," she answers.

"So, that's why Isalora said to seek out Dragonscale. He's the one under the sun?"

"Yes."

I change the subject as I look at Rory. "She hasn't stirred once since we've been talking. Can you see into Rory's mind?" I ask Cory.

"No. Not while she sleeps. I've already tried."

"What about you, Aunt Fran?"

"I'm afraid not. We will need to wait it out."

"She's right."

"So, what now?" I ask.

"We wait for Rory to wake. Nothing we can do. We're stuck here until she wakes up. She is our port out of here," Cory answers.

"How long will that be? King Zeelx will know I'm missing and come looking."

"And we will be ready. I have a plan," he says. "But for now, we should all get some sleep."

25
PORTING OUT

THE NEXT DAY, RORY finally wakes. At first, she doesn't know her surroundings. "Where am I?" She looks around. "Whose house is this? Last I remember I touched the Waxlily."

I give a slight giggle. "Cory conjured a tent. We're still at the lake," I say, relieved that she is out of her slumber. "He's outside, standing watch. Do you remember what happened?"

"Yes, all of it. I don't know how I got here, though." She sits up to look around more. Placing both her hands on her temples, she cries, "The pressure in my head is killing me."

"One of the side effects, I'm afraid," Fran cuts in.

Rory glances in the direction of Fran. "You-you're alive?" she stammers.

"No. Very much still... dead. The Waxlily cures the sight of the one who has been poisoned by Sea Spike, or in my case, Iknes Shaw poison. You get to have the wonderful inherited sight of seeing those who have passed."

"Is that supposed to be a rhetorical statement?" Rory replies, lying down against her pillow. "Does anyone have headache medicine, by chance?"

"Not meant to be, sorry," she replies. "It means you have become a seer like us." She goes to the cupboard in the kitchen to check on Rory's request.

"Us?" I ask.

"Yes, Wynter, you, myself, Isalora, and now... Rory." Distracted by our conversation, she adds, "Wow, Cory thinks of everything when he creates these tents.

What does he do, have it all itemized in a ledger of that brain of his? I found headache medicine." She reaches for the bottle, only she can't pick it up.

I laugh under my breath at her predicament. "Here let me help, Aunt Fran." I grab the bottle, along with a glass setting on the shelf, and fill it with water. "How is it you can open the cupboard door, but not be able to pick up items?"

"Hey, be nice, I'm still new at this," she contends. "Not every day one turns into a ghost."

Interrupting our candid conversation, Rory questions, "So, what you're saying is, I can see ghosts now? You do not appear at all like a spirit that has passed on, Fran."

"I suppose not. Apparently, I'm not solid enough yet to pick up simple things such as a bottle of pain pills, either." Her tone reveals frustration.

"Oh, Aunt Fran, I'm sure you will master the technique in time." I hand the glass and a pill to Rory. "Besides, Nyta said it would take a while."

Aunt Fran appears frustrated as she plops in a recliner next to the couch. "My sister has had years of practice, I suppose." She folds her arms in protest.

"I would venture to guess you're right. But don't go getting all senseless on us now. I'm the emotional one, remember?"

"So, tell us," Rory asks, "what's this story about the Waxlily?"

"Yes, Aunt Fran, you mentioned my mother was a seer, too?" I cross my arms, ready to hear this new bombshell. I mean, I know that since Aunt Fran has entered into her spirit form, she can see, everything living, and dead, I get that, Fran explained yesterday, but she saw ghosts like I do when she was alive, too. This doesn't make any sense.

"Right before you were born, Wynter, Moyer slipped poison into your mother's drink. It wasn't until Isalora began to develop the symptoms did I realize what was happening. I gave her a drop of serum I keep in my necklace."

Reflecting on the past, I say, "That day in the house, when they were coming for us, you were performing a ritual. It was the drop you placed in the bowl that allowed us to escape their capture, wasn't it?"

She smiles, continuing her tale, saying, "We were not sure what it would do to you in the womb, but if we did nothing, both of you would have died. Thankfully,

Jeoffrey was able to see enough into the future to know you would be fine. But he also saw Isalora's outcome. Knowing the probable consequences, we all prepared for the inevitable."

"So, you think somehow the reason I can see dead people is because of the Waxlily serum that was given to my mother when I was still in her womb?" I ask.

Fran nods. "Rory, you now have the same ability, too. It will take time to decode, but it may turn out to be very valuable to you. You may even be able to gain keen eyesight when using a bow and arrow."

"I must say," Rory adds, "it will be much easier to defeat Sarmira when she moves into her spirit form. I can help you fight her."

Cory walks into the tent. "I hate to interrupt, but since you have had time to wake up, do you feel up to porting us out of here?"

"Yeah, sure. I can try."

We gather our things and follow Cory outside. The morning sun shines bright, and the sky is a vibrant blue.

"Okay," Rory says, "let's get out of here."

Cory and I huddle close, waiting for Rory to cast.

A minute passes as nothing happens.

"Rory, we're ready when you are," I say.

"I'm trying."

"Deep breaths, my friend. Focus. Cancel out the noise and concentrate." Deep down I'm worried, but I don't dare tell her that.

Rory nods and closes her eyes.

Still nothing. We're standing in the exact spot as before.

"What's going on?" Rory looks at her hands. "I can't seem to teleport us out of here."

"Try doing your porting jumps," Cory encourages. "It will take us longer, but if it gets us out of here, then who cares, right?"

I smile, touching her shoulder. "It will be okay."

She nods. "Let's try that then."

Again, nothing happens.

"I don't understand. Why can't I port?" Her eyes fill with tears. "How is this possible?"

"I'm guessing," Fran says, "it's the side effects of the Waxlily."

"You mean I've lost my porting ability?" she asks as tears stream down her cheeks.

I feel her devastation. Her heartbeat quickens. It's the same beat I hear when people are afraid.

"How can she overcome this? We can't be trapped here, can we?" I ask.

Aunt Fran tries to reassure us, saying, "It may wear off. I've known of cases where people lost some abilities, but they came back in time. I don't know about porters, though. This is new to me. You three can't risk climbing out of here and up over those mountains; it will be nearly impossible. Besides, the Iknes Shaw live along these elevations, and going back through the mines will be a mistake."

"What about our whistles?" Cory suggests.

"I don't know. We are so far north they may not hear you," Fran says.

"Wait, stop. What are you two talking about?"

"Our dragon hybrids."

"Our what?"

"Half dragon, half horse. We call them dragongryphs. They can guide us to safety. Each hybrid is connected to us. As a resident of Storm Castle, we are given these dragons as a gift from Dragonscale."

"And you're just now telling me about these creatures?"

"Well," Cory says, "like Fran said, we are very far north, and it's never been tried. Besides, we were counting on Rory porting us out of here. Since that isn't an option, perhaps this is the only other choice we have."

"What if this doesn't work?" Rory asks.

"I think it will," he says.

"So, tell me more about these dragons, Cory?" I cross my arms, annoyed he hasn't mentioned one word about them before.

"When parents discover they're expecting, a dragon egg is given, and it lays next to the bed each night while the mother sleeps. When the egg begins to hatch, it's a clue that the baby isn't far behind. The small dragon hybrid is then like a sibling, sharing a common love. Much like humans when bringing home their bundle of joy to meet the family pet. The child and dragon grow together, bonding for life."

"Are you saying I have this creature you describe?"

"I fear I may have said too much," Cory says. "Blow your whistle, and let's find out. Perhaps your dragon will jog more memories?"

"Aunt Fran, why didn't you tell me about these creatures before?" I ask.

"I was planning on it. When the right time came around."

"I would say now is the right time."

"The night you were born we had your dragon egg with us. It began to hatch, and we knew Isalora would give birth to you anytime. We locked ourselves in the tower."

The three doors in the turret at the manor come to mind, where I was shown my room by Nora. "I was born in the same room I stayed in, at Storm River Manor, wasn't I?"

"Yes, your dragon hatched early. His head poked through the shell, and he was weak. With no magic on Earth, he wasn't strong enough to deal with the atmospheric changes. You two were connected. The plan was to escape Storm River Manor and port back to Ladorielle. We were running out of time, for both of you."

Aunt Fran takes a long pause. "Perhaps when we have more time, I can tell you more. What I can say is Sarmira set a trap, which is how you ended up being born on Earth."

I look at Cory. "You believe we can call our dragons?"

"I do." He nods.

"And where is this whistle?"

"You're wearing it."

"My necklace?" I glance down at the blue amulet and twist the chain between my fingers.

Cory adds, "If you will notice near the loop that the chain threads through, there is a hole. You blow into it."

"Wait," Fran interjects. "Do you think it is wise? They may find us for sure."

"Perhaps," Cory answers, "but what other choice do we have? If we fly through the mountains close to the ground while the sun shines, we might be able to stay out of the radar of the Trek and the Iknes Shaw. Besides, the dragons will be invisible."

"How would our dragons know what to do?" I ask. "I mean, I don't remember how to ride a dragon, either."

"When you ride a dragongryph, you're one with them. In the way you can speak to Fran," Cory explains.

"Well, we better think of something quick," Rory states. "I think I'm getting a vision now. At least that is what I think it is. There's an army flooding the tunnels in the mines."

"I take it your new abilities are kicking in, my friend?" I ask.

"If that's what this is? But we better get out of here fast. We have about ten minutes before they arrive at the mouth of the cave."

"Blow your whistles, you two," Fran says.

Cory pulls something small off his watch and puffs into it. "There's a small sound we can't hear, but the dragons hear it."

I flinch at the ear-piercing sound. "I heard it loud and clear. You didn't hear that?"

"No, not at all. That's weird. Guess your ears are keener than mine." He smiles. "Now, it's your turn."

I prepare for another ear-piercing sound and blow my whistle, too. "What about you, Rory?"

"Porters don't get dragons." She smiles.

"Right. Because you can port to a new location wherever you are," I reply.

"Yet, I no longer can," she says. "I'm sorry I am no use to you."

"Don't worry, you can ride with Wynter," Cory offers.

I hear a loud screech in the sky, and the amulet I wear, glows blue.

"They have arrived," he says.

26
DRAGONGRYPH

THEY'RE MASSIVE, GLIDING ACROSS the sky. One is turquoise having a lavender shimmer, while the other is a lavender-gray with a blue shine. They both have gold on the tips of their wings and talons.

As they draw closer, their shape reminds me of a Pegasus, except their wings and head are similar to that of a dragon, with their front legs as talons, and their hind legs of a Clydesdale. They don't have a coat like a horse, but rather scales that glimmer in the sunlight. Their enormous wingspan spreads far, bigger than the biggest bird I have ever seen, and their tails have a spiked ball on the end.

The blue dragon screeches as it lands. Cory reaches for her. "Hey, girl, I missed you." She makes a purring sound and lowers her head.

He smiles. "Meet Yssa."

"This is all too weird," I say. "Why don't I have any memory of these magical creatures?"

"You will, little by little." He climbs on her back. "I see that," he adds.

"Who are you talking to?" I ask.

Cory grins wide. "Yssa. Remember when I told you once you're on the back of a dragongryph, you become one?"

"Right." Intrigued, I smile. "What's she saying?"

"That we need to go. The mountains are surrounded by an army of Trek and goblins."

That grabs my attention and I look around trying to capture any movement among the trees above the cliffs, wondering if they can see us.

The other hybrid dragon lands, and as though it recognizes me right away, it gingerly approaches, purring louder than Yssa.

"He misses you," Cory says.

"I remember dreaming about this animal long ago as a child. We flew everywhere in my dreams, and I wasn't afraid of heights, either."

"It was probably a memory, Wynter. We need to hurry, though. Get on him," he says.

"Cory, how? I can't even climb a ladder without bursting into a cold sweat."

"He won't let you fall. Seriously, Wynter, when are you going to get over your fear of heights?"

"Probably never," I murmur.

"They're here." Rory points to the mouth of the cave we passed through last night after escaping the mines. "We should go. And I mean now!"

I scan the surrounding mountaintops again, and this time I spot an army of soldiers with weapons in their hands.

As though my dragon knows the danger, he takes his wing, and scoops both Rory and I onto his back. It all happens so fast I don't have time to react. Rory follows in behind me, grabbing onto my waist. Cory is already in the air, and we follow close behind.

Arrows fly, some making a direct hit to my companion, but they don't penetrate his thick scales.

I feel long hair wrap around me, as well as Rory. If I had to guess, I swear it was a horse's mane.

"Don't worry, you're safe," the voice inside my head says. *"I'm Namari, your dragon brother."*

The memories come flooding back as he speaks, and the fear of heights fades. *"I remember you."*

"I'm sure glad to hear that," my dragon replies.

"Can anyone else hear our conversation?"

"No, just us. You are free to let your thoughts roam. Unlike the humanoids, we dragons tend to keep our minds private. You are protected while riding. Not even Cory can hear you."

My mind is shielded at last.

"Maybe I should come to you when I want to hide my mind from intruders."

"You're always welcome to hide within the wings of my protection, dear princess."

My necklace is glowing again. It becomes brighter and brighter when I look up to see dragons approaching us. They're much bigger than the massive dragongryphs we ride.

I'm beginning to understand when this locket gleams dragons come flying. First on the ocean shore, when we were attacked the other day, and moments earlier when our dragongryphs arrived. Now it glows again, brighter than ever before. I sure hope they will be on our side and not the Treks.

Screeching sounds carry through the mountain range as they pass us. There are a couple dozen of them. They release fire toward the mountains where the arrows are coming.

"As you can observe, we brought reinforcements."

"I can see that."

"When you and Cory called us, the whistle beaconed to your location. We saw you two were at the Lake of No Return, which meant fighting a battle to get to you. Those who venture near these parts do not return home. Although, some are lucky enough to get through the mines, as it is the only way here. Unless you're a dragon, of course."

We soar through the sky, escaping once more from chaos. I breathe in the fantastic view below, hearing the sounds of a battle behind us. Soon the whizzing arrows cease, and we skate through the sky in silence with Rory continuing to cling to my waist.

"Your friend can let go of you, now. My mane will keep her from falling."

I repeat the words to Rory, but she still holds tight.

"Look who is scared of heights now," I tease.

Rory shakes her head. "Not letting go. If you fall off, we fall together."

"You're not going to fall, Rory. Namari won't let you."

"Is that his name? Well, how can you be so sure, huh?"

"You have never been on one of these dragons, have you?" It makes sense. She had a way to port to her destination before she was poisoned.

"No, not a dragon. I ride horses, remember?"

"It's going to be a long ride," Namari says. *"Sit back and enjoy."*

"Where are we going? Not back to Geneviève's Ranch?"

"No. To the castle, of course."

"When you say castle, are you referring to Storm Castle?"

"That would be the one."

"What about finding Geneviève and Dad?"

"You will find them. But it will not be at Geneviève's Ranch. Besides, if we took you there, it would be the first place the Trek will look."

"How do you know that?"

"We... dragongryphs have ways of knowing things. Now, sit back and enjoy the ride, princess."

"Namari, I'm confused. If it's such a long journey, then how did you come upon us so fast?"

"Yssa and I came from Ashengale. A one-way portal to the other side of the continent."

"Interesting that these whistles can be heard from so far away. Something odd happened when I blew into one. I heard an ear-piercing sound. Nobody else seemed to hear it."

"It's designed much like a dog whistle, only the one you and Cory carry are much softer."

"Didn't seem soft at all. Hurt my ears."

"Because you're a Deagon. All Deagons and the likes have sensitive ears."

"Cory seemed to not hear it at all."

"That's because he's a Storm."

As we fly, I think of the past dreams I've had and flip through them. I remember when I was not much older than twelve, I was playing where I shouldn't, and I was alone. I blew a whistle and Namari came within seconds.

"Tell me, Namari, what's so special about these trinkets anyway?"

"Each dragongryph has its own unique tone, responding to the call of the whistle. They're made from the shells we hatch from. It's very important to keep the shells; they're used for many purposes. A calling whistle is one of them. Part of it is ground to powder and used in recipes for specific ingredients to enchant items and to protect our riders."

"Like my necklace?" I question, realizing I'm finally getting clues as to why my chain is so protective.

"Yes."

"That's why my necklace glows when dragons approach, isn't it?"

"Indeed. It also is what protects you. Have you ever wondered why your necklace is so magical? Even in worlds other than Ladorielle?"

"I remember once Madame Moyer went to strike my throat, but she failed. The necklace jolted her backward, and she blamed Isalora for protecting me."

"That's because your necklace holds the magic of my shell. Nothing can destroy it."

"So, that's why Madame Moyer cannot find me?"

"Yes."

"It didn't stop the Trek from attacking us on the beach the other day."

"No, because the Trek, too, have dragons of their own. We may be able to hide from people, but we cannot hide from dragons. Good or evil."

"How do you protect yourselves?"

"By keeping invisible. Other dragons can sense us but cannot see us."

"It's all so fascinating."

"We have plenty of time to talk more, but now you should rest."

I feel like seconds have passed when Cory calls, "Wynter, wake up." I open my eyes to see we have landed in a field. "We're here," he says.

"Where are we?"

"Storm Castle."

"Here you are, My Lady," Namari says, and he lowers his neck to the ground, so I can slide down.

Rory climbs down first. "Get me off this thing," she says, as she jumps.

I laugh. "Can't wait to be on solid ground again, huh?'

She scowls.

"I'm never far, remember that," Namari says.

I lay my head down on his massive neck. *"Namari, I remember everything you and I did together. How could I have forgotten such wonderful memories?"*

"It was the way it had to be, My Princess. You must be protected at all cost. I'm glad to see you again. We shall ride together again, soon."

"I will not forget you a second time." I slide down off my gentle beast.

Our group stands in a field watching as both dragongryphs fly away toward a mountain in the far distance, erupting lava.

"Does that happen to be west?" I ask.

"Yes," Fran answers, *"that's Ashengale Mountain."*

"I remember him," I say. "All of it. And none of it was a dream."

"I knew some of your memories would come back if you rode Namari again," Cory says.

"How did you know?" I ask.

"Just a feeling I got." He pulls at my arm. "Come on, let's go see the queen."

"The queen?"

"And if my mom and Jeoffrey are here," Rory interjects, ignoring my question, "we need to find them, get that cuff off you, and kick some serious Trek butt. It's only a matter of time before they will come looking for you again."

27
LADORIELLE

GUARDS STAND AT THE entrance of a large gate not far from the open field where Yssa and Namari dropped us off.

"How do we get in?" I ask, and as if the drawbridge has ears, it lowers.

"Like that," Cory says, grinning.

I huff. "Right."

It isn't long before we reach a second gate, and the iron bars open up again, letting us pass. Inside, it's like a whole new world.

People walk about the courtyard while vendors encourage customers to buy their goods. Women pass by dressed in old-world attire of long hooped skirts, extravagant hats, and bright parasols while accompanied by gentlemen in suits. Some people are dressed in Western attire outfitted in leather pants, vests, and tunics, and still others, such as soldiers wear clad in armor. Some with quiver sets attached to their backs and a sword by their side. It's a setting much like Geneviève's Ranch. Horses are hooked to carts of hay with merchants riding on them, trotting across the cobblestone road, and more vendors line the walls selling food. Shops of all sorts line either side of the stone walkway, displaying items in the windows and having racks of merchandise set outside their shops. It's like entering an old-world market, yet still having an earthy modern atmosphere.

A massive clock tower is centered in the middle of a courtyard surrounded by a pool of water. A statue of a woman—looking much like the statue in the center courtyard at Storm River Manor—holds a pitcher of pouring water. A flower garden sprouts around the structure, and a path leads up to the steps where children throw coins into the fountain basin. Fruit trees line the edges of the circular park.

People are staring. "Am I paranoid, or is everyone looking at us?"

"You have the face of a princess, remember?" Rory answers.

"Funny girl. You have more jokes, I see."

"It's not a joke," she scoffs. "I'm being quite serious. Word travels fast when a royal comes to town." She points behind us to a painted mural above the gated entrance. There, a picture of a royal family stares back at me. It's my dad, Aunt Fran, and me with black hair, along with many faces I don't recognize. A man and a woman looking much like the wedding couple I saw in the foyer of Storm River Manor are also there, sitting in chairs.

I raise my brow. "Me?"

"How quickly you forget, My Lady, you're a Storm as well as a Deagon," Rory says.

"Yes, I seem to be continually reminded of that. So, where is this kingdom, anyway?"

Cory smiles. "It's all around you, Wynter. You're on the outskirts of Storm Castle. We're within the realm of Ladorielle."

"If I'm a princess, as you say, and to be the leader of this 'world,' who is currently taking my place?"

"The queen, of course," Rory says grinning, looking as though she enjoys watching me scratch my head trying to figure out the puzzle.

"Unbelievable," I say.

I nearly step in the path of someone on a horse, and Cory pulls me to his side. "Watch out for the riders. Follow me," he says, looking at us both.

I glance around at the fleeting looks of people as we tag close to Cory and follow him to a nearby stable where many horses graze in the grass.

A stable master greets us. "Good morning to you, Cory. Look at you!" he shouts in excitement. "You're all grown up.

"Good to see you, too, Lars," Cory replies. Lars pulls him in for a hug.

Lars tips his hat. "Good to see you again, too, Rory. How's your mother?"

"Not sure. We've come here to search for her."

"I haven't seen her."

Cory clears his throat. "Lars, I'd like to introduce you to a friend."

Lars glances toward me. "Friend indeed." He takes off his hat and bows. "My Lady."

"No need for that, sir, please," I say with embarrassment. "I hardly know anything about royalty, let alone finding out I'm a princess."

The man wears a look of shock.

"Lars, you will have to excuse Wynter," Rory interjects. "Fran placed a memory stamp on her to protect our kingdom from Sarmira. She hasn't any recollection of her past."

"I see..." He pauses as though that name isn't ever spoken in the kingdom. "Have you caught the wicked witch yet?"

"We're working on it now. Here to see the queen in fact," Rory answers.

"Is your mother missing?" Lars inquires.

Rory takes a deep breath. "No, not really—"

"What about Jeoffrey?" Cory asks. "Have you seen him?"

Lars shakes his head. "I haven't seen either of them." He turns to point at the animals grazing in the small field by the stable. "As you can see, their horses are still here, but they have not come to greet them since the day you left—" Lars gives a curious glance toward me.

"I left?" I question.

"Yes, with your aunt and father." He pauses, then squints, coming within inches of my nose, peering straight into my eyes, saying, "You haven't got a clue why you're here, do you?" It's like he's reading me as an open book.

Nervous from his abrupt manners I step back, saying, "No. I'm told the queen will have the answers."

"Ah, good, yes... she will be pleased to see all three of you, I'm sure." He bows again. "Would you like your horses, sir?" he asks, looking at Cory.

"That would be nice, yes."

Lars walks to the stalls where he instructs a boy to fetch the horses.

The lad brings me a white mare with a white braided mane and tail. The animal is magnificent. The tallest horse I've ever seen. The beast trots toward me, nodding its head, and the boy is having a hard time controlling her. The animal comes to me right away, as if it hasn't seen me for an eternity. "Easy girl," the boy says.

I give Cory a strange look, and he chuckles at my amazement. "This is Eluna." He smiles, appearing amused. "Seems she has missed you."

I look at Cory. "My horse?" I question, wishing I could remember having such a beautiful beast. The animal neighs. "She's quite large. How do I climb on? She's much bigger than the last horse I rode."

"You had no problem with Namari. What's the difference?" Rory snickers.

Eluna nuzzles my cheek and neighs again. I reach to scratch her forehead and a memory flashes before me of riding her through the trees. We're being chased. *"Wyndreana, you're going too fast,"* a voice calls. The memory quickly fades. "This is my horse?" I ask again, uncertain of the past moments I just experienced.

"Wynter, are you okay?" Cory asks, sounding concerned.

"I remember riding her through the meadow." I look at Cory. "And my name, it's different." I squint. "Wait a minute, you can see them?"

"I can't see your memories, only what you see presently." He smiles. "But this is good news. It sounds like your memories are returning. Wyndreana is your birth name, or so I'm told."

"What an odd name," I say.

"According to your parents, they thought changing your name would make it harder for Sarmira to find you."

"I see."

The stable boy gives me the reins. "My Lady," he says, "will you be riding her today?"

"What? You mean now?" I glance at Cory. "We aren't walking?"

Cory points to the castle up on the ridge. "Do you prefer to walk? That is why I requested the horses."

Seeing in the distance, a faint castle outline, I say, "It does look a bit far, doesn't it?" I take the straps from the boy. "Thank you, umm..."

"Thomas, miss." He smiles wide.

"Well, Thomas, it appears I will be riding after all."

The boy steps away, bowing, "Thank you, My Lady."

Cory smiles and flips a coin the boy's way.

"Gee, thanks." Thomas runs off to tell Lars.

"Shall we go meet the queen?" Cory climbs his horse. "Surely you haven't forgotten how to ride, have you?" he teases.

I reflect on the encounter at Geneviève's Ranch. My past self seems to remember riding and did quite well on the horse Rory brought. "Only one way to find out, isn't there?" I smirk.

"You seemed to do fine at the ranch," Cory says.

"Oh, Wynter. Where's your sense of adventure," Rory says, hopping on her horse.

"Right," I snap, "easy for you to say. You at least have a memory."

"Oh, stop being 'woe is me' and get on Eluna already."

I mount my horse with ease, bringing the reins to fit comfortably in my hands. Peering at Cory, I say, "Lead the way." But before we begin our travels, the Royal Guard rides in on a team of horses, stopping in our pathway.

The horses circle us, and some of the men riding them carry banners.

One man dressed in a royal uniform, and apparently the one leading, says, "By order of the queen, Her Royal Highness requests that Princess Wyndreana be escorted through Ladorielle to the castle."

"Are you serious?" I blurt. "There is no need for an escort. Cory is perfectly capable of leading the way."

"My Lady, we must insist. By order of the queen."

"I barely have the stomach to acknowledge I'm a princess, let alone have you chaperone my friends and me. And please call me Wynter. I'm not quite used to such a fancy name."

"As you wish, My Lady," he replies and turns his horse around.

"Wait," I call. "I don't know your name."

"Sir Simmons, My Lady. Now if you please, allow me to escort you and your friends." We follow him while the rest of his men trail behind us.

As we walk through the town, people step aside while our caravan of horses passes through.

People take notice, some giving shy glances, while others whisper and point. I don't know them, but they know me. Some smile wide while others scowl. Children hide behind their mother's skirts, and yet others wave with delight. I look around at the many people and ponder the thought of how many have gone to great lengths to protect me. How am I to defeat Sarmira? The power of this necklace I wear alone surely cannot stop her.

"You have been gone a long time, and they're all surprised you're here," Cory says, "It would be similar to seeing a celebrity walking down the sidewalk in a busy place."

While we ride through the cobblestone streets of town leading up to the castle, memories rush back again. A breeze blows through my hair, refreshing my senses. The familiar smells of the flowers that line our pathway wash over me. I remember everything in detail. Like déjà vu. I know I have seen this all before, whether in a dream or in real life, and it resonates deep within my soul.

"Aunt Fran, you have been quiet, are you still there?"

"Of course, I am." A breeze skates across my skin bringing goosebumps. *"You're never alone."*

Tree branches overhang the pathway, and bright wildflowers outline the road. As we follow Simmons up a narrow trail it twists and turns, and our horses slow their walk.

"Are you overwhelmed yet?" Cory calls over.

"When have I not been?" I huff.

"Look around, Wynter. This is your kingdom."

"My kingdom? Oh, Cory, no, I don't think so. I'm just a girl from Washington State. I wish I could remember all of this."

"You will, I'm sure."

My thoughts continue to wander. *Why are we coming here and not going to Dragonscale? He's, after all, the one we should be seeking.*

Once again, Cory reads my thoughts. *"Indeed, that is true. But we are not here for just that. We must find a way to bring back Cole, too. We can't possibly defeat her without him. Remember the second riddle?"*

Ignoring the fact that Cory is once again in my head, I nod. *"Yes, I do. 'The final step, before three can be one...' with Cole being the third."*

He nods. *"Then you know we must find a way to bring him back."*

"Yes." We continue to follow the trail toward the castle gates, passing more curious folks. "Why are we not flying up to the castle? Surely, we would reach the grounds faster than on horseback. At least then it would avoid all these uncomfortable stares from strangers."

Cory chuckles. "I thought it was important that you see the kingdom. Perhaps jog some memories."

We reach the entrance of the gate, and it opens automatically, as though we're expected. Trotting the horses near the stable area, we dismount and hand the reins over to the caretaker.

Sir Simmons dismounts, as well, and comes over, bowing. "My Lady, if you will please follow me this way."

Cory grins. "Someone has been dying to meet you."

I tilt my head. "More secrets?"

He smiles, nodding slightly. Rory tags close behind.

28
HAPPY ENDINGS?

DOES ANY OF THIS seem familiar to you?" Cory asks as we walk through the palace doors.

I shake my head. "Not yet." We pass the threshold of the giant wooden gates and travel inside the courtyard. Fruit trees line the stone fencing. "It looks a lot like Storm River Manor, except these grounds are more extravagant." Instead of expensive parked cars, there are horses decorated in lavish armor, hooked up to carriages, with drivers awaiting an escort.

Simmons leads us up the steps to the front door of the castle entrance while his group of soldiers stand guard at the gates.

"Such excessive treatment isn't needed, Sir Simmons. Cory can show us the way," I say.

"Certainly not, My Lady. He, too, deserves the royal treatment. He's a Storm, just as you are," Simmons argues.

We enter the hall. "Please wait here while I summon Arryn. She can guide you to Her Majesty," Simmons says.

"Who's Arryn?" I ask, turning to glance at Rory.

She shrugs, so I turn to Cory. He, too, rolls his eyes and shrugs.

We wait patiently in the center of the foyer. It looks identical to that of the manor.

"Please don't tell me I'm in a dream and about to walk right back into Storm River Manor?" I joke.

Cory chuckles. "I assure you this is your true home, not Storm River Manor. That place was built to make Lady Sara feel more at home while away from her true kingdom here. I should warn you, though, it's almost exactly the same... with perhaps a few different features you will soon discover."

The foyer is at least ten times larger than Storm River Manor. Cory's right, though, it's like looking at a near-exact replica. The same grand staircase leads to the upper levels, with the same dragon stone statues sitting on either side of the base of the stairs. Even the same-looking portraits hang on the walls. The floors are marble, too.

There is a slight difference on the lower level. Multiple doors line the walls on either side of the foyer, with each of them shut tight, unlike at the manor where all doors remained open—except the library.

Here, benches line up against the stone walls between each door, with a painting or portrait hanging above the pew. The Storm family crest banner overhangs on the balcony and the sound of a water fountain nestles in a corner below it.

A man approaches from behind one of the side doors, showing familiar features. I can't help but feel like I know him. He paces forward slowly. His tired face traces soft lines around his cheekbones, giving the appearance he's had a joyful yet weary life.

He bows his head, saying, "Welcome home, My Lady."

"Thank you," I say, furrowing a brow. He is all too familiar. Images flash before me but they're too fuzzy for a clear picture. Deep down, my soul knows him.

"Arryn appears to be tied up for the moment, so I've come to greet you myself." He has a gentle smile, with a beard covering his neckline, and his gray hair touches his collar. He wears clothes like he, too, is royal but doesn't at all seem to care that he's doing the job of hired help.

"Good to see you again, Charlie," Rory interjects.

Then it clicks. "Charlie?" My stuffed rabbit comes to mind, and I realize he's been forgotten with all the excitement.

Ignoring my question, Charlie says, "And you, too, my dear, Rory. How's your mother?"

"People seem to keep asking me that. Frankly, I don't know. Have you seen her?"

"She's not here if that's what you're asking."

He turns and smiles. "My dear Wyndreana, it's been so long since I laid eyes upon you, my child. My, how you have grown."

"Wynter, please," I respond. I look into his eyes, and a pleasant memory floats to the surface. I think I was about five. I'm climbing on the same rock I fell off when I broke my arm.

I look at Cory and then at Rory. Peering back at Charlie, I say, "I remember you. I lost my footing and fell. You rushed to my side to catch me."

Charlie smiles and nods. "Indeed, I did."

"It wasn't my teacher after all. I remember now. You ran with such speed through the forest, holding me in your arms."

"Yes. You broke your arm," he says, looking delighted, that I remember.

More moments surface and I slowly recall what happened. "The doctor that worked on me... It was Nyta, wasn't it. I remember her face now."

Both Cory and Rory grin from ear to ear.

"That's fantastic, Wynter," Rory exclaims, "you're getting some memory back."

"I remember you," I say, looking at Charlie. "You're my great-grandfather, and you gave me Charlie, my rabbit. You said we had to go away for a while. I didn't understand why."

The old man opens his arms, inviting a hug, shedding tears, and I run to his embrace.

"My dear child, I've missed you so much. We all knew you would be back."

"Tell me, Great Grandpa... why did we have to leave?"

His low grunt tells me it's a sad memory. "When you broke your arm, your screams were so loud, it sent a chill through the land so powerful that the Underworld heard you. The only way to protect you was to take you away."

A tear escapes, and I grab my necklace. "My dad told me a story once that this locket was made by you. But he called you Ailbert, not Charlie.

Charlie nods. "Yes, Ailbert is my first name. I suppose your father was worried if he told you the truth of my existence, that perhaps it would trigger a memory too soon. It was quite a feat to keep such a secret at bay."

He pauses to glance at Cory and Rory. "Come with me, there's much for you to see."

"More surprises?" I turn my head to Cory, and he smiles with a shrug.

"Perhaps more memories will come as you pass along these walls," Charlie adds.

We follow my grandfather around the grand staircase to the french doors behind the stairwell on the lower level, where two guards stand at the entry. "Step aside, please," Grandfather says.

The guards glance at each other and then to Charlie. They don't question his authority and move to the side, allowing us to pass.

We enter a majestic-looking room that reminds me of the ballroom, at Storm River Manor, except it resembles a church sanctuary. A few benches are set against the walls on either side of the room under stained glass windows. Ahead of us, two large chairs are set up on center stage. Come to think of it, the seats resemble thrones. I notice someone sitting in one of them. She holds a staff, dressed in royal attire, like my great-grandfather.

Charlie paces toward the queen, bending down near her face, kissing her cheek, and whispers, "She's here, my love."

We reach the base of the platform, where both Cory and Rory kneel. He nudges me to do the same. Not knowing how to act, I follow suit.

"My Queen," Charlie starts, "I bring with me Wynter Storm, daughter of Jeoffrey and Isalora Storm and great-granddaughter of Ailbert and Sara Storm."

"Oh, Charlie," she says, "there's no need for such formality."

"I couldn't agree more," Aunt Fran says.

The queen stares my way as though to hear our thoughts.

"Where have you been, Aunt Fran?" I can see her take form out of the corner of my eye.

"Hiding out. Watching from a distance."

"That will be all, my dear child. I can take it from here," another voice in my mind says.

"Who else is in my head?" I demand.

The queen stands and comes closer to us, bringing her staff with her. It has a crystal at the top, emitting a slight blue glow. Her hair is white like mine, and she wears a golden cloak that trails to the floor. A crème color gown hides beneath the lavish outer garment. Atop her head, she wears a simple crown, not like the big extravagant ones seen in the movies. Her features are soft, and she comes across as a gentle soul with a smile bright and eyes that seem to sparkle with delight. I first think the sunshine coming from the stained-glass windows makes her eyes shimmer, but then I see the tears, and I know then she's not of the physical world. Like Isalora, she's actually a spirit.

The queen comes to our side, grabbing my hands. "Let me take a good look at you." She has me twirl around, then hugs my frame with such a tight embrace I think I will burst.

She, too, must have an immortality spell cast upon her, for she is as real as any living being, but I see her true form.

I look deep into her eyes, saying, *"It's you, speaking inside my head, isn't it?"*

She ignores my question and smiles. "I see you have brought my great-granddaughter back safely." She glances at both Rory and Cory. "Please, stand like the rest of us. There is no need for formalities, as I said earlier." The queen lifts her hands gesturing for both of them to rise.

"Yes, it is me inside your head. Sara Deagon-Storm, your great-grandmother," she says.

29
THE TRUTH

STUNNED BY THE WORDS, I say aloud, "Then the rumors are true. You're... dead. Chad mentioned you and Aunt Isobel were poisoned. Do you have a spell cast, too, like my mother, to allow the living to see you physically and not as a ghost?"

Rory has an expression of shock, while Cory smiles. I know he can see what I see, but can Rory? She should be able to see the queen, too, shouldn't she? I mean, Rory could see Aunt Fran and even hear her. Can she not hear the queen inside my head?

"My Queen, please forgive me for not recognizing," Rory says, "I had no idea."

"There's no need to apologize," my great-grandmother answers. She directs her attention toward me. "My dear, I have been waiting years to finally see you again. My spirit is tired, yes, but the kingdom must believe I'm still alive, or else they will lose hope and Vothule will take advantage of the kingdom. We can't let that happen, now, can we?"

"No," I say.

She takes my hand. "I see you are at a loss as to what to say. No matter, in time all of your memories will return."

"This is all so confusing," I say. "The stories told at Storm River Manor say you died of poison."

She smiles. "Yes, well, one of the many stories that have not yet been told correctly. I have been waiting a long time, holding this palace together, making my people believe I'm still alive. My power shield is weakening, though, and it's time for me to pass it on to you. I'm exhausted. I need to rest these old bones of mine." She laughs. "My spirit, rather."

She continues, "When three become one, you will rule the whole land of Ladorielle, including Dragonscale Island. The territories will go back to having their houses, covens, or lands, whatever the people will want. The states of our world will again be as they were before Vothule came to destroy it."

I think of Blair and how much I have been told of her hurt and anger that Moyer took the life of Sara and Isobel, leaving Blair to wallow in pain. "But the stories? What about those who think you're dead?"

"Memory stamps. They work wonders, don't they? Blair thinks I died, yes... It was necessary for her at the time. My body lay in the crypt below the castle, as do Ailbert and your mother."

"My mother? You have her here, too?"

"Yes, another time, perhaps, we can share the stories."

"Another time? You spring this news on me and tell me I have to wait to hear more tales of my past?" Anger builds within me as I piece together this complicated puzzle.

"Watch your tongue, my child. I'm still queen and your great-grandmother."

"How can you sit there, knowing you have been the one to order the erasing of our family's memories? Blair loved you like a mother." I can't believe I'm defending Blair, but it doesn't feel right to play around with people's emotions like that.

"The stamps were placed for your protection, as well as the others. You have no idea the power you're dealing with, do you?"

"I do, a little, yes."

She squeezes my hand and smiles. "When you fell from the rock, a second stamp had to be placed."

"I remember I fell." I look at my grandpa. "You rushed me to Nyta's doctor's office. I remember all of it."

"And do you remember anything when you were younger?" she asks.

I think of the times when they taught me to ride Eluna. Namari was still a young dragon, young like me. We grew up together. "Yes," I say.

Twin boys come to the front of my mind, playing in a nearby field with their dragons, as my memories enact like a movie. Grandpa teaches me to ride Eluna, not far from them.

I look at Cory. "We were raised together when we were little."

"I know," Cory confirms. "The day you fell from that rock, my mother Blair, Cole, and I heard you all the way down the hillside by the river shore. My brother and I didn't know what was happening. Casey was out hunting with your father and Aunt Fran. They were over by the mountains, and they heard you, too."

"Within hours our kingdom was destroyed," Sara says." She circles to the throne and sits. "When Vothule realized you were gone, he executed us all." She smiles. "He didn't anticipate me casting the immortality spell, which is why you still see me here today. Nyta, of course, is good at what she does, and pulled out Charlie's heart and mine, placing them in coffers. It's the only thing that is keeping Vothule from overtaking the kingdom right now. You see, magic can be a wonderful thing, fooling even the King of the Underworld."

"That's what's in the second coffer, isn't it? The one that Isalora asked me to give to Nyta. It's not my mother's heart at all, but yours."

"Yes. But we haven't been able to find your great-grandfather's, nor your mother's." She places a palm on her husband's knee. Looking at Charlie, she smiles. "We think his may have been buried in the rubble during the last war."

"Where's my mother's coffer, then?"

Her stern look surprises me.

"You don't know where it is, do you?" I ask.

My great-grandmother dismisses my question. "We have been waiting a very long time for you, my dear." She looks at Cory. "We also hoped you might be able to find both Charlie and Isalora's coffers."

"I can try," he says. "I need something personal of yours, sir," he adds, glancing at Charlie, and then at me. "And your mother's."

My great-grandfather nods. "I can give you something of mine later. Our daughter may have something personal still here within the castle. I'll take a look. The more pressing matter is destroying Sarmira," Charlie says.

"And what about Vothule?" I ask. "If he thinks you were executed, then how are you keeping him away? I mean, he did witness your deaths, right?"

"You let us worry about him," my great-grandmother says. "Right now, the more important task at hand is to find the Sword of Valor. It's the only thing that can destroy Sarmira, and you are the only one who can wield the sword and see her in spirit form."

Cory interrupts, "My Queen, if I may speak?"

She nods.

"I can see the undead through Wynter's eyes. When the cuff was finally released from my ankles, my gifted powers returned." Cory pauses, adding, "But there's more."

"Well tell us, what is it?" Charles blurts with impatience.

"I can read the minds of every living creature. Not just the pictures of what they see, but also their thoughts."

Sara stands. "It appears we have a new advantage, doesn't it, Charles?"

"There's more," Rory butts in.

The queen turns to glance at Rory. "Well, aren't you all full of surprises? How lovely. Please tell us."

Nervous, Rory clears her throat. "I can also see the undead."

"How is that possible? You're not a Deagon, nor a Storm, not so much as a necromancer, either."

Rory swallows hard, her gulp audible. She glances toward me as though looking for approval.

"Go on, tell her," I coax.

"The other day, the Trek attacked us on the beach near Geneviève's Ranch. He flew in on a dragon, shooting poison arrows. Wynter knocked the rider from his mount, with water—"

"Wait," Sara interrupts, "did you say water?"

"Yes," Rory hesitates.

Sara smiles. "And you're positive it was water, not fire?"

"Oh, she can spout off some serious firepower, but no, Your Majesty, it was water."

"I saw it, too," Cory confirms.

The queen steps closer, looking directly into my eyes. "Is this true, my child?"

"Yes, Grandmother."

"Ailbert Charles, do you realize what this means?"

"I do indeed, my love."

"What? What does this mean?" I ask in a panic. "I don't understand any of it. This power, this change that has come over me, this—"

"Magic?" Sara says. "It means the time is near, war is coming, and you are the chosen one to take the place of Dragonscale."

"What? No, I-I can't. I don't know how to rule."

"My dear, you have no choice. It must be done."

"All the sword fights. That's why Dad had me practice." I take a step forward. "But why me? Why not Cory? Or Cole? I read the letter, the three must be one."

"Yes, the three must be one. But it isn't about just you, Cory, or Cole, no. It's about joining the continents as one kingdom once more, before Vothule took over the Underworld. He came to destroy our world. To grab it for his own."

"So, then what is our role, if we are not the three to be one?" Cory asks.

"You three are to take on the undead army that will erupt after the flesh of this world dies. The souls of humans, elves, witches, sorcerers, anyone whose body has been taken by the Underworld will be released in spirit form, and a battle of the undead and spirit of light will begin."

"So, this preparation of the Super Blue Blood Moon—"

"It only scratches the surface," she says.

"This war that's coming is much bigger than first assumed," Rory says. "How are we to defeat them?"

"With dragons," she says.

"Dragons? The Trek have dragons of their own?"

"Indeed, they do, but we have more." Great-Grandmother Sara smiles. "And the three of you. Four when you retrieve Cole from that wretched witch."

“That’s what the Sword of Valor is for, isn’t it?” I ask.

“Yes. You must find the Sword of Valor. It is the weapon needed to penetrate Sarmira’s withering spineless, evil soul, ridding her forever and will send her back to the depths of hell. In the meantime, I will have undead weapons made so they can help our soldiers defeat the wraiths. These enchanted armaments will destroy both the living and the dead.”

“What about steel arrow tips?” Rory asks.

“Excellent idea. However, there are only so many we can make. Choose your weapon wisely, Rory.”

“Perhaps not,” she argues. “Legend has it, our people know how to melt down the valiancium steel and enchant it.”

Sara pauses to come closer. “That would mean only one thing. Your grandmother, Queen Laveena, is still alive.”

Again, Rory swallows hard, as though she’s either afraid or has kept a hidden secret. “That she is, My Queen,” Rory says, “still alive, that is.”

“So, it appears she survived the massacre after all?” Sara lowers her voice. “This may rule to our advantage.”

“What about the Sword of Valor?” Cory interrupts. “Nobody knows its whereabouts.”

“No,” she says and looks at Cory.

“I get it. That’s where I come in,” he concludes. “I’ll need something personal from the knight that wielded it.”

“That can be arranged.” My great-grandmother’s expression shows delight.

“I still don’t understand how I’m the one to stop this?”

“Because you are a Deagon, and the only one left living with the blood of both dragon and necromancer blood running through your veins. You’re the only one who can withstand the heat of fire and put out the breath of a dragon.” She pauses, returns to her chair, and sits. “You are the glue that will put our world back together again.”

“But isn’t Dad of both bloodlines? Chad, too, for that matter. I read the stories of how you and Isalora broke the rules, marrying Storms, despite what people said.”

She takes a moment to respond, as though finding a way to answer my question delicately. "They are, indeed. But what I don't think you quite understand, Jeoffrey and Isalora had a forbidden love affair. They were first cousins. Conceiving you, blended the bloodlines together, making your power stronger than any Storm or Deagon."

I'm taken aback by her confession. It's beginning to make sense as to why I'm so desired by good and evil alike.

"So, what now?" Cory asks.

"Now, we prepare." She waves her hand, and I don't realize a guard is standing off to the side until he steps from the shadows. He bows as though he can read the queen's thoughts and walks off behind the stage to a hidden door. *He heard our every word.*

Appearing next to me, Fran says, *"Grandmother, she has come a long way."*

"My dear child, I must say, when I first saw you, standing next to Wynter, I thought my eyes were playing tricks on me, but now I must ask; what happened to you? This was not in the plans." Sara appears distraught.

"It was a giant that got the best of me, Grandmother. He had precise accuracy with a sword, piercing my heart." Aunt Fran bows her head and goes to her knees.

Ailbert stands, and Sara moves forward. *"Do not despair. You must have cast an immortality spell; else I would not be seeing you right now."*

"Yes, Grandmother." Fran glances at me and smiles. I fill in the pieces, realizing the connection.

30

THE KEY

"THE WAXLILY IS THE key, isn't it?" I blurt. "The antidote to poisons and the ingredient to the immortality spell. This whole time I thought I was looking for an actual physical key to unlock the mystery. This key was to lead us in destroying Sarmira once and for all, thereby releasing my grandmother Maura Moyer-Storm from Sarmira's clutches." My stomach churns thinking of this realization.

Cory looks as shocked as me while my Aunt Fran nods. Sara and Albert smile. Rory seems to be surprised, too.

"I used the last of the Waxlily to cast the immortality spell on me," Fran confesses.

"That day at our house in Washington—" I stop. My mind races to put the puzzle pieces together.

"Hold on a second," Cory says. "You mean the Waxlily is the crucial point?" Pacing back and forth, he puts his fingers to the bridge of his nose. After about a minute, he stops and looks over at Sara. "Nobody else knows about the Waxlily, do they? Else everyone would be harvesting it."

"Yes," Sara answers. "It wasn't planned to have you all travel to fetch the Waxlily from the Lake of No Return. It's not easy to get there. We had planned to take you once Wynter traveled back from Dragonscale Island. The roots for other recipes lay in low supply. The Waxlily ferns are needed to make more serum. Nyta tells me she instructed you to bring back one of the flowers with you?"

"Yes, I have it," Cory says.

"And the Waxlily," I cut in, "is that the antidote to keeping the kingdom alive? Anyone who dies will be kept immortal in spirit for as long as the heart is in the coffers. That's why Nyta had all those coffers on her shelves, isn't it?"

"And those that have fallen will fight the war with the undead," Sara adds, validating my questions.

"You mean, you've cast this spell on the whole kingdom?" Rory asks. "What about the Pine Willow Elves?"

"Too far, my dear. The Storm Castle, yes, but not the surrounding kingdoms of the other Houses. My power doesn't reach that distance, I'm afraid." Sara circles the three of us with her hands behind her back, pacing.

As though Sara can read my thoughts like Fran, Isalora, and Cory, she says, "Rest assured, Rory is safe from death." She glances at Rory and smiles. "She was here in the Kingdom when I cast the spell."

"Great-Grandmother? What happened to Great Aunt Isobel? Is she gone, too?" I ask.

The Queen chuckles. "She's very much alive, and somehow escaped death, too. You may find her around here somewhere, dancing about. My sister... has changed. She's not herself—she's no longer there if you know what I mean?"

"No, what do you mean?" Cory demands.

My great-grandmother looks at Cory, then at me. "The day we escaped, Storm River Manor – the same night as the cottage fire – the *poison* you know so much about, did, in fact, enter the veins of your great aunt Isobel and me. That part is indeed true. Lucky for us, we're Deagons, and the poison eventually solidified, but it did something to Isobel's brain. It changed her somehow. She's no longer the sister I once knew."

"But she's a Deagon," Cory says.

"Yes, my dear boy, which is precisely why she's still alive."

"Please, tell us what happened?" I ask.

My great-grandmother smiles. I can tell she's reluctant to elaborate. "Isobel was the first to take a drink from the craft brought in by Blair. Immediately, Isobel became sick."

"It's at that moment you knew the craft had been poisoned, am I right? I remember reading the journals," I say.

She nods. "The thoughts in Blair's mind showed me what I needed to know. I knew Blair had no idea, and as I trailed her steps back, I saw Nora standing next to her, looking innocent. To Blair, she's Nora the maid. To me, she's an Iknes Shaw, and one I've never trusted. This was before Blair knew Nora's true form. Seeing Nora, it wasn't hard to figure out where the poison came from."

"Wait," I say, "you can read minds in the physical form, too?"

Sara smiles wide. "All of the Deagon line can. You haven't learned to channel it properly. It's how our ancestors communicated. And it's how we were able to escape the grasp of Vothule... Sarmira, too. They cannot penetrate the minds of our bloodline."

My thoughts wander to Cole and the gift he bestows. The same gift Cole would have had, had Moyer not stolen it from him.

"I believe you're beginning to catch on," Sara says.

"Catching on to what? Right. You can penetrate my thoughts. I wish I could shield my head from everyone's intrusion."

She laughs. "Don't worry, I will teach you how to block out 'the outsiders' thoughts." She glares at Cory.

I snicker at them both, as Cory looks away in guilt.

"Now, where were we?" my great-grandmother continues. "Ah yes, I remember. You have a life here. This is your home, Wynter Storm. The home you belong to, the home you grew up in... and the home you're to reign. But first we must deal with the evil that has been bestowed on this family. Fear not, child, you will not need to worry. I will fight alongside you and help defeat the evil King of the Underworld and Sarmira."

"What can you tell me of them? I mean, I've read the journals you have written, but something tells me you have kept some secrets to yourself."

"I'm pleased to hear you have read the history of your past bloodlines." She motions for us all to come sit near her.

"There is still much more for you to learn. Much more history left untold," she says. "Perhaps it's best that we go somewhere more private?" She looks around the room and then to each of us. I glance at Rory, who has kept quiet through all of this news. "If you care to follow me, I will show you our Hall of Secrets."

"You're not talking about the same room behind the Iron Door of Secrets as at the manor, are you?" I ask in surprise.

"But of course, my dear."

"How is that possible? I mean, the Hall of Secrets is in a circular room, where the manor is located."

"Yes. I can see how this can confuse you," she says. "You may recall that all the doors circle the room, correct?"

"Yes." I nod, mesmerized by the thought that what had appeared as a room in Storm River Manor might not sit where I originally assumed. "And the Hall of History? Is it a corridor like here, too?"

She smiles. "Our Hall of History is the name of our library. I see your thoughts, Wynter, and I can say the door you saw to Ladorielle is the door to this palace, but you must be born of Ladorielle blood to pass through."

"So, are you saying even if Moyer somehow passes through the Hall of History at the manor, she cannot enter the pathway to this palace?" I glance at Cory. He smiles and seems intrigued like he hasn't heard this before.

"Yes, and no. Moyer was born on Ladorielle and a true native to the planet. Sarmira, on the other hand, as long as she possesses Maura Moyer's body, she cannot pass."

"So, either way, Sarmira is stuck at the manor?" I ask.

"In a manner of speaking, yes. But not entirely. She can still travel to her Underworld realm called Zhir. The only way to break her bond from Ladorielle is if she left Moyer's body. Unfortunately, there isn't any way to save Maura Moyer. Once Sarmira leaves her body, Maura Moyer will surely die."

Cory huffs a breath as if to insinuate it would be perfect if Sarmira did just that.

Sara shakes her head. "No, Sarmira will never leave Moyer's body. It will make her too vulnerable in spirit form. Plus, she risks the dynasty she's built over the centuries. When we fled Ladorielle years ago, Sarmira had not yet possessed a body. It's not that easy to do here on Ladorielle. With so much magic, people have the power to destroy evil and shield and protect themselves. The mistake we all made was fleeing to a whole new universe. It left the Storms and Deagons vulnerable and allowed evil to take hold of more power. Although, they, too, have limits to their abilities."

"That's how Sarmira took advantage," Cory blurts.

"If your faction lies with Vothule The Soul Reaper, King of the Underworld," Sara interjects, looking at me and then at Cory, "then yes, I suppose it would rule you." She pauses for a minute, turning as though she is about to speak to the guards. "But the House of Storm and the House of Deagon will not bow down to his discord. It was at that moment the decision needed to be made, either flee to save the bloodline or submit to Vothule's rule. Now enough of the chatter, shall we walk to the Hall of Secrets, so I can show you what each door represents?"

We all follow her. "Oh dear, I nearly forgot. I'm still in this formal attire. I do dislike such fluff I must wear when sitting in the throne room."

She calls to the sentries, "Guards, will you please bring an escort for our guests and have them meet me in the room behind the Iron Door of Secrets within the hour?"

They bow and one stands guard as the other leaves his post. And in a matter of minutes, the door opens and there appears a figure at the threshold.

Standing before me is someone I haven't seen before. She has white hair with lavender streaks, her ears are pointy, and her eyes a beautiful turquoise. A white tiger stands by her side.

"Hello, I'm Arryn. Her Majesty's huntress. This is Akira, my tiger." The cat purrs.

"Arryn, will you take Wynter and her guests to the Hall of Secrets?" Sara requests. "I must change. Introduce them, will you, to the others?"

"Others?" I ask.

"Yes, of course, Your Majesty," Arryn replies. "Follow me this way, will you please?" And she bows slightly, walking towards a door behind the throne, with her tiger next to her, with his tail twitching.

31
HEIGHT ISSUES

WE FOLLOW BEHIND ARRYN, entering a corridor very similar to that of the halls of Storm River Manor. There are multiple windows on one side and instead of doors on the opposite wall there are painted portraits, leaving the corridor much brighter.

"Queen Sara wishes us to guide you to the Iron Door of Secrets. This is the back way through to the hall. Your father and the others have required for you to be included in the expedition we have set to seek."

"My father? He's here?"

Arryn smirks. "No, but he did send word that we all must prepare for battle. Akira and I will be riding alongside you, as well as a handful of others."

"A handful of others will not suffice for the war that is coming," Rory protests.

I can feel Rory's heartbeat quicken. Cory steals a glance from me and asks Arryn, "And Geneviève, have you seen her?"

"We have not seen either of them. Are they in danger?"

"No," Rory remarks. "At least I don't think so."

"Rory, I haven't seen their spirits. They must still be alive," I say, trying to assure her.

She nods with an expression of hope.

"I haven't been to your other world before, nor do I have the desire to go, but Her Majesty has instructed me to go with you. I'm told it's much like this castle.

You may find as we walk, there are some similarities. We're headed to the library." Arryn opens a door to another hall. "This way."

"This place does look familiar," I say.

"It should. This is, after all, your home, Princess. You will notice all the paintings on the walls are of the royal court of past and present." She speaks with formality, like we're on a tour. "This is your mother."

I peer at a painting and swear I'm looking at myself. This young girl staring back at me in the portrait has black hair and not the platinum shade I wear now. "She—"

"Yes, it feels like you're looking in a mirror, doesn't it?"

I nod. "It's the first time I've seen my mother... I mean, I've seen Isalora in ghost form, and she looks like me, yes, but this portrait is like looking at a clone. How old was she in this picture?"

Arryn turns to continue down the hall. "Seventeen. About a month before she came into her magical powers." Arryn glances back at me. "Her hair turned white like yours, too."

We come to french doors with a plaque stating Hall of History above the door frame. Arryn opens the entry, and we walk into the room. There are ladders every few feet apart, to reach the top shelves of books of the first floor, and four spiral staircases in each corner of the room leading to a second level. A few differences set the two libraries apart, though, this one is much larger.

"It's like you mentioned, an exact replica," I say. "What's up there?" I ask, eyeing a catwalk above us that lines the perimeter of the large space.

"It leads to the council room," Arryn answers.

"It's like an upper-level loft in the center of the library," I say.

"Yes, I suppose you could say that. The circular room is supported by heavy chains suspended in midair." Arryn turns to face us. "I assure you; the room is safe."

I gulp. "You mean we're headed up there?" The thought of climbing an open space to the second story, away from solid ground, comes to mind.

"Of course. Believe it or not, that room is the safest place to be in all of Ladorielle." She guides us to one of the spiral staircases. "You might be familiar with the name: The Iron Door of Secrets. It's also known as the Keeper of the Realms."

"Wait, you mean like the Iron Door of Secrets at Storm River Manor?" I ask.

"As I said before, you will see some similarities. I've never been to Storm River Manor so I cannot answer that question. Perhaps one of your friends can confirm for you."

I look over at Cory and he nods.

"Shall we move on?" We trail behind her as she ascends to the upper level.

"Can we not meet down here instead?" I really hate being off the ground.

Arryn appears amused, ignores my concerns and climbs with ease, and her cat follows.

"It's not so bad," Cory teases. "No different than stepping up a ladder."

"Easy for you to say. You don't have a fear of heights."

"Neither do you." Pointing to his temple, he adds, "It's all in your head."

I huff. The anxiety fogs my logic. Deep down the inner voice says it will be okay, but my heart still pounds with fear. "I don't think I can do this."

Rory snickers behind me. "Oh, quit being such a baby." Rory leaps in front.

I glare at Rory's teasing.

"I swear, when Fran enforced that memory stamp, she must have added a few new features because you were never afraid of heights before." Rory gracefully springs up the staircase taking each step two at a time. Seconds later she waves at the top, calling, "Now your turn."

Arryn doesn't engage in our theatrics and continues onward down the catwalk.

I take a brief glance at the hovering room, then to Rory. Again, I ask, "Why can't we meet down here... on the ground?"

"Oh, come now, Wynter. It's all in fun."

"Suck it up," Cory says, nudging my arm. "It's like Rory said. You're not supposed to be afraid of heights anyway. Besides, if you fell, there wouldn't even be a scratch on you."

I stare at him. "How do you know that? It's two stories up, for Pete's sake."

"Yeah, and? It will be fine. You go first. I'll be right behind to catch your fall." He motions with his hand, allowing me to take my first step.

"I'm not in the mood for your teasing, either, Cory."

"What teasing? I mean it. I'll be right behind you."

Annoyed at them both, I push his hand aside. "I don't need either of you babying me." I ascend the stairs as fast as I can, trying not to look down.

"You're quicker than I first anticipated," Cory says, still standing on the first floor. "See, that wasn't so bad, now, was it?"

Somehow, I feel he suspected I would act the way I did to get me up the stairs.

Arryn ignores us as she rounds the corner of the top tier.

Cory catches up and whispers, "Let's see how you do, walking the catwalk. Don't look down." He grins.

"Right, you tell me not to look down. Don't you know that's the last thing you're supposed to say to a person who's afraid of heights?" I grip the side rail so tight that I bend the metal.

"I know, but you're so cute, acting this way. I can't help but tease." He smirks.

Without letting go of my grip, I jab him with my elbow.

"Ow," he huffs.

"Well deserved, I'd say," Rory remarks.

I try not to look down. By this time, Arryn has reached the mouth of the bridge leading to the suspended room. My stomach tightens in knots. Ignoring my inner fear, I say, "Here we go." At supersonic speed, I round the corner of the catwalk, catch up to Arryn, leaping over her and the tiger, and pass them both to the entrance of the Iron Door of Secrets in a matter of nanoseconds. Heaving in deep breaths, with my back against the door and arms stretched out, I look at them, saying, "There, I beat you all!" I smile in satisfaction. Pleased that I made it without a drop of vomit.

Rory and Cory soon trail behind. Arryn gives me a weird expression and shakes her head. "Are you always this odd?" Her tiger purrs. His rumbling hums release vibrations that shake the suspension bridge.

"Can you please not do that?" I ask as I hang onto the side of a post.

Akira's tongue droops out the side of his mouth like a dog, looking content.

Arryn ignores my concerns, saying, “If you don’t mind.” She gestures for me to move aside. “I’ll get the door.” She grabs a skeleton key from her pocket that resembles the one Cory had once back at the manor and opens the entrance.

32
THE PLAN

When we enter, I see many unfamiliar faces, yet for some odd reason, I feel like I already know them.

"There you are," someone says. "Wynter, come meet everyone. We may all look like strangers to you, but I assure you, we're not." The voice speaking cannot be located, as I look around the room to see twenty people or more. Many faces smile at us.

"Come sit down," one man says, standing. He's half my size, with dark brown wavy hair and a braided beard that falls halfway down his torso. He comes around the table to greet us, adding, "Hello, lass. It's been a long while since we've seen you. Do you remember me?" He puts out his hand.

I smile, feeling awkward shaking it and say, "I'm sorry, please forgive me, but I don't."

"It's okay. Lord Gottfried said it will come back at some point."

"Lord who?" I ask. My remark appears to stun him.

"He's referring to Jeoffrey, Wynter," the voice I still cannot locate, says.

"Who is that speaking? I'm sorry, but I can't see you."

The group around the table laughs, as though what I said has delighted them.

My question goes unanswered with the bearded man saying, "I'm Thomlun Dragonfoot." He points to a mirror image of himself sitting at the table. "Over there is my brother, Dhomlun Dragonfoot."

"Hello," Dhomlun says, waving. "You can call me Dom."

"And you can call me Thom for short," his brother says.

"My goodness, twins," I say. "How does one tell you two apart?"

"By our hats!" they both reply at the same time.

"I wear the red one," Thom states, taking his hat in his other hand and putting it back on. "I do like the color. It goes with the beard quite nicely, don't you think?"

"Oh, knock it off," Dom spats, slapping his green hat on the table, as though it has dirt he's trying to flick off.

"My apologies, My Lady," Thom says. "My brother tends to be overzealous at times. Come, we have seats for you near the head of the table."

They're both dressed in heavy attire, each having a shield by their chair and a sword at their hip. Although they're short, their physique appears strong, with muscles the size of both my legs put together. Thom steps aside, allowing us all to pass to our seats.

Cory sits next to me while Rory comes around to the other corner. Arryn remains standing by the door along with her cat Akira.

The atmosphere is beyond tense, giving me the feeling this meeting is way beyond important.

"Once the queen arrives, we will carry on. For now, shall we reintroduce ourselves to Wynter?" the voice calls out again. I look around the table, but not one of these men moves their lips.

Each member looks unique, sitting about the table. Some smile, some frown, while others sit against their chairs, not appearing to care who I am at all.

One man stands out among the rest, and to me he resembles Nora. He has the same lizard shaped pupils, and his skin is covered in scales. My immediate guess is he's an Iknes Shaw like her. When it comes to his turn for introductions, he announces, "I'm Zak. You may not remember me, but I'm Nora's brother. How is she, by the way?"

I'm taken aback by the news when I hear the strange voice say, "Let's hold off on the candid questioning for now, shall we? There will be plenty of time for chatter later."

Zak smiles as though he can read my thoughts. Or is it that he, like Nora, has a taste for Storms? The memory of Nora catching me in the hall before breakfast comes to mind.

He nods and the introductions continue on around the table until they come to me. "I imagine you know who I am."

Laughter flits around the room. "Indeed, we do, lass," comes a voice from the other end of the table. It's Dom.

A loud thud draws our attention to Arryn. Her tiger roars, as though he's the chiming bell like that of Daniel back at Storm River Manor when he wanted to grab the attention of the dining room guests.

"Her Majesty approaches. Please rise," Arryn announces.

THE DOORS SWING OPEN, and Sara enters. "Oh, please sit down," she says. "It's just us in the room. No need to be so formal."

She takes her seat at the other end of the table, and we all sit along with her. She doesn't look at all like a queen would now. She wears jeans, a white turtleneck, and a tan fur vest. Her brown leather boots accessorize her attire quite nicely. I feel like I'm staring at a hip grandma, keeping in with today's fashion on Earth.

I know I'm staring because she boasts, "What? Isn't a grandmother allowed to keep up with the fashion trends? Oh, bother." She laughs, adding, "You will soon learn I'm one that seems to always go against the grain. It doesn't matter what people do behind closed doors, right? I mean, why put up a show if you don't have to?"

I give her a bashful glance and nod. "I suppose you're right, Great-Grandmother."

"Oh, nonsense and get rid of the great, too. It makes me feel so old. I'm not nearly as ancient as Aoes over there," she jokes.

"Aoes?" I ask, confused.

"Greetings," a familiar voice says. From the shadows in one corner of the room, a tall man in a sea-green robe and holding a staff comes forward.

"You must be the one speaking earlier," I remark.

"I am." He nods and comes closer. "I'm Aoes, the Wizard of Time."

"The Wizard of Time?" I gasp. "I never knew there was such a thing."

"Oh, my dear, it's a thing indeed. Me." He grins, showing ivory teeth and one gold one that can barely be seen on the side. "I will accompany you on your journey to Storm River Manor. I'm the shield that will protect this group should we need *time* to escape. My abilities can stop the enemy from pursuits. I can also open certain portals, jumping us from one area to another. This shall be rather fun, don't you think?"

"Aoes, don't scare the poor girl," my grandmother says. "He can port to other worlds and jump ahead of time. Kind of like the day you were being chased in the car, remember?"

"How do you know that?" My head hurts with all this newfound information.

"See that staff Aoes holds in his hands?" she remarks.

I glance at the plain-looking cane that seems to be helping the old man stand. Nothing in the slightest indicates it's anything out of the extraordinary.

"Look closer," she coaxes.

It's then I see the illusion of the staff change to a crystal rod, with a glowing bulb setting atop the weapon. It has a circular gem secured by spiral prongs.

"What do you see when you peer into the sphere?" Aoes asks.

A vision appears in the gem and when I look closer, I can see Moyer in the basement taking yet another life. My stomach regurgitates its juices, and the bile travels up my throat. I fight the burn and push the pain down so I don't spew all over the table in front of us.

"Moyer has gained a power like Aoes? To manipulate time?"

"Not time, per say, but she can jump from place to place," Aoes replies. "She has found someone that can port from Earth to here."

"So, the boy last week... in that chair." I point at the crystal globe. "Is that how she gained her power? Is that what you mean? The day I was kidnapped, are you saying she put a porter in there, and that is how she was able to catch up to us so quickly?"

"The boy last week didn't have much power, more for vanity purposes than anything. She keeps herself young that way. Taking the essence of life." Aoes pauses a few seconds before continuing, "You're right, yes. She did, indeed, acquire a Druid's power to steal the ability to jump through time, though."

"At least that's the assumption," Sara adds.

"I didn't see her the day of the accident."

"And why would you? You think Moyer wanted to be seen? Gracious, no. When she saw that you all were indisposed, hanging upside down in the car, she left the rest to Chad, Dexter, and Blair to handle your return to Storm River Manor to continue with more important things."

"Like what?"

"To groom you, of course. However, we seemed to be a tad bit smarter than she."

"What do you mean?"

"I mean, when you were trapped in your dream while Moyer had you in her grasp, keeping you in that dungeon cell, she and Vothule were no match for the magic of Ladorielle." She pauses and smiles. "Or me."

"What are you saying?"

"I'm saying I was able to give Isalora what she needed to warn you, to help you through the escape. To be able to help you through the tunnels. Your father and Chad devised a scheme to get you out of there without tipping Moyer off to the plan. I was able to bring you out of that comatose state Moyer had put you in long enough to allow you to flee through the tunnels," Sara says.

"The pocketknife Chad threw me... he knew about the hole in the cell, didn't he?"

"Perhaps." She smiles.

"It's Sarmira doing all the damage, though, isn't it? I mean, Moyer is the innocent soul she possesses," one of the men at the table intervenes.

"I don't know about Moyer being innocent, exactly," Sara says. "She's had her share of dishonesty. After all, Maura is the one who put herself in this situation in the first place."

"What do you mean by that?"

"Have you not read the journals?"

Aoes clears his throat.

"Is there something you would like to add?" she asks him.

"Just that Your Majesty, the girl wouldn't know this for those journals are here in this library and not at the cottage."

"Ah, yes. Right. I do remember now. You see, Wynter, Sarmira has bigger plans than just raising an army. When your father and Fran took you when you were a baby, they brought you to Ladorielle."

She goes on, "For every year spent on Ladorielle, it's about twelve years past on earth. By the time you were five, Sarmira had built an empire on Earth, concocting new species, blending powers. Years had gone by before she realized. This is why it's so important we find the Sword of Valor and why we must bring Cole home and back to the light."

I quickly do the math in my head. It had been about four days since we stepped onto Ladorielle lands. "This means when we get back to Earth it will be—"

"Not entirely," Sara interrupts. "I know what you're thinking. That we will be too late, and the Super Blue Blood Moon will have already passed, but we have Aoes here who can manipulate time."

"When we return to Earth, I can jump us back to the precise time you first stepped through the portal to Ladorielle. It would be as though you never left," Aoes explains.

"But there's a catch," Sara adds.

"What's the catch?" Cory asks.

"I can only jump back time by a few weeks before it erases for good. Sort of like purging. Even the memory of time has its limits.

Rory speaks up, "If I'm hearing you right, once Moyer is destroyed, Sarmira will be lost on Earth, powerless, and forced to port to the Underworld. And in order to stop her, we must jump backwards before the eclipse on Earth?"

"If she can port to our world, she will be more powerful than ever," Zak states.

"She's accumulated much power over the centuries with many stolen gifts from others. Including Cole's," another member at the table adds.

"Why hasn't she already come back to Ladorielle?" Dom asks.

"What's stopping her from killing her host and leaving?" Thom questions.

"She has all the power she needs now. What if she were to suddenly appear here on Ladorielle," another member explains.

"Please settle down, everyone," Sara orders. "We can only assume it has something to do with Wynter." She glances at me. "You're now eighteen and no longer in danger of her stealing your power. She has something more sinister up her sleeve." Sara takes a deep breath. "What I can tell you is if she's stabbed with the Sword of Valor her spirit form is destroyed, and she can never possess another soul again."

"In theory," Cory interrupts, "Sarmira wants Aoes's magic."

"Over my dead body," Aoes remarks.

"Precisely what I'm implying."

"We don't know if once she leaves her host she's rendered powerless, or if she becomes more powerful," Sara inserts.

"What about the watch?" I ask. "What if we were able to slip it on Cole? Will his powers come back?"

"It's a good concept, Wynter. Not sure how we didn't think of that before," Cory says.

"Cory, do you think you would be able to slip it on him?" Sara asks.

"Well, I don't know. I suppose it's worth a shot. However, Cole claimed he could see the watch I wear."

"What do you mean?" Sara has a look of concern.

Cory clears his throat. "Cole was working on seducing Wynter, and we sort of had a disagreement."

"I see. Go on," she says.

"Well, after a few choice words..."

More like a scuffle.

"That's when he asked about the watch. Apparently," Cory adds, "he obtained one like it to do an experiment. Moyer noticed he wore it, yet Cole couldn't figure out why Moyer couldn't see mine."

"This means there's hope," Sara says. "Cole isn't a lost cause as I first thought. It also means he is fighting the demons within him."

"So, what do we do now?" I ask, looking at my grandmother.

"The only thing we can do. If what you say is true, Cory, getting Cole away from the manor is our top priority."

"But what about finding the Sword of Valor?" Zak questions.

"We will find it." Dom and Thom say together.

"But how? The dragons will burn you to a crisp," Zak persists.

Dom adds, "The dwarves have an alliance with them. We are protected, but how are Wynter, my brother, and I able to get through to the castle? Everyone else will be charred to the bone."

"My fellow friends, calm yourselves," Aoes says. "The dragons are our allies, true and they will not harm us, but we need to act carefully and swiftly."

"It's the Elves the Dragons do not trust," Thom says, glancing toward Rory.

Rory glares back. "Do you really want to start down this road again, Thom?"

He firms his lips, but Dom says, "If your people hadn't stolen from us in the first place, there wouldn't be this war between our people."

"That was thousands of years ago and you know it!" Rory snaps.

Sara slams her fist on the table. "Calm yourselves. I will not have this bickering in my presence," Sara commands. "Now, it seems we have come into some fascinating information. We need to find Cole and bring him back from that wretched place at Storm River Manor."

"But how? We're not prepared to invade Storm River Manor yet," Rory protests. "And then there is my sister to contend with. How are we to get her and Casey back?"

"We will split the mission into two groups. Rory, you will work on getting Redmae out. And see if you can also manage to grab Cole while you're at it." Sara veers her attention to the twin dwarves. "You two will go with her."

"But, Your Maj—"

She cuts him off, holding up her hand. "I've made my decision. We all need to work as a team. We're all on the same side here, are we not?"

Both dwarves bow their heads.

"My sister won't leave without Casey," Rory says.

"I know it will not be easy, but you must get her back here to receive the antidote before the Super Blue Blood Moon rises, or she will remain a dire wolf forever," Sara warns.

I'm beginning to realize finally how I play into all of this. "I was the key to her plans, and when I escaped it foiled her strategy, didn't it?"

My great-grandmother gives a pleasing smile. "Yes, Sarmira is having to readjust her strategy. It would have been easier for her to steal your power at the stroke of midnight on your birthday, but we all know that didn't go according to her plans. Now, she's preparing for an alternative approach."

"Trying to steal my power wasn't enough?"

"Oh, my dear, no, that was her best option. You took that from her when you escaped. Now, she's on the hunt for the Sword of Valor, too. She will use every possible means to get it back. She will search everywhere to find it, with the help of Vothule, of course."

"But no one knows where the Sword of Valor is," Cory says. "I thought Dragonscale knew its whereabouts?"

Sara pauses as she makes eye contact with everyone in the room. "When Bryce stabbed Sarmira with the sword, shattering her to a million pieces, it landed in the ground and the sword was forgotten for a moment as the knight lay near death and his beloved lay alongside him. When she touched him with her healing ability, transferring her power to his, it sent him into a deep sleep for a long while. When he awoke, he had found the news that his wife had sacrificed her life for his. This drove Bryce to protect his boys from magic. You might find it strange, that in this world compared to the human one, a spirit can walk among the living and look as though they are of flesh and bone. You cannot see them with the natural eye, but they are all around you. If one bestows the gift of seeing the undead, they can see them as plain as day." Sara smiles. "It's hard, even for someone holding these gifts to differentiate whether they're seeing a ghost or a physical person."

I try to wrap my head around this. "And these… spirits. Are they aware they're dead?"

"Most of them, yes. And many of Ladorielle wear items such as jewelry to embed the magic needed to see them."

The men around the table lift their hands, showing a ring around each of their fingers.

"This shows me your Aunt Fran, standing behind your chair right now," Thom says.

"What?" I turn around and she is right behind me.

She smiles, saying, "Hello."

I stand up and back away from the table.

"Thom, I do believe you have startled my poor niece," Fran replies.

"She must learn sooner or later the power she possesses," Sara interrupts. "How else are we ever to defeat Sarmira?"

"I should have sensed your presence, Aunt Fran."

"Like I have been warning you all along, Wynter, coming into your power will take time," Fran says.

"You can hear her, too?" I ask the rest of the men.

"Of course, we can," they say in unison.

Sara holds up a ring on her hand. "Although, I, too, am of spirit form, the ring allows me to display as human flesh as long as the ring remains on my body."

"What do you mean?" I ask, confused.

"It's on my body, child. In the crypt," Sara says. If the ring is taken off the finger of my corpse, I will vanish back to a spirit. This ring, like the similar ones these men wear, will allow those alive to see spirits.

The puzzle pieces are coming together. "Wait, so to clarify these rings hold a special insight?"

Sara nods. "The men in this room can see me as long as they wear the Ring of Insight."

"And you have a Ring of Insight on your body?"

"Yes," she answers. "You already have the innate ability of insight."

"I think I understand. And where is this crypt?" I ask.

"Below the castle where all the Storms and Deagons rest after death."

I sit back down, scooting my chair up to the table. "This is all too much to process." I look at Aunt Fran's hands and don't see any such jewelry on her fingers, and ask, "The necklace around your neck... is that what is allowing you to show as though you're of flesh and bone right now?"

She smiles. "Sort of. My body will take time to fully regenerate. The arrow that pierced my heart damaged it badly. Of course, I wouldn't be able to do this on Earth. The immortality spell you have heard us mention preserves the body, allowing us to keep our form. The hearts in the coffers keep us alive, and the jewelry allows us to form as a solid body."

I'm in awe hearing her admissions.

"Give yourself some time to think. In the meantime," my great-grandmother cuts in, "I will have the battle knight master prepare you for your teachings in the coming week."

"My teachings?"

"There's much more to learn before the final battle." Sara stands, and we all stand with her. "Aoes, I presume you know what to do from here. I have a few tasks I must attend to."

He nods, bowing his head and Sara leaves the room.

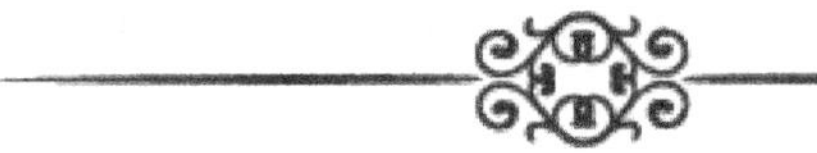

"Now that we have that settled, our second problem still lies in wait," Aoes says, turning to sit at the table bench behind him.

"Second problem?"

"The sword of Valor. Nobody knows where it is, remember?" Fran answers.

"Right."

We all sit around the table, talking among ourselves, brainstorming ideas, and setting plans.

Thom says, "Sarmira will put up a fight to protect Moyer."

"Not to mention," Dom says, "we have no powers on Earth. Only the innate ones we are born with according to our lineage."

"And she will have my brother heavily guarded," Cory adds.

"Wynter must travel to Dragonscale, first," Aoes replies, glancing toward me.

I raise a brow, concerned. "Training, now? Grandmother said in the coming week."

A door opens behind Aoes within the Halls of Secrets, showing a new world on the other side. "You're going through another portal to Dragonscale," he answers. "He will guide you through the right choices. She must begin her training. Shall we get started?"

The many surrounding the table do not seem alarmed at all by the sight and stand to leave. I hear one say under his breath, "Guess it's time we prepare." He exits the room.

Rory grabs my hand, pulling me in for a hug. "I'll be down by the archery area practicing waiting for your homecoming. You can tell me all about your adventure when you get back."

"Adventure? Wait, you mean you're not coming with me?" I ask.

"Not this time." She winks and leaves the room.

"I wasn't expecting to go so soon."

Cory takes my hand. "We go together," he says, smiling.

Aoes puts his hand up. "No, she must go it alone. The path she is taking only allows the blood of a dragon to enter."

"Why can't we find a Druid and port there?" I ask.

"Because Geneviève is the only one left with a rune to take those there, other than a dragon of course. Ashengale is where it's safe, but not the Island surface."

"We're not going with her, are we?" Thom and Dom say together.

"No, not this time, my friend. As I've said, she must take this journey alone." Aoes smiles and takes my hand, placing a gem inside my palm. "This will help you on your expedition."

"What do you mean?" I ask, looking at the blue glowing stone. "How will I know where to go?"

"I will be with you, my niece."

I turn to Cory and smile. He gives me a kiss on the cheek. "You'll be fine with Aunt Fran. Apparently, this is the famous portal to Ashengale. If I go with you, I'll die, and something tells me you may want to keep me around a little while longer."

"It's hard to let you go like this. We've done everything together up to this point."

"I'll be fine. Besides, I can see you no matter where you are. Rest assured, I'll be watching from a distance." This time, he takes my hand and pulls me in, kissing my lips. "Don't be too long, or I will come in after you, though." He smiles. "You wouldn't want me to die, now, would you?"

There aren't any words I can express. I know I would do the same for him and I nod. "I'll not be long. I promise."

"I'm holding you to that promise."

"I know I can keep it," I say, and I step through the dark portal backward, watching Cory's face as I slip through to the other side.

33
DRAGONSCALE ISLAND

IMMEDIATELY, INTENSE HEAT HITS the surface of my skin and the heaviness of the hot air fills my lungs. I'm suffocating. The air burns as I inhale. It's so severe I fight to breathe, and I take the collar of my jacket to cover my mouth. The atmosphere is sultry, and flakes float around in the air. At first, I think it is snow, but when it lands on the surface of my skin, it burns.

"Relax, my niece. You're not going to die. Trust me. Focus on steady breathing. The intensity will subside."

"The ash. It's so overpowering."

She points. *"Yes, from that volcano over there."* Bright orange lava erupts from a nearby mountain. Screeches above my head alert me to look up at the blood orange sky to see dragons circling.

"These lands have the deep scars of war," my aunt says.

"My skin feels like it's burning underneath my protective armor."

"I can understand your discomfort. I've traveled the surface many times."

All around me is red glowing hot rock with lava bursting through the holes in the ground with fissures of lava spewing everywhere and although my flesh feels like it's burning against hot coals, my skin remains the same as before entering through the portal. A numbing feeling takes hold and coats my entire body. The discomfort soon dissipates. *"So, this must be what Aoes meant when he said nobody can step through to this world,"* I say.

"Yes, and the spirit form is unaffected."

I smile knowing I have her here with me to take this courageous journey. I stop, noticing she appears different. "Wait, you're not translucent anymore."

She giggles. "So, you noticed," she says aloud.

"You're like in a human body again? I mean sure, you appeared physically visible back in the hall, but you really look—alive."

Fran grins. "The perks of being on Dragonscale Island."

I squint. "Hmm, quite the pleasant surprise, indeed."

"Come on, there is more to see underground and it's less tumultuous. Plus, speaking out loud will suck up our stamina and we need to conserve our energy, so it's best to continue telepathically until we're out of the heat of danger."

We walk toward the mountains ahead where lava flows down one side and into the ground below. *"Where does that lead?"* I ask.

"To the lava caverns. I'll show you how we can enter the lava mountain safely."

Ash falls through the air, and the smell of burning flesh bleeds through the atmosphere. The dragons above us continue to circle, paying no attention to us intruders.

"The smell is awful," I say.

"It's the smell of trespassers who dare to cross onto Ashengale," Fran answers.

"If people know not to cross, that sounds like a foolish move if you ask me. Can you tell me more about Ashengale?"

She grunts. *"That leads to a long story. A tale so long ago, it's almost a legend."*

"Is there a short version?"

She smiles. *"Rumor has it there is treasure below the surface that will make one rich beyond belief. There's always some genius devising the best armor to withstand the burning heat of Ashengale."* She turns and smiles. *"Can you imagine such nonsense?"*

"But the armor I wear is withholding just fine."

"Yes, of course, it is. You're a Deagon."

"Right," I retort.

We travel around a large lava rock that leads to a stone path. Fran points. *"See that."*

A dark opening sets in the distance. *"Another cave?"*

"Trust me, you will be able to breathe much easier once inside." She pushes forward and I follow.

Fran's right, once inside the dark hollow cavern I can breathe much easier. Oddly enough, instead of feeling the molten lava surrounding the island, I can now hear the trickling of water coming down from inside the cave. I can't see nearly as well as I did in the Grengore mines, though.

"Stop for a minute," she says. "You might need to give yourself a few minutes to adjust to the darkness. Close your eyes." My aunt takes a few steps. "I want you to concentrate on my voice." She takes a few more steps. "Visualize where I might be by the sounds of my words and follow that sound."

"That sounds a bit intimidating, I confess.

"Trust me, Wynter, I wouldn't steer you toward danger. Listen to your body."

"Okay." I walk blind through the cave, trusting where her voice takes me. In the background, the sound of water becomes more prevalent.

"We're almost there," she adds.

"You sound as though you have this cave memorized," I say.

"Long ago, before Sarmira came to hunt our family down, when I was a little girl, I played in these tunnels with friends."

The brush of her fingers takes my hand. "You should be able to see, now."

I open my eyes. There is a dim light ahead.

"It's not far," Fran says.

The closer we step the brighter the light becomes, and the outline of vines hanging over the exit become visible. We draw closer and Aunt Fran parts them so we can pass through. "Here's your underground paradise. Welcome to Ashengale."

I'm awestruck. Fran and I stand high above on a cliffside overlooking a beautiful city. The cavern opens up to a massive cave. "It's a cave within a cave."

"Sort of. We're inside the large mountain you saw above the surface."

A waterfall grabs my attention to the left of us. I can tell there is more to see hiding behind the shrubs that cling to the edge of the cliff.

Fran notices my intrigue, saying, "The Druid circle is over there."

"It's surrounded by a double waterfall."

Fran nods and points. “The second waterfall lands down there in the healing pool.”

“Healing pool?”

Fran smiles. “Come on, this way. There will be time to show you later.”

As we walk in the opposite direction of the waterfall down a winding trail, I take in the abundance of nature. “It’s amazing how much beauty is underneath considering the surface of the island.”

“It’s one of the best defenses this land has.”

“I never would have guessed something like this existed here, that’s for sure.”

“Pleasantly surprised, I take it?”

“Yeah, you could say that.” I take note of the white castle in the center of the town.”

Fran says, “From where we stand the palace is big but wait until you get into town. Come, I’ll show you the way.”

Light comes through the opening above the cave, with dragons circling.

“They’re the Guardians of Ashengale,” Auth Fran says, steps forward down the trail. “Shall we move on? It’s time you meet Dragonscale.”

As we pace closer down the path to the city below, I can’t help but think this looks all too familiar. Large birds fly through the cavern and trees seem to flourish. Flowers grow out of the side of the cliff in some areas, as well as many ferns. The opening of the tunnel that we passed through now closes, with a wall appearing in its place.

“It’s to keep the outsiders out, should anyone dare to get this far,” Fran answers. “Most of Ladorielle don’t know of this city’s location. It’s only recently that the enemy knows of its existence. The city is on high alert at present. Closing off the protective gate is an added safeguard.”

“I see.”

Drawing closer as we talk, I feel a sense of familiarity.

“In time you will learn to hone your abilities,” Fran says. “And you will soon learn to read every mind imaginable like Cory, too.”

“I can’t wait to master that.”

Fran smiles. "I can imagine your frustration. Your ability to see ghosts is a gift, but there is much more to discover."

"Like what?"

"Like, all Deagons can read minds." She grins bigger. "It's not something that everyone needs to know, of course, so we hide it by saying it's a 'gift.' If this secret fell into the wrong hands, it may pose as leverage to the enemy."

"You mean you lie to your people?"

"They're your people too... and no, not exactly. People of Ashengale know of this sworn secret."

"Sworn secret? You mean the reading of minds thing?"

Fran nods.

"What about the Storms? Do they know?"

"Only a select few, like Sara and Ailbert. Cory doesn't even know who you really are."

"And who am I, exactly?"

Fran avoids my question. "You'll find out soon enough."

"I feel like I've been here before."

"Well, you should. This is your home."

A distant memory plays out. "I was quite little, and I remember playing down by the creek when I saw another little girl playing alongside me. We splashed in the water and played along the rocks, hopping over them from one side to the other. I fell in, and the current carried me away. I heard the other girl yell and run alongside the bank to keep up with me. A waterfall was coming near, and I was close to its edge. Right before I was about to fall, I was scooped up by Namari."

"This alcove is where you played all the time. When you fell from the rock at Storm Castle and Charlie ran to you, your screams alerted Vothule to your whereabouts. We had no other choice but to protect you and the rest of the family. You hid here for a short while."

"Who was the little girl with me?"

"Rory. You two were always together. She won't remember this place. She too, has a memory stamp of her own. It was to protect you both should plans fail and

Sarmira capture you. The longer you are here, more of the memories will come back."

"Tell me again why the others couldn't come with us."

"Because you need a porter that has the Stone of Ashengale to enter. Only those who are of Dragon blood can withstand the heat from the outer island."

"And because you are of spirit form, you can withstand the heat, correct?" I ask.

"Well, that is true, but there is much more to that story than you know."

"And you're not going to share that bit of information with me, are you?"

She shakes her head. "No, not yet."

I can tell Aunt Fran wants to tell me more, and although my curious mind is intrigued, I'm not going to press the issue now. I'm too mesmerized by the beauty surrounding me and the memories coming back.

"Tell me something, Aunt Fran. I've been curious about how Cory and I are related. He's obviously not a Deagon, else he would have been on this journey with us. Where does he fit in with all this mess?"

"He's a Storm. A story that doesn't have time for an explanation right now."

There is an archway made of trees, flowers, and ferns ahead. Behind it are more trees and another narrow pathway.

"Beyond this gate is the city of Ashengale. I must warn you. People will recognize who you are. We must race to the castle doors as fast as we can, do you understand?"

"Not exactly, no. Why the secrecy?"

"Remember the memory stamp?"

I nod. "Yeah, and I'm still not happy you planted it there."

"It needed to be done to protect you. But that's not the point right now. Some of these people may trigger a memory, stop you, and say something. If you don't remember the past moment already, you will risk being paralyzed in time with that memory and never recover it. Dragonscale is the only one who can retrieve your memories safely."

"Kind of like the birds in the meadow waking one from sleep?"

"Something like that, yes. Your Aunt Isobel is lost in the past, from the memory that was prematurely awakened."

"Great-Grandmother said it was the poison that caused it."

"Indeed, it was. When one takes a poison from the Iknes Shaw, like the Birds of Songbird Meadow, it places a memory stamp upon you. Where do you think the memory stamps come from, anyway?"

"Where's the invisibility potion when you need one."

"It will be fine," she says. "You have the speed of a vampire. I know you can hear sounds in the distance, and you can see exceptionally well. So can the others in the city. Most that live here are either refugees from past wars and choose to stay in this peaceful place, or they have dragon bloodlines themselves. Keep your eyes on me, and we can race to the front doors of the castle before anyone notices you. Just stay focused and don't lose sight of me. Are you ready?"

"Wait, but you don't have the speed of a vampire."

"Very true. But unlike anywhere else, here on Dragonscale Island, I'm granted the speed like any other with the ability. Plus, now I'm a ghost," she says, grinning. "I'm faster than the speed of light now."

I smirk. "Well, what are we waiting for then?"

Fran takes off, and I follow, racing close behind her. We speed through the town, and I sense some people notice when we approach while others seem to think it's the wind flowing through their hair, but it isn't long before someone detects us.

"Aunt Fran?"

His speed matches mine. "Well, well, who do we have here," he says. "If it isn't—"

He's cut off by a brush of what I think is wind, except it's Aunt Fran knocking him to the ground. He looks dazed.

"Let's go," she says. *"We're almost there."*

We are off again, whizzing through the town before we stumble upon large doors fit for a giant to walk through. She tugs at the hanging rope. "We made it." A bell from inside rings.

In seconds, a large eye shows from the peephole. It's oval in shape and yellow in color, looking much like a lizard's eyeball.

"Who disrupts the palace of a king?" a gruff voice says from beyond the door.

"Garrick, it's me. Drelanda."

"Who is that you have with you? Bringing strangers here is not something in your character, Fran."

"She isn't a stranger. She's Wynter Storm, of House of Storm."

Garrick doesn't answer, instead, I promptly hear the unlocking of the doors. "Stand back," she warns, and we both step aside, allowing the gate to open quickly and we pass through it.

Once inside, we're in another large space resembling a courtyard. The large eye that peered out at us is nowhere to be found, but a man comes forward, stepping out of the shadows near a corner wall to greet us.

"It's good to see you, Fran," he says. "Although you look different. Turn around." He shakes his head. "Oh, my... no. What happened?"

"A giant got me when I was trying to save Wynter."

"I see."

The atmosphere suddenly feels awkward, and I don't know what to think. Who's this man standing before us? He looks familiar.

"There is no time for small talk, Garrick. We've come to see Dragonscale," Fran says.

There are guards up top on the rafters. Two more guards stand on either side of the gate. Then behind me the doors slam shut, making a loud thud that echoes through the grand hall.

"He's gone to meet with the council and will not be back until tomorrow."

"I see. Well, we will wait until he returns. Is Mother here?"

"Wait. What?" I question, in shock.

Fran smiles. "Some things need to be kept secret from the outside world," she whispers.

"Yes, she's here. Follow me," Garrick interjects. "It's time for some proper introductions, Princess Wyndreana."

METAMORPHOSIS

He takes the valiancium cuffs off my wrists and ankles and I feel a sudden power surge within my frame. The force feels overwhelming. "My veins burn! What is going on with me? I can't control it!" I scream.

"Yes, you can. Concentrate," he says.

"You say that, but it's easier said than done. It's too overpowering," I cry.

My skin feels like it's about to rip from my body and peel away from my bones. The agony is so painful. "Make it stop!"

"The change is inevitable. Trust me, the first time is always the hardest." He pauses to bend down to my level, looking me in the eyes. "It was painful for me, too, but I know you can do this."

I kneel on the floor as my feet grow, pushing out nails that look like talons. My spine feels like it's about to break into a million pieces and I double over in pain.

"Why do you think that the poison given to me all those years ago as a child didn't kill me?" Aunt Fran questions as she stands against the wall, witnessing my agony. "Or Sara, for that matter? Have you ever thought why Sarmira stole your mother's heart from her chest in the first place? Wynter, think! Use your intuition." I sense the frustration from my aunt.

My trainer comes forward, laughing as though I'm ignorant. "Don't you get it? You're a Deagon."

"You all keep telling me that." I breathe a heavy and exhausting breath. "But I still don't see what it has to do with this." More pain erupts through my skin, as it breaks open, revealing black scales with a shimmer of gray. I scream in pain.

He touches my forehead with his thumb, and flashes of the past come racing in, a power of strength coming with it. My body lifts as my whole frame changes. The heat builds and the winds kick up, like a tornado. I feel like I can't control the power that's overriding my soul. I think of the past: rage, happiness, sadness, it all consumes me like a vacuum. I feel all my emotions line up, as though each piece falls together like a missing puzzle — lost pieces of my life suddenly found. I gasp in confusion.

Aunt Fran smiles and Garrick smirks.

"See, I told you she could do it," Garrick boasts. "I knew you had it in you, Wynter, the first day I saw you enter the palace, I knew."

Dragonscale, my trainer, sits back watching me, as I explore the *new me*. He joins my thoughts, saying, "You've awakened."

My mind becomes clear and I say, "I remember—everything."

JOIN EMMY'S NEWSLETTER

I hope you enjoyed reading Different Shade of Wynter
Want to read more books by Emmy?
Book 3 Wynter Reign is the next book in the series.
Want to be notified the minute Emmy releases her next book? Sign up for her **newsletter** to get sneak peeks of cover reveals, exclusive content, and new release announcements.
Visit erbennettbooks.com

OTHER BOOKS BY EMMY R. BENNETT

Storm Bloodline Saga

Book 1: Eyes of Wynter

Book 2: Different Shade of Wynter

Book 3: Wynter Reign

Book 4: Wynter's Fury

Prequel: Eye of the Raven

Book 5: Wynter Eclipse (Coming Soon)

House Trilogies

Vol 1: House of Shadow Raven

Part of the Storm Bloodline Saga

Mirror of Fate

Mirror of Souls (coming soon)

Mirror of Darkness (coming soon)

Middle Grade

The Fairy Mermaid and the Crystal Key

GLOSSARY

The Storms

Ailbert Storm: The middle sibling of the three Storm brothers, Gavin and Bram. His Wife: Sara Deagon. Their Son is Ian. Great grandfather to Wynter Storm.

Arik Storm: Son of Gavin Storm and Isobel Deagon - Storm Wife: Maura Moyer.

Blair Storm: Mother is Drena (Vampire). Father is unknown, but she knows she's Storm. Adoptive Mother: Madame Moyer. Her sons; Casey, Cole and Cory. Born a vampire.

Bram Storm: The youngest son of Bryce and Petra Storm. His wife is Clarice. Their sons are Derek and Daniel.

Bryce Storm: The knight that killed Sarmira's original body, causing her to exile her remaining years as a wraith. Bryce is married to Petra. They have three sons: Gavin, Ailbert and Bram.

Casey Storm: Son of Blair. Born deformed. Redmae's best friend. Father unknown at this time. Cory and Cole's older brother.

Chad Storm: He is the son of Madame Maura Moyer-Storm and Arik Storm. Jeoffrey's younger brother. Wynter Storm's uncle.

Clarice Storm: Married to Bram Storm. Died in childbirth.

Cole Storm: Son of Blair and twin brother to Cory. Born a vampire father unknown.

Cory Storm: Son of Blair and twin brother to Cole. Born a vampire. Father unknown.

Daniel Storm: The son of Bram and Clarice Storm and Derek's older brother.

Derek Storm: He is the Son of Bram and Clarice Storm. Daniel's younger brother.

Eleena Storm: Married to Ian. Mother to Isalora and Francesca Storm. Grandmother to Wynter Storm.

Francesca Deagon-Storm (Fran): Older sister to Isalora and Daughter to Eleena and Ian. Sara Deagon Storm is her grandmother. Wynter Storm's aunt. Her formal name is Drelanda.

Gavin Storm: Oldest brother to Ailbert and Bram. Parents are Bryce and Petra Storm. Son is Arik.

Ian Storm: Son of Ailbert and Sara Storm. Husband to Eleena. Their daughters are Francesca and Isalora. Wynter Storm's grandfather.

Isalora Deagon-Storm: Mother to Wynter Storm and wife to Jeoffrey Storm. Her parents are Ian and Eleena Storm. Her grandmother is Sara Deagon-Storm. Younger sister to Fran.

Isobel Deagon-Storm: Sara's younger sister. Wife of Gavin Storm and mother to Arik Storm. She's the grandmother to Jeoffrey and Chad Storm. Both sisters married Storms in secret. Causing a great scandal among the Houses.

Jeoffrey Storm: Son of Madame Maura Moyer-Storm and Arik Storm. Husband of Isalora Deagon-Storm. Chad's brother. Wynter Storm's father.

Madame Maura Moyer: Married to Arik. Mother to Jeoffrey and Chad. Adopted mother to Blair. Grandmother to Wynter Storm. Possessed by Sarmira.

Petra Storm: Wife to Bryce. Mother to Gavin, Ailbert, and Bram.

Sara Deagon-Storm: Married to Ailbert Storm. Mother to Ian Storm. Grandmother to Isalora and Fran, and Great grandmother to Wynter Storm. Oldest sister to Isobel. Her father is the slain king of Ashengale. Her father was killed during the great battle.

Wynter Storm: Daughter of Jeoffrey Storm and Isalora Deagon-Storm.

*****First cousins**: Arik, Ian, Derek, and Daniel.

Ladorielle Characters

Aoes: (Eh-yo-s) The wizard of time.

Drena: Elven daughter to Gage was turned into a vampire. Blair's mother.

Gage: Elven; Drena's father.

Geneviève Fernshadow: The Royal Storm's porter. Her father is Gage and mother is Laveena (Dryads).

Gretta: A Dryad.

Kyla: Gretta's sister, also a Dryad.

Laveena: Geneviève's mother.

Namari: (Naw – mar- ee) Wynter's familiar.

Nora: Iknes Shaw. Wynter's Lady's Maid, and a Shadow Walker

Nyta: (Nigh-ta) One of the last of Sara's court. The medical doctor for the Storm Castle and its surrounding people. High Priestess to the castle. A Diviner of magic.

Redmae: A wolf.

Rory: Wynter Storm's best friend.

Stella: Wynter's friend from Storm River Manor.

Zak: Nora's brother.

Ladorielle Community

Ashengale: City of dragons.

Elleirodal: (Elle- ir - o - dal) Elleirodal and home of Zhir and the twin planet to Ladorielle.

Giant Country: A heavy mountainous terrain where giants and Iknes Shaw live among each other.

Geneviève's Ranch: An elven city.

Grengore Mines: Area where minerals are located and the tunnel to the Lake of No Return.

Ladorielle Territory: An area that is at war with the Underworld that's trying to overtake the land.

Ladorielle: (La- door - ē – elle) Twin planet to Elleirodal. Ladorielle is divided into three continents. Ladorielle Territories, Storm Castle Realm, and Dragonscale Island. The Storms once ruled all of Ladorielle, with Dragonscale Island coexisting on the same planet. Elleirodal realm and the house of Zhir plan to take over both realms.

Pine Willow Valley: The place where Geneviève's ranch is located.

Scale Rock: The crevasse cavern where the Iknes Shaw live.

Shadow Vine Forest: The home of the Dryads, and haven for fairies.

Songbird Meadow: The meadow where the killer birds sing their prey to sleep.

Storm Castle: Where the Storm family resides.

Underworld

Iknes Shaw: Snake-like creatures that are of a humanoid form. They have the head and arms of a human, and a body of a snake. They have the ability to look like a human.

Sarmira: A powerful necromancer sorceress: Ultimate power of evil. Has the ability to raise the dead, create chemistry poisons, and read the minds of anyone. Often places memory stamps on her victims. Necromancers see the undead and can possess the bodies of others. As long as they breathe the essence of life they can live forever. Weakness is Labradorite.

Trek: Ogre-like creatures that can have skin shades from green to a pale white. They have the innate ability to shift into anything.

Vothule: King of the Underworld. Sarmira's superior.

The Houses

Dragonscale: Ruler of the universe, and the balance of power with good vs. evil.

The Council: the circle of balance: the ruler of each realm seats at the table of balance. They are the high courts of the universe. Each house has their own set of rules, and leaders. If a decision cannot be made, it is brought up to the council for a vote.

House of Storm ~ Nytemires (hybrid Vampire/Necromancer)

House of Deagon ~ Dragons

House of Fernshadow ~ Elves

House of Fae 'Oria ~ Dryads

House of Grengore ~ Trek (aka ogres and goblins)

House of Zhir ~ Vothule's Underworld and Sarmira's home. (necromancer)

House of Silverback ~ The wolves

House of Bloodbane ~ Vampires

House of Ashburn ~ Light Witches

House of Shaw ~ Iknes Shaw snake people

House of Dhor ~ Giants

House of Odewyn ~ Wizards

House of Ironstone ~ Dwarves

House of Shadow Raven ~ Dark Witches

ACKNOWLEDGEMENTS

I hope you enjoyed reading book two of the Storm bloodline Saga: Different Shade of Wynter

This book was a challenge to write. I've always had a plan for how this saga would begin, and end, but I had no clue how I would write the second book into the mix. It was a— fly by the seat of my pants, kind of story. My muse seemed to know what to do and it ended up flowing exactly like I'd hoped.

I would first like to thank God. Without him I can do nothing. Thank you to my husband who has been a complete gem. Without his constant support I'm not sure how I could have gotten through writing another novel. Thank you to my children who have consistently supported me throughout this process and cheering me on.

Thank you, Lesley Donaldson-Reid, for brainstorming with me through the developmental editing. You're fabulous at what you do.

To my editors: Rebecca Jaycox, and Gail Delaney thank you for editing this story and making it the best it could be.

To my alpha readers: Sharon, Olivia, and Denise: thank you for your support and help through the awful first couple of drafts. Your input is very valuable, and I appreciate your feedback. To my beta readers Tiffany, Melonie, Kelsey, Brianna, and Gracie: thank you for taking on the task of beta reading, I'm thrilled to have you a part of the reading team. To Veronica, and Laura, thank you so much for volunteering, to help catch the last-minute errors.

Finally, to the readers: thank you for your support.

ABOUT THE AUTHOR

Emmy R. Bennett lives in the Pacific Northwest and grew up in Washington State in a Lutheran household. Although she's strong in her faith, she believes everyone has the right of free will, in their beliefs.

When she isn't at her desk writing, she's spending time with her family, gardening, crafting, or reading.

She loves to study genealogy and her family line has been traced back to the Vikings. It's one of the many inspirations from which she's drawn to write.

©2018 Photography by Mel Sabarez

Made in the USA
Las Vegas, NV
26 October 2023

79677615R00163